Night
Fears

-

Weird Tales in Translation

Paradise Edition No. 2
*

ISBN: 979-8-9875626-1-1
Cover Image: Captain Brodie, English street preacher,
circa 1911 by Unknown

Night Fears

-

Weird Tales in Translation

-

Edited
by
Eric Williams
-
Paradise Edition No. 2
MMXXIII

Contents

Tales from Beyond

Introducing...the Weird Translation

by Eric Williams

Aside from indulging a perverse enthusiasm for old magazines, what justification can there be for yet another collection of stories from *Weird Tales*? After all "The Unique Magazine" has been mined extensively in the century since it first went to print; its stories fill numerous anthologies and collections, while its more famous contributors like H.P. Lovecraft and Robert E. Howard have left their mark on global popular culture through the Cthulhu Mythos and Conan the Barbarian. For connoisseurs and even casual readers of horror, fantasy, and science fiction, *Weird Tales* is hardly an unknown quantity. So what's our angle?

Introducing...

Night Fears collects translated fiction and poetry that appeared in the magazine during the influential editorship of Farnsworth Wright, who held the position from 1924 to 1940. The fact that *Weird Tales* devoted a sizable portion of its pages to work in translation is, in itself, notable, cutting against the stereotyped image of the magazine (and of the pulps in general) as a purely philistine venture. Also notable is the fact that Wright was himself a polyglot translator, whose engagement with world literature—to borrow Goethe's phrase—had begun years before he assumed his position at *Weird Tales*. These translated works were more than just one editor's personal indulgence, however; they are, as we will argue, key to understanding the development of the magazine and the genre it birthed.

Before proceeding further, some taxonomy might be in order. What is this weird fiction stuff? Giving a definitive answer is no simple task, and not for lack of trying; debates have raged since *Weird Tales* made its debut. In the July 1927 issue of the magazine, Farnsworth Wright cited Lafcadio Hearn's essay on Poe's use of the word "weird" as a foundational definition. Hearn, who attributed Poe with rescuing the word from the dustbin of Anglo-Saxon lexicography, also argued that he had deepened its meaning to encompass both "the ghostly" as well as the presence of alien or occult forces. This concern with defining "weirdness" in literature was clearly on the minds of many, since in August of the same year H.P. Lovecraft published his influential essay "Supernatural Horror in Literature," famously specifying that the weird tale is something "more than secret murder, bloody bones, or a sheeted form clanking chains according to rule." Rather, for Lovecraft:

> A certain atmosphere of breathless and unexplainable dread of outer, unknown forces must be present; and there must be a hint, expressed with a seriousness and portentousness becoming its subject, of that most terrible conception of the human brain—a malign and particular suspension or defeat of those fixed laws of Nature which are our only safeguard against the assaults of chaos and the daemons of unplumbed space.

Subsequent writers and critics have come to explicitly identify concepts like awe, transgression, sensory derangement, and the limitations of human perspective as being at the core of "the weird". This demarcation from mere scary stories is important, and reflects an evolution that began when disparate material was first assembled into a magazine devoted solely to the subject. But how did this magazine decide which authors and stories to include? Which to exclude? From what time and which places? This book uses the broad and somewhat imperfectly polished lens of translation to help answer those questions, as well as provide a quantity of stories to entertain and frighten.

Wright used his bully pulpit to shape this new genre, publishing translated fiction alongside the usual fare of modern English-language stories. This helped him to define an aesthetic by connecting the magazine to older, more established literary traditions. That was not done by fiat, however; Wright, like all pulp editors, had to contend with an active and participatory fandom who made their voices heard in readers' letter sections. These sometimes contentious conversations about the merits (and deficiencies) of the stories in *Weird Tales* created the critical framework that allowed people to read and write in a new genre. Wright midwifed weird fiction through its difficult birth with his own unique taste and strongly exercised editorial authority.

But this is not the consensus position in literary scholarship, either of the genre as a whole or of *Weird Tales* in particular. No less a critic than S.T. Joshi dismissed the influence of the magazine in his monumental study *The Weird Tale*, calling the magazine a "dubious watershed" that published "inconceivably wretched" stories. Indeed for Joshi, *Weird Tales* offers very little of value for understanding the origin and history of the weird tale—it was, so the argument goes, merely a commercial venture, where the mercenary instincts of publishers and editors were antithetical to the artistic pursuits of the genre's true practitioners.

This is demonstrably false; before the magazine there was, in fact, no such thing as weird fiction. It was in the pages of *Weird Tales* that the genre was constructed, its scope defined, its conventions codified, and a framework for the interpretation and evaluation of its corpus created. Wright was intensely aware that his magazine was the spearhead of a new pulp literary movement. Much of this creation took place in *The Eyrie*, a regular column in which Wright and the magazine's readership discussed and argued about the state of the genre. The grist for this mill was always the stories themselves, and Wright's choice to publish fiction in translation alongside modern English-language stories can best be understood as a deliberate attempt to influence the taste and shape the aesthetics of both the authors and readers of *Weird Tales*.

"...a poet and the soul of whimsy"

The polyglot second editor of *Weird Tales* was born in Santa Barbara, California on July 29th, 1888. He assumed leadership of the magazine in November 1924 and died from complications related to Parkinson's disease on June 12 1940, mere months after his departure from the publication; it was, without much exaggeration, the work of his lifetime. There is no comprehensive biography of Wright, who, like many in the pulps, toiled in relative obscurity. The most detailed description of his life is found in John Locke's history, *The Thing's Incredible: The Secret Origin of Weird Tales*, taken mostly from the written recollections of *Weird Tales* authors themselves (in particular, from affectionate essays by E. Hoffman Price). Readers interested in the details are directed there; instead, we'll focus on Wright's experience with languages other than English and with his editorial work.

Wright's linguistic talent first arose in his college years at the University of Nevada, Reno, where he initially studied in the Department of Italian as an undergraduate. There he became deeply interested in Esperanto, an artificial language created in 1887 with the idealistic goal of facilitating global communication and overcoming cultural chauvinism through a universal second language. Esperanto's appeal was also probably partly political for Wright; as president of the Social Democrat Club in college, Wright would have been intimately involved with the grassroots of progressive politics. His fascination with the artificial language followed him to the University of Washington, where he would give presentations about Esperanto on campus while pursuing a degree in journalism. He also published literary translations from English in some of the leading American Esperantist magazines. These included the poetry of William Blake, Robert Herrick, and William Cullen Bryant along with prose such as Mark Twain's *Captain Stormfield's Visit to Heaven* and the "Battle of the Ants" section from Thoreau's Walden. The choice of these prose pieces is worth noting, both of which have themes and plot elements in common or at least adjacent to the future genre of weird fiction.

The Twain novel describes the eponymous Captain Elias Stormfield's journey to the afterlife. According to its fictive cosmology, Heaven is not a spiritual dimension but rather an exaggerated mirror of the physical universe, one that requires many long years of travel through interstellar space to reach. And because such a vast universe must be inhabited by many alien beings, there are separate heavens for each inhabited planet. When Captain Stormfield finally arrives at the celestial counterpart to Earth, he is taken aback to learn that it teems with a cliquish populace obsessed with biblical celebrities like Adam and Elijah. A characteristic example of Twain's satire, the story also contains genre tropes that would become staples of weird fiction, such as the portrayal of figures from myth and religion as alien beings who are incomprehensible to the human mind. Similarly, the "Battle of the Ants" exemplifies the perspective-shifting that the subtlest of weird fiction strives after. Observing a brutal and furious war of "red republican" and "black imperialist" ants raging over a woodpile, Thoreau shows how the life-and-death struggles of a civilization can, to cosmic eyes, recede into minuscule vanities. Its language and humor (particularly the darkly comedic calendrics Thoreau uses to situate the battle in time) would fit particularly nicely with the sardonic stories of Lovecraft or Clark Ashton Smith. In addition to their fantastic flavor, both of these works are by authors deeply established in the canon of American literature. That Wright would translate them for national Esperantist magazines presages his editorial work at *Weird Tales*; in both cases, translations of older works create aesthetic associations and boundaries for readers. And while his Esperantist efforts reflected concerns with the literal construction of language,

Wright's work as the editor of *Weird Tales* was correspondingly focused on building a shared body of stories and ideas, a corpus, that would sustain his magazine in the crowded world of the pulps.

Along with Esperanto and Italian, Wright would also at some point gain proficiency in German, Spanish, and Latin, as well as fluency in French, a language in which he was capable of punning. His skill in the latter language was sufficient for him to serve as an interpreter in France during and after World War I, staying a year post-Armistice to work in the Sarthe Department for the Army. One can't help but wonder what his reading habits were like in a country whose literature had been so influenced by Baudelaire's translations of Poe.

Wright's earliest exposure to the magazine that would define his legacy came after the war, when he had moved to Chicago and taken a position as the music editor for the Chicago Herald-Examiner. The first editor of *Weird Tales*, Edwin Baird, had placed numerous solicitations for stories in various trade magazines, and Wright submitted two pieces of fiction, both of which were accepted ("The Closing Hand" in the very first issue in March 1923, and "The Snake Fiend" in April's second issue). It was sometime shortly after April 1923 when Wright was hired on as an editorial assistant by Baird, probably as much for the fact that he was living in Chicago, where *Weird Tales* had its offices, as for his competent writing.

Wright's eventual assumption of the editorship of *Weird Tales* in 1924 was marked by a strange and somewhat confusing series of events; the primary sources consist of gossipy letters by secondary parties, many of whom were *Weird Tales* contributors themselves (for a detailed description, see Locke's *The Thing's Incredible!* and Weinberg's *The Weird Tales Story*). As near as can be ascertained, in early 1924 the magazine's founder, J.C. Henneberger, sold his interest in his publishing company's other magazines (*Real Detective Stories* and *College Humor*, both very profitable) to his partner in exchange for sole ownership of *Weird Tales*, which was hemorrhaging money. Baird, who had a stated preference for crime and detective fiction, stepped away from *Weird Tales* and went to *Real Detective*. At that time, Wright was appointed interim editor of the magazine while Henneberger secretly (and unsuccessfully) began sounding out H.P. Lovecraft for the job.

However, by the summer of 1924 Wright had become acquainted with the depth of financial troubles the magazine was facing, including a staggering $40,000 debt to the B. Cornelius printing company. In July 1924, Wright announced his resignation from *Weird Tales* in the pages of the trade magazine *The Author & Journalist*. In this deeply indignant letter, Wright complained that not only had his salary as an editor gone unpaid for months, but *Weird Tales* also owed nearly $5000 to various authors whose work had already been published. Furthermore, he claimed that Henneberger had instructed him to settle with those authors for 33¢ on the dollar, effectively reducing their previously contracted rates, an insult that Wright refused to be party to. Immediately following this break with Henneberger and *Weird Tales*, Wright began circulating among his author friends his intention to begin a rival magazine, provisionally titled *The Weird Story Magazine*. This would never materialize—Henneberger would soon lose majority ownership of *Weird Tales* as part of a deal that saw B. Cornelius assume control of the magazine in lieu of payment of the $40,000 owed to them; in this reorganization Wright would return as a full and independent editor in the autumn of 1924. It's worth noting, however, that in the midst of all this wrangling, Wright was willing to both start his own magazine dedicated to weird fiction and then return to *Weird Tales* when the opportunity arose, despite the trouble he'd encountered there. His commitment to the nascent genre was clearly a deep and sincere one.

As the editor of *Weird Tales*, Wright put a solicitation in the October 1924 issue of *The Author & Journalist* where, in addition to promising to pay authors still waiting for their money and expressing a never-to-be-realized hope that the magazine would implement a pay-on-acceptance model, he also made a call for new submissions:

> *Weird Tales* especially wants pseudo-scientific stories; tales of science, invention and surgery; tales of the bizarre and unusual; occult and mystic tales and tales of the supernatural, preferably with a rational explanation; good humorous and romantic tales with a weird slant; tales of thrills and mystery; unusual tales of crime and a few tales of horror, but nothing sickening or disgusting.

The Weird Translation

Quite a list, and one that suggests that Wright envisioned an interestingly wide scope for the magazine. For one thing, the inclusion of "romantic tales" and "tales of crime" suggests that perhaps Wright saw "weirdness" as an aesthetic that could be incorporated into existing genres. What this weirdness was and how best to use it would be a major part of the discourse in his editorial column.

Translating Weirdness

Hot on the heels of a raging controversy over C.M. Eddy's story of necrophilia "The Loved Dead" in the bumper May/July 1924 issue, Farnsworth Wright announced in *The Eyrie* that *Weird Tales* would soon begin publishing reprints of "the great weird stories of the past." It is significant that this decision happened during an intense period of discussion about what was appropriate for the genre. Battles, for instance, over the inclusion of gory or "nauseating" stories and the role of humor in weird fiction had been a major focus of the letters received; what better way to circumscribe a new genre than by finding authoritative, influential, and illustrative works from the past? But of course these works were written in a time before the genre existed; no writer (or reader for that matter) would have viewed them through a unified generic lens. So what then is a classic weird story? Wright begins the discussion, as always, by situating it within the discourse of the readership itself. "Hardly a week passes," wrote Wright, "without the receipt of several letters calling attention to some old masterpiece." He goes on to name E.T.A. Hoffman, Wilkie Collins, Theophile Gautier, and Walter Scott among the most requested names. Interestingly, in a later paragraph he bars the better known stories of Poe, Bierce, and Fitz-James O'Brien from the reprint series since "every lover of weird fiction" would already be acquainted with them. He goes on to once again call for the readers to recommend stories, saying that he has decided only on the first entry of the *Weird Story Reprints*, Alphonse Daudet's "The Three Low Masses".

The choice of Daudet for a "reprint" is interesting, since it isn't a reprint at all—Farnsworth Wright translated the story himself for *Weird Tales*. Originally published in French newspapers, it was then included in Daudet's collection *Letters from My Windmill* in 1869. And though readers of *Weird Tales* with a more literary bent might have recognized the author, it's hard to imagine anyone putting him in a list of the great writers of strange or eerie tales. The majority of his work remains firmly realistic, to the point of him being regarded, along with Émile Zola, as a major exponent of naturalism, the 19th century literary movement that rejected Romanticism in favor of emotional detachment, scientific objectivity, and social realism. As a scholar of language and literary history, Wright may have well seen the irony in publishing a naturalistic writer in a pulp magazine; he might have, as an editor, deemed this haunting (and haunted) tale of damnation as particularly well-suited for the magazine; or he simply might have been fond of the story on a personal level. Motivations for editors, as for everyone else, are rarely unmixed.

Weird Story Reprints was popular with the readers and would continue through the years, relying heavily though not exclusively on translations. A collection of ghost stories from 1890 called *Modern Ghosts* would be mined, with almost every story from it appearing in *Weird Tales*. Translated works by Balzac, Gautier, Flaubert, Pushkin, and Turgenev would all be part of the reprint series, along with classic Anglophone writers like Poe, Wilde, Hawthorne, and Walter Scott. But importantly, translated works weren't merely relegated to the reprint series; sometimes these were announced as having been specifically commissioned for *Weird Tales*, such as four short stories by Gaston Leroux, best known today as the author of The Phantom of the Opera. Other translations would have been difficult to identify as translations at all, with no attribution to the translator or even a hint of the original's language, as in the heavily edited adaptations of "John Flanders"; these were originally published in French by the Belgian writer Jean Ray and all were translated by Roy Temple House, although that information is never shared in the pages of the magazine.

During Wright's sixteen years as editor, at least forty-eight translations were published in *Weird Tales*, a surprising amount of material for which there is no real precedent in the pulps. And while that's only a fraction overall of the stories in *Weird Tales*, an important point bears repeating: they were never isolated or categorized apart from the main body of work in the magazine. There was no *Weird Translations* section, for instance; rather, they were either presented as "classics" and "reprints" or, equally common, they were simply another weird story, fully integrated into the issue right alongside the most recent work of Greye la Spina or Seabury Quinn. While not in keeping with contemporary publishing ethics of crediting the translator or even of seeking out the rights holder for permission, this catch-all approach was a strong editorial decision on the part of Wright. For him, these stories merited inclusion because of their artistic value as exemplars of "the weird", a synthesis of languages and authorial voices that could comfortably fit alongside his stable of contemporary writers.

Among the most prominent of these was Clark Ashton Smith, who shared with Wright an affinity for French literature. After teaching himself the language in the mid-1920s, Smith embarked on the ambitious project of rendering Baudelaire's *Flowers of Evil* into English, from which three poems are included in this collection. Smith's translation career would continue with versions of Victor Hugo, Theophile Gautier, and Paul Verlaine, as well as Spanish-language poets such as Amado Nervo and Jorge Issacs. Smith's relationship with Wright could be fraught, particularly over the rejection of his longer original prose works, but Wright's commitment to publishing his translations was durable, lasting throughout the latter's tenure as editor.

Another notable figure edited by Wright was Roy Temple House, a professor of modern languages at the University of Oklahoma. House translated from German and Russian for *Weird Tales*, and along with his renditions of writers such as Maxim Gorky and Franz Nabl he also wrote a nonfiction account of telepathy for the magazine in its issue of June 1937. Contemporaneous to his pulp magazine contributions, House was also emerging as a pioneer in the academic fields of comparative literature and translation studies. In 1926, he founded the journal *Books Abroad* with the aim of fostering a "universal world literature" as Goethe envisioned, quoting an essay by the German poet and dramatist in the masthead, "there can be no question of the nations thinking alike, the aim is simply that they shall grow aware of one another, understand each other, and, even where they may not be able to love, may at least tolerate one another." It was the goal that Wright, an Esperantist and progressive activist, would have understood well. House's academic legacy has also proved enduring and, in an institutional sense, outlasted *Weird Tales* by a significant margin. His journal, *Books Abroad*, is still published by the University of Oklahoma under the name *World Literature Today*.

Night Fears

The stories selected for this volume are only a small portion of the translated material that appeared in *Weird Tales*. Wright translated from German and French; consequently, works from these languages make up a large proportion of the translations, both in *Weird Tales* and in this collection. Exceptions include "The Tall Woman" by Pedro Antonio de Alarcón, a Spanish story taken from *Modern Ghosts*, and some particularly striking Russian tales. Following Wright's precedent, a decision was made to exclude some of the more famous material from *Night Fears*; Guy de Maupassant's "The Horla" is a classic and would be printed (and reprinted) in *Weird Tales* several times and can be found in many other collections. We have had to similarly make hard choices about some of the more well-known writers who appeared in the magazine, excluding a number of the great names in literature due to length considerations, even though there are few things more enjoyable than seeing, say, Theophile Gautier on the same table of contents as H.P. Lovecraft and Robert E. Howard (February 1928, if you're interested).

Also left out are several stories illustrative of the well-known dark side of pulp magazines in the early 20th century. Indeed, this uncomfortable history led to the decision to cut two stories initially considered for this collection, Bodo Wildberg's "The Snake-Skin Cigar Case" (July 1936,) and Gustav Meyrink's "The Violet Death" (July 1935). Wildberg's story is described in *Weird Tales* as "an unusual tale about a dread experience in the tropics" and was translated by Roy Temple House. In it, a casually colonialist European overseer of a snake-skin processing factory in Indonesia recounts a harrowing tale where a "native girl" (made worthy of affection by the inclusion of some "Dutch blood" in her parentage) is subjected to the dark magic of a "medicine man" who, you can imagine, is described in excruciatingly caricatured and racist detail. Wildberg, who edited volumes of poetry with his friend Rilke, is an able writer and handles the ironic denouement well, but it is not enough to save what can only be described as a classically orientalist story. Meyrink's tale, "The Violet Death" (also translated by House) is truly weird, hinging around a mysterious tone that, when uttered, transforms people into cones of purple dust. Meyrink was most famous for *The Golem*, a novel concerning the mystical automaton of Jewish folklore, widely lauded as one of the best supernatural novels ever written. But again, the story is marred by crudely racist caricatures, in this case of Tibetans who, with the "unearthly ugliness of [their] faces, which were naturally hideous…" threaten the clean, adventurous Europeans who have heroically penetrated the Himalayan wilderness.

The fact that both of these stories are set in Asia is probably not a coincidence. The readers of *Weird Tales* were very enthusiastic about "oriental stories", which were almost always clash-of-civilization narratives about two-fisted white men doing battle with inscrutable and exotic villains. Indeed, they were so popular that Wright would create and edit a short-lived sister publication to *Weird Tales* called *Oriental Stories*, a magazine that tended towards more straightforward adventure tales. It is telling that Wright would happily, indeed eagerly, publish these and other "oriental stories" in *Weird Tales* while neglecting the classic literature and folklore of Asia, which was then just becoming widely available to American readers. A particularly striking omission is that of Lafcadio Hearn's translations and adaptations of folktales and ghost stories. Hearn was of course known to Wright; aside from being a major figure in 19th century literature, Wright published Hearn's translation of Theophile Gautier's "La Morte Amoureuse" as "Clarimonde" in the February 1928 issue of *Weird Tales* and also excerpted Hearn's lecture on Poe in the pages of *The Eyrie*. Familiarity with that work means Wright would have been aware of Hearn's 1904 book *Kwaidan: Stories and Studies of Strange Things*, a hugely important and very well known work of folklore and translation that compiled weird stories full of ghosts and monsters and strange magic from Japan. It would have been a perfect fit for the magazine! For that reason alone, its absence in *Weird Tales* would be notable, but the fact that its editor was a translator himself with a demonstrable interest in world literature makes it remarkable. What explains this?

Without documentary evidence we are limited to conjecture, but it seems reasonable to posit that Wright simply didn't see value in the folkloric stories Hearn had adapted into English, at least not in terms of the weird tale as a new genre. This could be simply due to the regrettable compartmentalization of folklore as something other than literature, which also explains why, by the same token, there wasn't any European folklore or "weird history" published in *Weird Tales* either. This was another editorial decision made by Wright, since histories of European witchcraft or medieval occultism were among the common requests from readers in *The Eyrie* that he consistently ignored. For Wright, weird fiction meant just that: imaginative fiction that trafficked in weirdness. There was no room for actual occultism, historical anecdotes, odd news stories, or folklore in an exclusively literary genre, even though his authors mined this material obsessively to build their original creations. There is, of course, also simple racism—multilingualism doesn't necessarily imply racial egalitarianism, even in a progressive like Wright, and the idea of stories told from non-western and non-white perspectives might simply have been too much for him and his readership. The simple fact is that the racism, sexism, and nationalism of the age were all reflected in the pages of *Weird Tales* (an explanation but not an excuse), and anyone plunging into its pages should go in forewarned. This is not at all surprising, as even the most casual reader of H.P. Lovecraft can attest, but recognizing the time and place of the creation of the weird fiction helps elucidate the role these prejudices played in its history. We can (and must) be active in our reading of these texts, cognizant of their history and understanding of their context, even though as the genre has been further enlarged and enriched in the century since its birth.

Anatomizing the Weird

What motivated the choices made for *Night Fears* is the belief that each story represents an interesting and provocative point in a continuous mediation on what constitutes the weird. Wright often used *The Eyrie* to highlight specific subjects and themes, referencing for instance "pseudo-scientific" tales (precursors to the then yet-to-be-codified genre of science-fiction), tales of black magic and witchcraft, "horror" (meaning stories with notably violent or gruesome content), and occult detective stories as some of the specific areas where weirdness was a distinguishing quality. Wright called these out as ways to identify some of the trappings of the nascent genre, though they were subservient to a broader and more meaningful distinction: weird fiction was an imaginative literature, directly in opposition to "the stark school of realism" that insisted "that true literature must be tied to the sordid experiences of everyday life." As for the magazine itself, it was the beachhead of a revolutionary literary movement, revolutionary in that weird fiction militated against the contemporary artistic status quo as well as represented a return to an older conception of literature.

> Other magazines put up the bars against stories that wander very far from the experiences of the life about us, and thus inevitably they publish much that is humdrum, much that is commonplace. This very conservatism robs them of some of the most brilliant stories that are written.

The stories in *Night Fears* were selected to illustrate Wright's commitment to literary invention. Our selections are organized thematically into four sections, broad subcategories of strange or inexplicable human experience that point towards how weird fiction developed and evolved.

Our first section, Tales of Malediction, encompasses stories of supernatural curses, a popular subgenre in *Weird Tales*. Some of the stories, like Daudet's "The Three Low Masses," concern curses earned through bad choices or evil behavior, whereas others, like de Alarcón's "The Tall Woman" or de Maupassant's "On the River" suggest the inexplicable machinery of forces beyond human comprehension,. A third typology of the curse is suggested in the haunting "Lazarus" by Leonid Andreyev: the curse of sanity-blasting knowledge not meant for mere humanity, a favorite theme of weird fiction.

"The Three Low Masses" nicely illustrates Wright's desire to set weird fiction in opposition to the fashionable and, per Wright, "sordid" realism of his day. Daudet, a champion of naturalism, nonetheless provides an evocative ghost story, one concerning a gormandizing priest who rushes through his ceremonies to partake in a Christmas feast; clerical hypocrisy is certainly not uncharted literary territory, and the loving, almost Rabelaisian recitation of sumptuous dishes certainly grounds the character of Dom Balaguère in a realistic and very material gluttony; but the haunting (in a literal sense) coda of the story provides a deeper spiritual resonance, one anchored to landscape and history in the visceral way that only a ghost story can achieve.

Introducing...

This supernatural realism underpins Alarcón's "The Tall Woman" as well, a story of an engineer haunted by a malevolent specter of unknown provenance. Again, this is well-mapped country, a staple of horror literature. But "The Tall Woman" also presents something deeper and more elusive than the usual gothic window dressing. Otherwise normal and unspectacular city streets, Madrid in this case, suddenly become the haunt of something deeply and existentially menacing. The story's idyllic frame introduction sets a tonal counterpart to the main narrative while voicing its overriding thematic concerns. A group of gentleman naturalists take a rest in the mountains near the Escorial palace. They engage in a spirited discussion on the difficulties of squaring rationalist thought with the vagaries of experience, a challenge embodied, as the gentlemen come to realize, in the eponymous Tall Woman. The sober, scientific mind encountering the inexplicable is a core trope of weird fiction, and Alarcón's story illustrates that perfectly.

Guy de Maupassant's "On the River" deftly demonstrates its author's mastery of atmosphere and narrative pacing. A bracingly efficient piece packed with evocative imagery, it concerns a boatman on the Seine and his finding of a mysterious corpse. Outwardly, very little happens other than close observation of a river, but the details compound in such a way as to make the boatman's macabre discovery both inevitable and surprising. Wright's inclusion of it in *Weird Tales* could be linked as much to its technical perfection as its subject matter. The swift and jarring conclusion is illustrative of a key frisson at the heart of the weird tale, where the characters' (and by extension the readers') knowledge of what is happening is suddenly and irrevocably shown to be deficient.

The final story in Tales of Malediction is Leonid Andreyev's "Lazarus," a grim tale of existential horror that elicited much praise from readers in *The Eyrie*. It expands and retells a central passage from the New Testament, the raising of Lazarus from the dead by Jesus in the Gospel of John, but with the miracle inverted. The resurrection of Lazarus, instead of filling him with awe and gratitude, robs him of all savor of life, a condition that he can transmit with a glance. The story communicates a central theme of weird fiction, the terror of mortality and concomitant suspicion that there are fates worse than death. It also shows how menace can be conveyed with simple description, in mundane phenomena such as a frown or a frayed piece of cloth.

Second comes our Tales of Madness section. Early on, *Weird Tales* singled out themes of madness and delusion as worthy of special attention, reflecting a foundational assumption in the fragility of human happiness and mental wellbeing. Extreme behaviors, morbid obsessions, and the social consequences of madness have a long history in literature, but the style and structure of the weird tale is uniquely suited to its exploration (or exploitation). Wright recognized that sensational tales would attract readers, but there's a subtler aspect of the genre illustrated by the stories included in this section: the skewed reality that weird fiction evokes forces the reader to reevaluate the mental preconceptions they bring to the story, the rigid binary that separates madness with sanity. This psychological, even psychoanalytical approach was firmly established in the earliest stories published in *Weird Tales* and is an important part of its literary lineage.

Sologub's "The White Dog," further illustrates the way weird fiction can suspend readerly expectations of mental cause and effect. A Russian peasant woman, reacting to the harsh gossip in her village, begins to take on the doglike aspects imputed on her by fellow villagers. Is this the result of occult intervention or the acting out of a disturbed woman? No answer is given. A powerful and enigmatic atmosphere of oppression and struggle is evoked in this brief story, and its disjointed language and mysterious events crack open what might otherwise be a reductive narrative of the rigid class and gender roles in Russian society. The mad and the sane, outcast and insider, these dichotomies are collapsed in a terse climax.

A more urban and industrial horror, that of confinement with strangers, is the subject of the second story of this section, "On a Train with a Madman," by an obscure German author, Hermann Plahn, pseudonymously writing as Pan-Appan. Once again, this tale dramatizes how thin the veneer of sanity is, both for the individual as well as society at large. A rail passenger is accosted in a private compartment by a quack, who attempts to perform an improvised eye operation on him. After he beats away his assailant, the passenger realizes to his horror that they are not the only ones on the train to have acted out the same encounter. A straightforward account of medical horror gives way to something more troubling, a meditation on how the orderly functioning of society is, ultimately, as fragile as the small, breakable little animals that seek shelter under its umbrella.

"A Masterpiece of Crime" by Jean Richepin is a story of arbitrary cruelty that expands into an almost- or perhaps pre-postmodernist meditation on art and identity. Here, a failed writer takes de Quincey at his word and treats murder as an art to be perfected. So devoted is Richepin's narrator that he sacrifices his entire sense of selfhood for absolute mastery of both violence and its resultant narrative reconstruction.

Our third section concerns Tales of Revenge, broadly construed. Wright had specifically requested "unusual tales of crime" in his call for submissions to *Weird Tales*, and the stories in this section reflect this interest. Crime fiction was one of the most popular genres of the day, and the pulps could confidently point to the origin of the hard-boiled detective story in their pages. Brutal violence, casual nihilism, and suffocating despair were therefore already well-established in the literary landscape; but what separated *Weird Tales* from competing magazines such as *Black Mask* was its emphasis on the unexplained, and the fickle, fundamentally irrational beliefs that undergird morality both public and private.

A translation of Gaston Leroux's "The Mystery of the Four Husbands" was commissioned specifically for *Weird Tales*, a story of mysterious murder and thwarted passion that ends with Leroux's characteristic grand-guignol excess. The author reverses, inverts, and ultimately upends the classic fable of Bluebeard here, unleashing a serial killer of husbands. The violence unfolds within an elaborate narrative frame, which, like the act of oral storytelling itself, is modified and improvised in its own performance. The tale plays on pulp audiences' expectation of the occult and the supernatural, with the characters themselves indulging in useless speculation about the origins of the crime, setting up an ultimately more mundane (though certainly twisted) anticlimax to events in the story. "The Mystery of the Four Husbands" neatly encapsulates Wright's literary and editorial philosophy: pragmatically, a tale well-told by a famous and spectacular author was always welcome, but of equal interest is a work that also explores and comments on the very genre being created in the pages of *Weird Tales.*

Wilhelm Hauff's "The Severed Hand" relates the nightmarish adventure of a Byzantine merchant-doctor in Florence, who is unwittingly transformed into a tool of vengeance for an act he doesn't understand by a person he'll never know. This story shows that weirdness needn't always be a riot of tentacular cosmicism—the operation of our fellow humans is sufficiently weird when their motives and histories are impenetrable. It conveys a sense of smallness of man in the face of incomprehensible forces that is as weird and poignant as anything found in Lovecraft.

Alexander Pushkin's "The Queen of Spades" furnishes an ideal example of the literature that captivated

The Weird Translation

Farnsworth Wright, fantastically imaginative and yet connected to the mainspring of the classic European literary tradition. The story is a moody meditation on greed, obsession, and vengeance. It follows the attempts by an aristocratic adventurer to wrest gambling secrets from a geriatric countess and the misfortune that befalls him when he succeeds. The tale is underscored by the doom-laden portentousness so prominent in the romantic literary tradition. As pure literature, it is a remarkable example of the power of ambiguity, forcing the reader to ask whether Hermann's experiences are real or imagined, the vengeance that falls upon him supernatural or merely psychological? Viewed through the lens of weirdness being articulated in *Weird Tales*, however, this dichotomy dissolves. Pushkin's imaginative story becomes one about a man trying to pervert the orderly functioning of the universe, the same goal of mad sorcerers or bloodthirsty cultists found in the magazine's more conventional fare.

The last section of *Night Fears* is reserved for what readers likely think of as the typical expression of the genre, what we've termed Tales from Beyond. These are often the most highly imaginative expressions of the weird genre, stories of the inexplicable or truly alien, where the horror defies not merely description but comprehension itself. This particular subgenre bloomed under the influence of the modern scientific age in the 19th and early 20th centuries, when rationalist faith in progress and explicability of the universe were undermined by new discoveries in physics and new theories about human psychology. It

Introducing...

was perfected by H.P. Lovecraft in the pages of *Weird Tales* and has come to typify the genre to this day. At its core, it represents a rejection of both banal realism and pedestrian supernaturalism; the "real" world with its familiar and understandable rules and logic and mechanistic laws is shown to be an illusion, replaced not by mere supernatural agency but rather by alien and incomprehensible logic that seems to us, limited as we are, an unfathomable chaos.

Franz Nabl's "The Long Arm" has an eerie and unique image at the center of its narrative of uncontrollable psychic powers. Stylistically, the story captures the careful tightrope act of much successful weird fiction, where the weirdness must be simultaneously explicit to the reader but hidden from the characters. It rests on the self-loathing of the psychic Banaotovich as he confesses his numerous crimes to a childhood friend. What begins as a simple account of parapsychology run amok turns into something more complicated and threatening. It's not just his powers that make Banatovich a monster, but his all-consuming need to be believed and to have others understand his condition, an instinct that leads him to attack even those closest to him. The story is a showpiece for weird fiction's pessimism regarding human agency and altruism.

At first blush, Wright's inclusion of Honoré de Balzac's "A Passion in the Desert" may seem like the purest indulgence of a literary Francophile. Indeed, Balzac's finely observed characters and sharply described social relationships are credited as the wellspring of French realism, so it may seem odd, more so than even Daudet, that Wright would include the story among his usual, unabashedly speculative fare. After all, hadn't Wright excoriated realism and planted his flag firmly in opposition to all it stood for? Superficially a colonial adventure tale, in which a marooned French soldier befriends a lion in the desert, there are no ghosts or ghouls to be found, no psychics or even the conventionally insane. But a closer reading of "A Passion is the Desert" reveals the same thoroughgoing epistemic skepticism and indifference to human motivations that Lovecraft would champion. The story's paradoxically lush descriptions of the desert provide a scaffolding for intense, perhaps bestial emotional outbursts. The reality of the marooned soldier and his animal companion are as divorced from the experience of an everyday Frenchman as an explorer on the surface of the moon. In this story, Balzac once again proves his metier in showing how normality can be thrown askew by the unexpected.

Alexander Kielland's tale "Siesta" has, appropriately enough for the pulps, a convoluted textual history. Originally published in English in *Modern Ghosts*, it was relayed through a German version of the Swedish original. The story describes a fashionable party in Paris and its interruption by a mysterious musician. The piece might be entirely atmospheric if not for its biting satire of the moneyed class, but it also embodies a theme perennial in weird fiction, that of the uncanny power of art, even and perhaps especially over those who think themselves above its influence, a sentiment that Farnsworth Wright, as an editor, translator, and music critic would have appreciated deeply. "Siesta" also captures the way weird fiction can achieve its goals with suggestion and insinuation. Not every horror story needs to include some masked lunatic or slavering globular entity from transdimensional space; sometimes, and in a very true-to-life way, you can find the inexplicable during an occasion as mundane as a dinner party.

"A Ghost" closes out our collection with another example of Maupassant's command of the short story along with his sense for the ominous and macabre. The story begins classically enough; friends are gathered for an evening's entertainment, with one guest recounting a particularly strange and harrowing experience of his long-gone youth. An acquaintance, having experienced the death of his bride, asks the narrator to deliver a sealed message to his former estate. There, in a ruined mansion in the countryside, he encounters an entity whose own request is as banal as it is frightening and inexplicable, the brushing of hair. "And in fifty-six years I have learned nothing more," he concludes, "I never found out the truth." A fitting coda for any of the stories in the collection.

Defining the Weird

With circulation in the tens of thousands, these strange and subversive stories almost certainly had their greatest exposure to English-language audiences in *Weird Tales*. This, along with the coherent and considered editorial focus behind their inclusion, shows that we need to take seriously the literary merits of the pulps. These translations offer a uniquely clarifying view of Wright's aspirations for his magazine. Far from Joshi's "dubious watershed," *Weird Tales* was the handiwork of a thoughtful (if not always tasteful) editor. Wright envisioned the weird tale as part of an imaginative, romantic tradition of literature, one that emphasized heightened emotions, the sublime terror and viscerality of uncanny experience, as worthy aesthetic goals in themselves. He did not construct this new genre haphazardly; before the magazine, there were ghost stories, horror stories, tales of the occult, mystery stories, gothic romances, all written in a variety of styles and pursuing different topics or exploring different themes. Given the amount of back-and-forth in the letters to *Weird Tales*, the idea of what constituted weird fiction was always foremost in both Wright's and the readers' minds. Reading and translating in multiple languages and with a clear affinity for outré literature, Wright used his position to forcefully and tirelessly argue for a particular vision of the weird tale, and one of his great innovations was publishing work in translation as a way to simultaneously legitimize the genre, argue for its global scope, and create a unified aesthetic that would define it.

In addition to Wright's articulation of a new imaginative literature focusing on weirdness, there is a second and related aesthetic illustrated by the translated fiction in *Weird Tales*: that of "telling the tale" itself. It is notable that so many of these stories are framed as a character giving an account to other characters within the narrative. For example, the botanizing naturalists in

"The Tall Woman," the circus-goers in "A Passion in the Desert," the Judge in "On a Train with a Madman," the fisherman in "On the River," the old sea dogs in "The Mystery of the Four Husbands," and the Marquis de la Tour-Samuel in "A Ghost." This framing reflects more than a convenient narrative device; it imbues these stories with a specific kind of immersion and verisimilitude that is uniquely important to weird fiction. Similarly, these tales are full of numerous asides and incidents where a character pauses the action to nest a second (or third, or fourth) story within the larger narrative, as in the tale of the countess's adventure with the Count St. Germain in "The Queen of Spades". With some latitude, you can even stretch this tale-telling structure further, including first-person narratives that are, within the framework of the story, effectively being told to the readers, as in "The Severed Hand" or "The Long Arm." This complex and sometimes confounding discursiveness mirrors the general difficulties of humans as they fumble towards the truth. For all their investigative doggedness or intellectual rigor, the narrators of these tales often come up short. Ultimate proof eludes them and, by extension, the readers as well, and only the salience of memory remains. These stories represent Wright trying to communicate this key experiential aspect of weird fiction, where the extraordinary and unprecedented events of a tale are made highly personal and intimate by the narrative structure itself.

Much has been made of the weird fiction reflecting 20th century concerns around modernity:

decentered humanity, the precariousness of "civilization," Promethean and seemingly limitless science, the existential threats posed by new technological warfare. To express these concerns, weird fiction developed a set of specific literary and aesthetic tools, and in this Farnsworth Wright played an out-sized role, linking the weird genre to a tradition of imaginative literature. Nowhere is this more evident than in the translated fiction that he published in the magazine. Russian romanticism, French naturalism, German expressionism; the stories shared here in *Night Fears* represent a primer on the imagery and techniques championed in the pages of *Weird Tales*. It is no coincidence that the most influential modern writers of weird fiction, H.P. Lovecraft, Robert E. Howard, and Clark Ashton Smith, all consciously and actively wrote in a romantic style, using the idiom and artistry of older styles for their own explorations into the uncanny. Likewise their appearance within the pages of *Weird Tales* was no accident; as an editor, Farnsworth Wright actively encouraged that exact kind of work, leaving his mark on a genre that left behind simple "goose-flesh stories" in favor of a dynamic and sophisticated literary approach that revolutionized popular fiction, and popular culture, forever.

Tales of Malediction

Le Revenant

by Charles Baudelaire

May 1929 (vol. 13, no. 5)
Translated from the French by Clark Ashton Smith

Like an ill angel tawny-eyed,
I will return, and stilly glide
With shadows of the lunar dusk
Along thy chamber aired with musk.
And I will give thee, ere I go,
The kisses of a moon of snow.
And long caresses, chill, unsleeping,
Of serpents on the marbles creeping.
When lifts again the bloodless dawn.
From out thy bed I shall be gone—
Where all, till eve, is void and drear:
Let others reign by love and ruth
Over thy life and all thy youth,
But I am fain to rule by fear.

The Three Low Masses:
A Ghost-Tale of Old Provence

by Alphonse Daudet

July 1925 (vol. 6, no.1)
Translated from the French by Farnsworth Wright

1.

"Two stuffed turkeys, Garrigou?"

"Yes, Reverend, two magnificent turkeys stuffed with truffles. And I ought to know, too, for I helped stuff them myself. One would think their skins would crack while they were roasting, they are stretched so tight."

"Jesus and Mary! I who love truffles so much!… Quick, Garrigou, give me my surplice…And besides the turkeys, what else did you see in the kitchens?"

"Oh, all sorts of good things! Ever since noon we have been plucking pheasants, hoopoes, hazel-hens and heath-cocks. The feathers filled the air. And then from the pond they brought eels, goldfish, trout, and—"

"How big were the trout, Garrigou?"

"So big, Reverend! Enormous!"

"Oh, good Lord! I can fairly see them…Did you put the wine in the vases?"

"Yes, Reverend, I put the wine in the vases. But heavens! it's nothing like the wine you will have later, when you come from the midnight Mass.[1] Oh, if you could only see the dining hall, all the decanters blazing with wines of all colors! And the silverware, the chased centerpieces, the flowers, the candelabra! Never was there seen such a Christmas supper! The marquis has invited all the lords of the neighboring estates. There will be at least forty of you at the table, without counting the bailiff or the notary. Ah! you are fortunate in being one of them, Reverend! Only from sniffing those wonderful turkeys, the odor of truffles follows me everywhere. Mmmm!"

"Come, come, my boy! Heaven preserve us from the sin of gluttony, above all on this night of the Nativity!…Hurry off, now, and light the tapers and ring the first call for Mass, for it will soon be midnight and we mustn't be late."

This conversation took place one Christmas night in the year of grace sixteen hundred and something, between the Reverend Dom Balaguère, former prior of the Barnabites and present chaplain of the Sires of Trinquelage, and his little clerk Garrigou—or at least him whom he believed to be

---

1. A Low Mass is a simplified version of the ceremony, performed without a choir, deacon, the use of incense, or chanting by the priest.

the little clerk Garrigou, for let me tell you that the devil, that evening, had assumed the round face and uncertain features of the young sacristan, the better to lead the reverend father into temptation and make him commit the frightful sin of gluttony. So while the so-called Garrigou (hm! hm!) rang out the chimes from the seigniorial chapel, the reverend father slipped on his chasuble in the little vestry of the castle, and, his imagination already excited by Garrigou's gastronomical descriptions, he kept muttering to himself as he got into his vestments:

"Roast turkeys…goldfish…trout, so big!"

Outside, the night wind blew and spread abroad the music of the bells. Lights began to appear in the darkness on the sides of Mont Ventoux,[2] on whose summit the old towers of Trinquelage upreared their heads. The neighboring farmers and their families were on their way to the castle to hear midnight Mass. They climbed the mountain singing gayly, in groups of five or six, the father leading the way with his lantern, the women following, wrapped in great dark coats, under which the children snuggled to keep warm. In spite of the cold and the late hour of the night, all these good people walked along merrily, cheered by the thought that on coming from the Mass they would find, as usual, a great supper awaiting them down-stairs in the castle kitchen. From time to time, on the rough ascent,

---

2. A mountain in Provence, which at 1,909 m (6,263 ft) is the highest in the region outside the Maritime Alps. The poet and humanist scholar Petrarch wrote of summiting it with his brother 1336. Their ascent, made for the view alone, is often cited as an early example of mountaineering. The chateau and estate of Trinquelage are fictional.

the carriage of some lord, preceded by torch-bearers, showed its glimmering windowpanes in the moonlight; or a mule trotted along shaking its bells; or again, by the gleam of the great lanterns wrapped in mist, the farmers recognized their bailiff and hailed him as he passed:

"Good evening, good evening, Master Arnoton!"

"Good evening, good evening, my children!"

The night was clear; the stars seemed brightened by the frost; the northeast wind was nipping; and a fine sleet powdered all these cloaks without wetting them, preserving faithfully the tradition of a Christmas white with snow. On the very crest of the mountain the castle appeared as the goal, with its huge mass of towers and gables, the chapel steeple rising straight into the blue-black sky, and a crowd of little lights moving rapidly hither and thither, winking at all the windows, and looking, against the intense black of that lordly pile, like the little sparks that run through the ashes of burnt paper.

After passing the drawbridge and the postern, in order to get to the chapel one had to cross the first court, full of coaches, footmen and sedan-chairs silhouetted against the flare of the torches and the glare from the kitchens. One could hear the creaking of the turning spits, the clatter of pots, the tinkling of glassware and silver, as they were laid out for the banquet; and above it all floated a warm vapor smelling of roasted meats and the pungent herbs of elaborate sauces, which made the farmers, as well as the chaplain, the bailiff, and everybody say:

"What a wonderful midnight supper we are going to have after the Mass!"

2.

Ding-a-ling-ling ! Ding-a-ling-ling!

The midnight Mass has begun. In the chapel of the castle, which is a miniature cathedral with its intercrossed arches and oaken wainscoting up to the ceiling, all the tapestries are hung, all the tapers lighted. What a crowd of people! And what sumptuous costumes! Here, in one of the carven stalls that surround the choir, is the Sire of Trinquelage, clad in salmon-colored silk; and around him all the noble lords, his guests. Opposite them, on velvet fall-stools, kneel the old dowager marchioness, in a gown of flame-colored brocade, and the young lady of Trinquelage, wearing on her head a great tower of lace puffed and quilled according to the latest fashion of the French court. Farther down the aisle, all dressed in black, with vast pointed wigs and clean-shaven chins, sit Thomas Arnoton the bailiff and Master Ambroy the notary, two somber spots among these gaudy silks and figured damasks. Then come the fat majordomos, the pages, the outriders, the stewards, and Dame Barbe, with all her keys dangling at her side on a great keyring of fine silver. On the benches in the rear is the lower service—the butlers and maids, the farmers and their families; and last of all, back by the doors, which they half open and discreetly close again, come the cooks to take a little nip of the Mass between two sauces, and bring an odor of the Christmas supper into the bedecked church, which is warm with the light of so many tapers.

Can it be the sight of these little white caps that diverts the reverend father's attention? Is it not rather Garrigou's bell?—that fiendish little bell that tinkles away at the foot of the altar with such infernal haste and seems to say all the time:

"Hurry up! Hurry up! The sooner we've finished, the sooner we shall be at supper."

The fact is that every time this devilish little bell peals out, the chaplain forgets his Mass, and his mind wanders to the Christmas supper. Visions rise before him of the cooks running busily hither and thither, the ovens glowing like furnaces, warm vapors rising from under half-lifted lids, and through these vapors two magnificent turkeys, stuffed, crammed, mottled with truffles…Or then again, he sees long files of little pages carrying great dishes wrapped in their tempting fumes, and he is about, to enter the dining hall with them for the feast. What ecstasy! Here stands the immense table, laden and dazzling, with peacocks dressed in their feathers, pheasants spreading their bronzed wings, ruby-colored flagons, pyramids of luscious fruit amid the green foliage, and those wonderful fish that Garrigou spoke of (Garrigou, forsooth!) reclining on a bed of fennel, their pearly scales looking as if they were just from the pond, and a bunch of pungent herbs in their monsterlike nostrils. So vivid is the vision of these marvels that Dom Balaguère actually fancies all these glorious dishes are being served before him, on the very embroideries of the altar cloth, and two or three times, instead of *Dominus vobiscum*[3] he catches himself saying the *Benedicite*.[4] But except for these slight mistakes the worthy man rattled off the service conscientiously, without skipping a line or omitting a genuflection; and all went well to the end of the first Mass. For you must know that on Christmas the same officiating priest is obliged to say three Masses consecutively.

"And that's one!" said the chaplain to himself with a sigh of relief; then, without losing a second, he motioned to his clerk, or him whom he believed to be his clerk, and—

Ding-a-ling-ling! Ding-a-ling-ling!

The second Mass has begun, and with it Dom Balaguère's sin.

"Quick, quick! let us hurry!" says Garrigou's bell in its shrill, devilish voice, and this time the unfortunate priest, possessed by the demon of gluttony, pounces upon the missal and devours its pages with the avidity of his over-excited appetite. He kneels and rises frantically, barely catches the sign of the cross and the genuflections, and shortens all his gestures in order to get through sooner. He scarcely extends his arms at the Gospel, or strikes his breast at the *Confiteor*.[5] Between

3. "The Lord be with you," a traditional salutation and blessing given at the beginning of Holy Mass.
4. The Benedicite (also Benedicite, omnia opera Domini or A Song of Creation) is a hymn used in the Liturgy of the Hours. It can be used as a call for thanksgiving at Mass, but at the end rather than the beginning.
5. The Confiteor (named from its first word, Latin for "I confess" or "I

him and the clerk it is hard to tell who mumbles the faster. Verses and responses leap out and jostle each other. The words, half uttered between their teeth—for it would take too long to open their lips every time,—die out into unintelligible murmurs.

"*Oremus...ps...ps...*"[6]

"*Mea culpa...pa...pa...*"[7]

Like hurried vintagers crushing the grapes in the vats, they both splashed about in the Latin of the service, spattering it in every direction.

"*Dom...scum!*"[8] says Balaguère.

"*...Stutuo!*"[9] replies Garrigou; and all the time the accurst little bell jingles in their ears like the sleigh-bells that are put on stage-horses to make them gallop faster. You may well believe that at such speed a Low Mass is soon hurried out of the way.

"And that's two," says the chaplain, all out of breath; then, red in the face, perspiring freely, without taking time to breathe he goes tumbling down the altar steps and—

Ding-a-ling-ling! Ding-a-ling-ling!

The third Mass has begun. There are only a few steps between him and the dining hall; but alas! as the time approaches, the unfortunate Dom Balaguère's fever

---

acknowledge") is one of the prayers that can be said during the Penitential Act, a general confession of sinfulness spoken during Mass.

6. "Let us pray."

7. "My fault," words of confession spoken during the Penitential Act.

8. A careless mumbling of *Dominus vobiscum,* "The Lord be with you", ancient liturgical salutation of the Church.

9. A mumbling of the customary response by the congregation: *Et cum spíritu tuo,* "And with your spirit".

of impatience and greediness grows. His imagination waxes more vivid; the fish, the roasted turkeys, are there before him…he touches them…he—good heavens!—he breathes the perfume of the wines and the savory fumes of the dishes, and the infernal little bell calls out frantically to him:

"Hurry, hurry! Faster, faster!"

But how on earth can he go faster? —his lips barely move; he no longer pronounces his words—unless, forsooth, he chooses to cheat the good Lord and swindle him out of His Mass. And that is just what he does, the wretched man! Yielding to temptation after temptation, he begins by skipping one verse, then two; then he finds the Epistle too long, so he leaves it unfinished; he skims over the Gospel; passes the *Credo* without entering: jumps the *Pater*; salutes the preface from afar; and by leaps and bounds he plunges into eternal damnation, followed by that infamous Garrigou (*Vade retro, Satanas!*),[10] who seconds him with marvelous sympathy, holds up his chasuble,[11] turns the pages two at a time, jostles the lectern, upsets the vases, and constantly rings the little bell faster and louder.

It would be impossible to describe the bewildered expression of the congregation. Compelled to follow, mimicking the priest, through this Mass of which they cannot make out a single word, some get up while others kneel, some sit while others stand; and all the phases of this singular service are jumbled together along the benches in a confusion of varied postures.

---

10. "Get thee behind me, Satan!"
11. The outermost liturgical vestment worn by a priest celebrating Mass.

The Christmas star on its celestial road, journeying toward the little manger yonder, grows pale at seeing such a frightful confusion.

"The abbe reads too fast; one can't follow him," murmurs the old dowager marchioness, her voluminous headdress shaking wildly. Master Arnoton, with his great steel spectacles on his nose, hunts desperately in his prayerbook to find where on earth is the place. But at heart, all these good people, whose minds are equally bent upon the Christmas supper, are not at all disturbed at the idea of following Mass at such breakneck speed; and when Dom Balaguère, his face shining, faces them and cries out in a thundering voice, "*Ite, missa est*,"[12] the congregation answers with a "*Deo gratias*,"[13] so joyous, so enthusiastic, that one might believe they were already at the table for the first toast of the Christmas supper.

3.

Five minutes later, the assembled lords, with the chaplain in their midst, had taken their seats in the great hall. The castle, brilliantly illumined from top to bottom, echoed with songs and laughter; and the venerable Dom Balaguère planted his fork in a capon's wing, drowning the remorse for his sin in floods of old wine and the savory juice of meats. He ate and drank so heartily, this poor holy man, that he died in the night of

---

12. "Go, the dismissal is made," the concluding words of the Mass from the priest.

13. "Thanks be to God," the response from the congregation.

a terrible attack of indigestion, without even having time to repent. By morning he reached heaven, his head still swimming from the odors of the supper; and I leave you to imagine how he was received.

"Get thee gone from my sight, thou wretched Christian!" said the Sovereign Judge, the Master of us all. "Thy sin is great enough to wipe out the virtues of a lifetime! Ah, thou hast stolen from me a midnight Mass! Very well, then: thou shalt pay me three hundred Masses in its place, and thou shalt not enter into paradise until three hundred Christmas Masses have been celebrated in thine own chapel, in the presence of all those who sinned with thee and through thee."

And this is the true legend of Dom Balaguère, as it is told in the land of the olive-tree. The castle of Trinquelage has long ceased to exist; but the chapel stands erect on the crest of Mont Ventoux, in a clump of evergreen oaks. The wind sways its unhinged door, the grass grows over the threshold; there are nests in the angles of the altar and on the sills of the high ogive windows, whose jeweled panes have long ago disappeared. Still, it seems that every year, on Christmas night, a supernatural light wanders among the ruins; and the peasants, on their way to midnight Mass and the Christmas supper, see this specter of a chapel lighted by invisible tapers which burn in the open air, even in the wind and under the snow. You may laugh if you will, but a vinedresser of the district, named Garrigue, no doubt a descendant of Garrigou, has told me that on one particular Christmas night, being somewhat in liquor, he lost his way on the mountain somewhere near Trinquelage, and this what he saw.

…Until 11 o'clock, nothing. Everything was silent and dark. Suddenly, toward midnight, the chimes rang out from the old steeple—old, old chimes that seemed to be ringing ten leagues away. Soon lights began to tremble along the road that climbs to the castle, and vague shadows moved about. Under the portal of the chapel there were faint, footsteps, and muffled voices:

"Good evening, Master Arnoton!"

"Good evening, good evening, my children!"

When they had all gone in, the vinedresser, who was very brave, softly approached, and, looking through the broken door, beheld a singular spectacle. All those shadows that he had seen pass were now seated around the choir in the ruined nave, just as if the old benches were still there. There were fine ladies in brocades and lace head-dresses, gayly bedecked lords, peasants in flowered coats like those our grandfathers wore; all of them old, dusty, faded, weary. Every now and then some night-bird, a habitual lodger in the chapel, awakened by all these lights, would flutter about the tapers, of which the flame rose erect and vague as if it were burning behind a strip of gauze. And what amused Garrigue most was a certain gentleman with great steel spectacles, who constantly shook his huge black wig, on which perched one of those birds, its claws entangled and its wings beating wildly.

The Three Low Masses

A little old man with a childlike figure knelt in the center of the choir and frantically shook a tiny bell that had lost its clapper and its voice, while a priest clad in vestments of old gold moved hither and thither before the altar repeating orisons of which not a single syllable could be heard.

Without doubt, this was Dom Balaguère in the act of saying his third Low Mass.

The Tall Woman

by Pedro Antonio de Alarcón

February 1929 (vol. 13, no. 2)
Translated from the Spanish by Rollo Ogden

1.

"How little we really know, my friends; how little we really know!"

The speaker was Gabriel, a distinguished civil engineer of the mountain corps. He was seated under a pine-tree, near a spring, on the crest of the Guadarrama. It was only about a league and a half distant from the palace of the Escurial,[1] on the boundary line of the provinces of Madrid and Segovia. I know the place, spring, pine-tree and all, but I have forgotten its name.

---

1. The Royal Site of San Lorenzo de El Escorial is a historical residence of the King of Spain, located outside the town of San Lorenzo, about 45 kilometers (28 miles) northwest of Madrid. Built between 1563 and 1584 on the order of King Philip II, it functioned as a basilica, library, museum, university, royal palace, and hospital, among other roles.

The Tall Woman

"Let us sit down," went on Gabriel, "as that is the correct thing to do, and as our program calls for a rest here—in this pleasant and classic spot, famous for the digestive properties of that spring, and for the many lambs here devoured by our noted teachers, Don Miguel Bosch, Don Maximo Laguna, Don Augustin Pascual, and other illustrious naturalists. Sit down, and I will tell you a strange and wonderful story in proof of my thesis, which is, though you call me an obscurantist for it, that supernatural events still occur on this terra-queous globe. I mean events which you cannot gel into terms of reason, or science, or philosophy—as those 'words, words, words,' in Hamlet's phrase, are understood (or are not understood) today."

Gabriel was addressing his animated remarks to five persons of different ages. None of them was young, though only one was well along in years. Three of them were, like Gabriel, engineers; the fourth was a painter, and the fifth was a *litterateur* in a small way. In company with the speaker, who was the youngest, we had all ridden up on hired mules from the Real Sitio de San Lorenzo to spend the day botanizing among the beautiful pine groves of Pequerinos, chasing butterflies with gauze nets, catching rare beetles under the bark of the decayed pines, and eating a cold lunch out of a hamper which we had paid for on shares.

This took place in 1875. It was the height of the summer. I do not remember whether it was Saint James' day or Saint Louis'; I am inclined to think it was Saint Louis'. Whichever it was, we enjoyed a delicious coolness at that height, and the heart and brain, as well as the stomach, were there in much better working order than usual.

When the six friends were seated, Gabriel continued as follows:

"I do not think you will accuse me of being a visionary. Luckily or unluckily, I am, if you will allow me to say so, a man of the modern world. I have no superstition about me, and am as much of a Positivist as the best of them, although I include among the positive data of nature all the mysterious faculties and feelings of the soul. Well, then, apropos of supernatural, or extra-natural, phenomena, listen to what I have seen and heard, although I was not the real hero of the very strange story I am going to relate, and then tell me what explanation of an earthly, physical, or natural sort, however you may name it, can be given of so wonderful an occurrence.

"The case was as follows. But wait! Pour me out a drop, for the skin-bottle must have got cooled off by this time in that bubbling, crystalline spring, located by Providence on this piney crest for the express purpose of cooling a botanist's wine.

2.

"Well, gentlemen, I do not know whether you ever heard of an engineer of the roads corps named Telesforo X______; he died in 1860."

"No; I haven't."

"But I have."

"So have I. He was a young fellow from Andalusia, with a black mustache; he was to have married the Marquis of Moreda's daughter, but he died of jaundice."

"The very one," said Gabriel. "Well, then, my friend Telesforo, six months before his death, was still a most promising young man, as they say nowadays. He was good-looking, well-built, energetic, and had the glory of being the first one in his class to be promoted. He had already gained distinction in the practice of his profession through some fine pieces of work. Several different companies were competing for his services, and many marriageable women were also competing for him. But Telesforo, as you said, was faithful to poor Joaquina Moreda.

"As you know, it turned out that she died suddenly at the baths of Santa Agueda, at the end of the summer of 1859. I was in Pau when I received the sad news of her death, which affected me very much on account of my close friendship with Telesforo. With her I had spoken only once, in the house of her aunt, the wife of General Lopez, and I certainly thought her bluish pallor a symptom of bad health. But, however that may be, she had a distinguished manner and a great deal of grace, and was, besides, the only daughter of a title, and a title that carried some comfortable thousands with it; so I felt sure my good mathematician would be inconsolable. Consequently, as soon as I was back in Madrid, fifteen or twenty days after his loss, I went to see him very early one morning. He lived in elegant bachelor quarters in Lobo Street —I do not remember the number, but it was near the Carrera de San Jerónimo.

"The young engineer was very melancholy, although calm and apparently master of his grief. He was already at work, even at that hour, laboring with his assistants over some railroad plans or other. He was dressed in deep mourning.

"He greeted me with a long and close embrace, without so much as sighing. Then he gave some directions to his assistants about the work in hand, and afterward led me to his private office at the farther end of the house. As we were on our way there he said, in a sorrowful tone and without glancing at me:

"'I am very glad you have come. Several times I have found myself wishing you were here. A very strange thing has happened to me. Only a friend such as you are can hear of it without thinking me either a fool or crazy. I want to get an opinion about it as calm and cool as science itself.

"'Sit down,' he went on when we had reached his office, 'and do not imagine that I am going to afflict you with a description of the sorrow I am suffering—a sorrow which will last as long as I live. Why should I? You can easily picture it to yourself, little as you know of trouble. And as for being comforted, I do not wish to be, either now, or later, or ever! What I am going to speak to you about, with the requisite deliberation, going back to the very beginning of the thing, is a horrible and mysterious occurrence, which was an infernal omen of my calamity, and which has distressed me in a frightful manner.'

"'Go on,' I replied, sitting down. The fact was, 1 almost repented having entered the house, as I saw the expression of abject fear on my friend 's face.

"'Listen, then,' said he, wiping the perspiration from his forehead."

3.

"'I do not know whether it is due to some inborn fatality of imagination, or to having heard some story or other of the kind with which children are so rashly allowed to be frightened, but the fact is, that since my earliest years nothing has caused me so much horror and alarm as a woman alone, in the street, at a late hour of the night. The effect is the same whether I actually encounter her, or simply have an image of her in my mind.

"'You can testify that I was never a coward. I fought a duel once, when I had to, like any other man. Just after I had left the School of Engineers, my workmen in Despeñaperros revolted, and I fought them with stick and pistol until I made them submit. All my life long, in Jaen, in Madrid, and elsewhere, I have walked the streets at all hours, alone and un-armed, and if I have chanced to run upon suspicious-looking persons, thieves, or mere sneaking beggars, they have had to get out of my way or take to their heels. But if the person turned out to be a solitary woman, standing still or walking, and I was also alone, with no one in sight in any direction—then (laugh if you want to, but believe me) I would be all covered over with goose-flesh; vague fears would assail me; I would think about beings of the other world, about imaginary existences, and about all the superstitious stories which would make me laugh under other circumstances. I would quicken my pace, or else turn back, and would not get over my fright in the least until safe in my own house.

"'Once there I would fall a-laughing, and would be ashamed of my crazy fears. The only comfort I had was that nobody knew anything about it. Then I would dispassionately remind myself that I did not believe in goblins, witches, or ghosts, and that I had no reason whatever to be afraid of that wretched woman driven from her home at such an hour by poverty, or some crime, or accident, to whom I might better have offered help, if she needed it, or given alms. Nevertheless, the pitiable scene would be gone over again as often as a similar thing occurred—and remember that I was twenty-four years old, that I had experienced a great many adventures by night, and yet that I had never had the slightest difficulty of any sort with such solitary women in the streets after midnight. But nothing of what I have so far told you ever came to have any importance, since that irrational fear always left me as soon as I reached home, or saw anyone else in the street, and I would scarcely recall it a few minutes afterward, any more than one would recall a stupid mistake which had no result of any consequence.

The Tall Woman

"'Things were going on so, when, nearly three years ago (unhappily, I have good reason for knowing the date, it was the night of November 15-16th, 1857), I was coming home at three in the morning. As you remember, I was living then in that little house in Jardines Street, near Montera Street. I had just come, at that late hour, a bitter, cold wind blowing at the time, out of a sort of a gambling house—I tell you this, although I know it will surprize you. You know that I am not a gambler. I went into the place, deceived by an alleged friend. But the fact was, that as people began to drop in about midnight, coming from receptions or the theater, the play began to be very heavy, and one saw the gleam of gold in plenty. Then came bank-bills, and notes of hand. Little by little, I was carried away by the feverish and seductive passion, and lost all the money I had. I even went away owing a round sum, for which I had left my note behind me. In short, I ruined myself completely; and but for the legacy that came to me afterward, together with the good jobs I have had, my situation would have been extremely critical and painful.

"'So I was going home, I say, at so late an hour that night, numb with the cold, hungry, ashamed, and disgusted as you can imagine, thinking about my sick old father more than about myself. I should have to write to him for money, and this would astonish as much as it would grieve him, since he thought me in very easy circumstances. Just before reaching my street, where it crosses Peligros Street, as I was walking in front of a newly built house, I perceived something in its doorway. It was a tall, large woman, standing stiff and motionless, as if made of wood. She seemed to be about sixty years old. Her bold and malignant eyes, unshaded by eyelashes, were fixed on mine like two daggers. Her toothless mouth made a horrible grimace at me, meant to be a smile.

"'The very terror or delirium of fear which instantly overcame me gave me somehow a most acute perception, so that I could distinguish at a glance, in the two seconds it took me to pass by that repugnant vision, the slightest details of her face and dress. Let me see if I can put together my impressions in the way and form in which I received them, as they were engraved ineffaceably on my brain in the light of the street-lamp which shone luridly over that ghastly scene. But I am exciting myself too much, though there is reason enough for it, as you will see further on. Don't be concerned, however, for the state of my mind. I am not yet crazy!

"'The first thing which struck me in that *woman*, as I will call her, was her extreme height and the breadth of her bony shoulders; then, the roundness and fixity of her dry, owlish eyes, the enormous size of her protruding nose, and the great dark cavern of her mouth; finally, her dress, like that of a young woman of Avapiés[2]—the new little cotton handkerchief which she wore on her head, tied under her chin, and a diminutive fan which she carried opened in her hand, and with which, in affected modesty, she was covering the middle of her waist.

---

2. A working-class district in Madrid, now called Lavapiés. The women of the area were known for their distinctive polka-dot skirts and headscarves, a tradition continued into the present during festive occasions.

"'Nothing could be at the same time more ridiculous and more awful, move laughable and more taunting, than that little fan in those huge hands. It seemed like a make-believe scepter in the hands of such an old, hideous and bony giantess. A like effect was produced by the showy percale handkerchief adorning her face by the side of that cut-water nose, hooked and masculine; for a moment I was led to believe (or I was very glad to) that it was a man in disguise.

"'But her cynical glance and harsh smile were those of a hag, of a witch, an enchantress, a Fate, a— I know not what! There was something about her to justify fully the aversion and fright which I had been caused all my life long by women walking alone in the streets at night. One would have said that I had had a presentiment of that encounter from my cradle. One would have said that I was frightened by it instinctively, as every living being fears and divines, and scents and recognizes, its natural enemy before ever being injured by it, before ever having seen it, and solely on hearing its tread.

"'I did not dash away in a run when I saw my life's sphinx. I restrained my impulse to do so, less out of shame and manly pride than out of fear lest my very fright should reveal to her who I was, or should give her wings to follow me, to overtake me—I do not know what. Panic like that dreams of dangers which have neither form nor name.

"'My house was at the opposite end of the long and narrow street, in which I was alone, entirely alone with that mysterious phantom whom I thought able to annihilate me with a word. How should I ever get home? Oh, how anxiously I looked toward that distant Montera Street, broad and well lighted, where there are policemen to be found at all hours! I decided, finally, to get the better of my weakness; to dissemble and hide that wretched fear; not to hasten my pace, but to keep on advancing slowly, even at the cost of years of health, or life, and in this way, little by little, to go on getting nearer to my house, exerting myself to the utmost not to fall fainting on the ground before I reached it.

"'I was walking along in this way—I must have taken about twenty steps after leaving behind me the doorway where the woman with the fan was hidden, when suddenly a horrible idea came to me—horrible, yet very natural nevertheless—the idea that I would look back to see if my enemy was following me. One thing or the other I thought, with the rapidity of a flash of lightning: either my alarm has some foundation or it is madness; if it has any foundation, this woman will have started after me, will be overtaking me, and there is no hope for me on earth. But if it is madness, a mere supposition, a panic fright like any other, I will convince myself of it in the present instance, and for every case that may occur hereafter, by seeing that that poor old woman has stayed in that doorway to protect herself from the cold, or to wait till the door is opened; and thereupon I can go on to my house in perfect tranquility, and I shall have cured myself of a fancy that causes me great mortification.

"'This reasoning gone through with, I made an extraordinary effort and turned my head. Ah, Gabriel! Gabriel! how fearful it was! The tall woman had followed me with silent tread, was right over me, almost touching me with her fan, almost leaning her head on my shoulder.

"'Why was she doing it?—why, my Gabriel? Was she a thief? Was she really a man in disguise? Was she some malicious old hag who had seen that I was afraid of her? Was she a specter conjured up by my very cowardice? Was she a mocking fantasm of human self-deception?

"'I could never tell you all I thought in a single moment. If the truth must be told, I gave a scream and flew away like a child of four years who thinks he sees the boogeyman.[3] I did not stop running until I got out into Montera Street. Once there, my fear left me like magic, in spite of the fact that that street also was deserted. Then I turned my head to look back to Jardines Street. I could see down its whole length. It was lighted well enough for me to see the tail woman, if she had drawn back in any direction, and, by heaven! I could not see her, standing still, walking, or in any way! However, I was very careful not to go back into that street again. The wretch, I said to myself, has slunk into some other doorway. But she can't move without my seeing her.

---

3. El Coco or La Coca is a mythical ghost-like monster found in Iberia and many Latin American countries. The monster is said to come to the houses of disobedient children and make them disappear.

"'Just then I saw a policeman coming up Caballero de Gracia Street, and I shouted to him without stirring from my place. I told him that there was a man dressed as a woman in Jardines Street. I directed him to go round by the way of Peligros and Aduana Streets, while I would remain where I was, and in that way the fellow, who was probably a thief or murderer, could not escape us. The policeman did as I said. He went through Aduana Street, and as soon as I saw his lantern coming along Jardines Street I also went up it resolutely.

"'We soon met at about the middle of the block, without either of us having encountered a soul, although we had examined door after door.

"' "He has got into some house," said the policeman.

"' "That must be so," I replied, opening my door with the fixed purpose of moving to some other street the next day.

"'A few moments later I was in my room; I always carried my latch-key so as not to have to disturb my good José. Nevertheless, he was waiting for me that night. My misfortunes of the 15th and 16th of November were not yet ended.

"' "What has happened?" I asked him in surprize.

"' "Major Falcon was here," he replied, with evident agitation, "waiting for you from eleven till half-past two, and told me that, if you came home to sleep, you had better not undress, as he would be back at daybreak."

"'Those words left me trembling with grief and alarm, as if they had predicted my own death to me. They knew that my beloved father, at his home in Jaen, had been suffering frequent and dangerous attacks of his chronic disease. I had written to my brothers that, if there should be a sudden and fatal termination of the sickness, they were to telegraph Major Falcon, who would inform me in some suitable way. I had not the slightest doubt, therefore, that my father had died.

"'I sat down in an armchair to wait for the morning and my friend, and, with them, the news of my great misfortune. God only knows what I suffered in those two cruel hours of waiting. All the while, three distinct ideas were inseparably joined in my mind; though they seemed unlike, they took pains, as it were, to keep in a dreadful group: They were: my losses at play, my meeting with the tall woman, and the death of my revered father.

"'Precisely at 6:00 Major Falcon came into my room, and looked at me in silence. I threw myself into his arms, weeping bitterly, and he exclaimed, caressing me: "Yes, my dear fellow, weep, weep." '"

4.

"M y friend Telesforo," Gabriel went on, after having drained another glass of wine, "also rested a moment when he reached this point, and then he proceeded as follows:

"'If my story ended here, perhaps you would not find anything extraordinary or supernatural in it. You would say to me the same thing that men of good judgment said to me at that time: that everyone who has a lively imagination is subject to some impulse of fear or other; that mine came from belated, solitary women, and that the old creature of Jardines Street was only some homeless waif who was going to beg of me when I screamed and ran.

"'For my part, I tried to believe that it was so. I even came to believe it at the end of several months. Still, I would have given years of my life to be sure that I was not again to encounter the tall woman. But, today, I would give every drop of my blood to be able to meet her again.'

"'What for?'

"'To kill her on the spot.'

"'I do not understand you.'

"'You will understand me when I tell you that I did meet her again, three weeks ago, a few hours before I had the fatal news of my poor Joaquina's death.'

"'Tell me about it! Tell me about it!'

"'There is little more to tell. It was five o'clock in the morning, it was not yet fully light, though the dawn was visible from the streets looking toward the east. The street lamps had just been put out, and the policemen had withdrawn. As I was going through Prado Street, so as to get to the other end of Lobo Street, the dreadful woman crossed in front of me. She did not look at me, and I thought she had not seen me.

"'She wore the same dress and carried the same fan as three years before. My trepidation and alarm were greater than ever. I ran rapidly across Prado Street as soon as she had passed, although I did not take my eyes off her, so as to make sure that she did not look back, and, when I had reached the other end of Lobo Street, I panted as if 1 had just swum an impetuous stream. Then I pressed on with fresh speed toward home, filled now with gladness rather than fear, for I thought that the hateful witch had been conquered and shorn of her power, from the very fact that I had been so near her and yet that she a not seen me.

"'But, soon, and when I had almost reached this house, a rush of fear swept over me, in the thought that the crafty old hag had seen and recognized me, that she had made a pretense of not knowing me so as to let me get into Lobo Street, where it was still rather dark, and where she might set upon me in safety, that she would follow me, that she was already over me.

"'Upon this, I looked around and there she was! There at my shoulder, almost touching me with her clothes, gazing at me with her horrible little eyes, displaying the gloomy cavern of her mouth, fanning herself in a mocking manner, as if to make fun of my childish alarm.

"'I passed from dread to the most furious anger, to savage and desperate rage. I dashed at the heavy old creature. I flung her against the wall. I put my hand to her throat. I felt of her face, her breast, the straggling locks of her gray hair, until I was thoroughly convinced that she was a human being—a woman.

"'Meanwhile she had uttered a howl which was hoarse and piercing at the same time. It seemed false and feigned to me, like the hypocritical expression of a fear which she did not really feel. Immediately afterward she exclaimed, making believe cry, though she was not crying, but looking at me with her hyena eyes: "Why have you picked a quarrel with me?"

"'This remark increased my fright and weakened my wrath.

"' "Then you remember," I cried, "that you have seen me somewhere else."

"' "I should say so, my dear," she replied, mockingly. "Saint Eugene's night, in Jardines Street, three years ago."

"'My very marrow was chilled.

"' "But who are you?" I asked, without letting go of her. "Why do you follow me? What business have you with me?"

"' "I am a poor weak woman," she answered, with a devilish leer. "You hate me, and you are afraid of me without any reason. If not, tell me, good sir, why you were so frightened the first time you saw me."

"' "Because I have loathed you ever since I was born. Because you are the evil spirit of my life."

"' "It seems, then, that you have known me for a long time. Well, look, my son, so have I known you."

"' "You have known me? How long ?"

"' "Since before you were born! And when I saw you pass by me, three years ago, I said to myself, *that's the one.*"

"' "But what am I to you? What are you to me?"

"' "The devil!" replied the hag, spitting full in my face, freeing herself from my grasp, and running away with amazing swiftness. She held her skirts higher than her knees, and her feet did not make the slightest noise as they touched the ground.

"'It was madness to try to catch her. Besides, people were already passing through the Carrera de San Jerónimo, and in Prado Street, too. It was broad daylight. The tall woman kept on running, or flying, as far as Huertas Street, which was now lighted up by the sun. There she stopped to look back at me. She waved her closed fan at me once or twice, threateningly, and then disappeared around a corner.

"'Wait a little longer, Gabriel. Do not yet pronounce judgment in this case, where my life and soul are concerned. Listen to me two minutes longer.

"'When I entered my house, I met Colonel Falcon, who had just come to tell me that my Joaquina, my betrothed, all my hope and happiness and joy on earth, had died the day before in Santa Agueda. The unfortunate father had telegraphed Falcon to tell me—me, who should have divined it an hour before, when I met the evil spirit of my life! Don't you understand, now, that I must kill that born enemy of my happiness, that vile old hag, who is the living mockery of my destiny?

"'But why do I say kill? Is she a woman? Is she a human being? Why have I had a presentiment of her ever since I was born? Why did she recognize me when she first saw me? Why do I never see her except when some great calamity has befallen me? Is she Satan? Is she Death? Is she Life? Is she Antichrist? Who is she? What is she?'"

5.

"I will spare you, my dear friends," continued Gabriel, "the arguments and remarks which I used to see if I could not calm Telesforo, for they are the same, precisely the same, which you are preparing now to advance to prove that there is nothing supernatural or superhuman in my story. You will even go further; you will say that my friend was half crazy; that he always was so; that, at least, he suffered from that moral disease which some call 'panic terror,' and others 'emotional insanity;' that, even granting the truth of what I have related about the tall woman, it must all be referred to chance coincidences of dates and events; and, finally, that the poor old creature could also have been crazy, or a thief, or a beggar, or a procuress—as the hero of my story said to himself in a lucid interval."

"A very proper supposition!" exclaimed Gabriel's comrades; "that is just what we were going to say."

"Well, listen a few minutes longer, and you will see that I was mistaken at the time, as you are mistaken now. The one who unfortunately made no mistake was Telesforo. It is much easier to speak the word 'insanity' than to find an explanation for somethings that happen on the earth."

"Speak, speak!"

"I am going to; and this time, as it is the last, I will pick up the thread of my story without first drinking a glass of wine."

6.

"**A** few days after that conversation with Telesforo I was sent to the province of Albacete in my capacity as engineer of the mountain corps. Not many weeks had passed before I learned, from a contractor for public works, that my unhappy friend had been attacked by a dreadful form of jaundice; it had turned him entirely green, and he reclined in an armchair without working or wishing to see anybody, weeping night and day in inconsolable grief.

"This made me understand why he had not answered my letters. I had to resort to Colonel Falcon as a source of news of him, and all the while the reports kept getting more unfavorable and gloomy.

"After an absence of five months I returned to Madrid the same day that the telegraph brought the news of the Battle of Tetuán.[4] I remember it as if it were yesterday. That night I bought the indispensable *Correspondencia de España*, and the first thing I read in it was the notice of Telesforo's death. His friends were invited to the funeral the following morning.

"You will be sure that I was present. As we arrived at the San Luis cemetery, whither I rode in one of the carriages nearest the hearse, my attention was called to a peasant woman. She was old and

---

4. The Battle of Tetuán was fought on 4 to 6 February 1860, near Tetuán, Morocco, between a Spanish army sent to North Africa and the tribal levies which at the time made up the Moroccan Army. The battle was part of the Spanish-Moroccan War of 1859–1860.

very tall. She was laughing sacrilegiously as she saw them taking out the coffin. Then she placed herself in front of the pall-bearers in a triumphant attitude and pointed out to them with a very small fan the passageway they were to take to reach the open and waiting grave.

"At the first glance I perceived, with amazement and alarm, that she was Telesforo's implacable enemy. She was just as he had described her to me—with her enormous nose, her devilish eyes, her awful mouth, her percale handkerchief, and that diminutive fan which seemed in her hands the scepter of indecency and mockery.

"She immediately observed that I was looking at her, and fixed her gaze upon me in a peculiar manner, as if recognizing me, as if letting me know that she recognized me, as if acquainted with the fact that the dead man had told me about the scenes in Jardines Street and Lobo Street, as if defying me, as if declaring me the inheritor of the hate which she had cherished for my unfortunate friend.

"I confess that at the time my fright was greater than my wonder at those new coincidences and accidents. It seemed evident to me that some supernatural relation, antecedent to earthly life, had existed between the mysterious old woman and Telesforo. But for the time being my sole concern was about my own life, my own soul, my own happiness —all of which would be exposed to the greatest peril if I should really inherit such a curse.

"The tall woman began to laugh. She pointed at me contemptuously with the fan, as if she had read my thoughts and were publicly exposing my cowardice. I had to lean on a friend's arm to keep myself from falling. Then she made a pitying or disdainful gesture, turned on her heels, and went into the cemetery. Her head was turned toward me. She fanned herself and nodded to me at the same time. She sidled along among the graves with an indescribable, infernal coquetry until at last she disappeared forever in that labyrinth of tombs.

"I say forever, since fifteen years have passed and I have never seen her again. If she was a human being, she must have died before this; if she was not, I rest in the conviction that she despised me too much to meddle with me.

"Now, then, bring on your theories! Give me your opinion about these strange events. Do you still regard them as entirely natural?"

Lazarus

by Leonid Andreyev

March 1927 (vol. 9, no. 3)
Translated from the Russian by Anonymous

1.

When Lazarus left the grave, where for three days and three nights he had been under the enigmatical sway of death, and returned alive to his dwelling, for a long time no one noticed in him those sinister things which made his name a terror as time went on. Gladdened by the sight of him who had been returned to life, those near to him made much of him, and satisfied their burning desire to serve him, in solicitude for his food and drink and garments. They dressed him gorgeously, and when, like a bridegroom in his bridal clothes, he sat again among them at the table and ate and drank, they wept with tenderness. And they summoned the neighbors to look at him who had risen miraculously from the dead. These came and shared the joy of the hosts. Strangers from far-off towns and hamlets came and adored the miracle in tempestuous words. The house of Mary and Martha was like a beehive.

Whatever was found new in Lazarus' face and gestures was thought to be some trace of a grave illness and of the shocks recently experienced. Evidently the destruction wrought by death on the corpse was only arrested by the miraculous power, but its effects were still apparent; and what death had succeeded in doing with Lazarus' face and body was like an artist's unfinished sketch seen under thin glass. On Lazarus' temples, under his eyes, and in the hollows of his cheeks, lay a deep and cadaverous blueness; cadaverously blue also were his long fingers, and around his fingernails, grown long in the grave, the blue had become purple and dark. On his lips, swollen in the grave, the skin had burst in places, and thin reddish cracks were formed, shining as though covered with transparent mica. And he had grown stout. His body, puffed up in the grave, retained its monstrous size and showed those frightful swellings in which one sensed the presence of the rank liquid of decomposition. But the heavy corpselike odor, which penetrated Lazarus' grave-clothes and, it seemed, his very body, soon entirely disappeared, the blue spots on his face and hands grew paler, and the reddish cracks closed up, although they never disappeared altogether. That is how Lazarus looked when he appeared before people, in his second life, but his face looked natural to those who had seen him in the coffin.

In addition to the changes in his appearance, Lazarus' temper seemed to have undergone a transformation, but this circumstance startled no one and attracted no attention. Before his death Lazarus had always been cheerful and carefree, fond of laughter and a merry joke. It was because of this brightness and cheerfulness, with not a touch of malice and darkness, that the Master had grown so fond of him. But now Lazarus had grown grave and taciturn, he never jested, nor responded with laughter to other people's jokes; and the words which he very infrequently uttered were the plainest, the most ordinary, and necessary words, as deprived of depth and significance as those sounds with which animals express pain and pleasure, thirst and hunger. They were the words that one can say all one's life, and yet they give no indication of what pains and gladdens the depths of the soul.

Thus, with the face of a corpse which for three days had been under the heavy sway of death, dark and taciturn, already appallingly transformed, but still unrecognized by anyone in his new self, he was sitting at the feast-table among friends and relatives, and his gorgeous nuptial garments glittered with yellow gold and bloody scarlet. Broad waves of jubilation, now soft, now tempestuously sonorous surged around him; warm glances of love were reaching out for his face, still cold with the coldness of the grave; and a friend's warm palm caressed his blue, heavy hand. Music played—the tympanum and the pipe, the cithara and the harp. It was as though bees hummed, grasshoppers chirped and birds warbled over the happy house of Mary and Martha.

2.

One of the guests incautiously lifted the veil. By a thoughtless word he broke the serene charm and uncovered the truth in all its naked ugliness. Ere the thought formed itself in his mind, his lips uttered with a smile: "Why do you not tell us what happened yonder?"

All grew silent, startled by the question. It was as if it occurred to them only now that for three days Lazarus had been dead, and they looked at him, anxiously awaiting his answer. But Lazarus kept silence.

"You do not wish to tell us," wondered the man; "is it so terrible yonder?"

And again, his thought came after his words. Had it been otherwise, he would not have asked this question, which at that very moment oppressed his heart with its insufferable horror. Uneasiness seized all present, and with a feeling of heavy weariness they awaited Lazarus' words, but he was sternly and coldly silent, and his eyes were lowered. As if for the first time, they noticed the frightful blueness of his face and his repulsive obesity. On the table, as if forgotten by Lazarus, rested his bluish-purple wrist, and to this all eyes turned, as if it were from it that the awaited answer was to come. The musicians were still playing, but now the silence reached them too, and even as water extinguishes scattered embers, so were their merry tunes extinguished in the silence. The pipe grew silent; the voices of the sonorous tympanum and the murmuring harp died away; and as if the strings had burst, the cithara answered with a tremulous, broken note. Silence.

"You do not wish to say?" repeated the guest, unable to check his chattering tongue. But the stillness remained unbroken, and the bluish-purple hand rested motionless. And then he stirred slightly and everyone felt relieved. He lifted up his eyes, and lo! straightway embracing everything in one heavy glance, fraught with weariness and horror, he looked at them—Lazarus who had arisen from the dead.

It was the third day since Lazarus had left the grave. Ever since then many had experienced the pernicious power of his eye, but neither those who were crushed by it forever, nor those who found the strength to resist in it the primordial sources of life, which is as mysterious as death, never could they explain the horror which lay motionless in the depth of his black pupils. Lazarus looked calmly and simply with no desire to conceal anything, but also with no intention to say anything; he looked coldly, as one who is infinitely indifferent to those alive. Many carefree people came close to him without noticing him, and only later did they learn with astonishment and fear who that calm stout man was that walked slowly by, almost touching them with his gorgeous and dazzling garments. The sun did not cease shining, when he was looking, nor did the fountain hush its murmur, and the sky overhead remained cloudless and blue. But the man under the spell of his enigmatical look heard no more the fountain and saw not the sky overhead. Sometimes he wept bitterly, sometimes he tore his hair and in frenzy called for help; but more often it came to pass that apathetically and quietly he began to die, and so he anguished many years, before everybody's eyes, wasted away, colorless, flabby, dull, like a tree silently drying up in a stony soil. And of those who gazed at him, the one who wept madly sometimes felt again the stir of life; the others never.

"So you do not wish to tell us what you have seen yonder?" repeated the man. But now his voice was impassive and dull, and deadly gray weariness showed in Lazarus' eyes. And deadly gray weariness covered like dust all the faces, and with dull amazement the guests stared at each other and did not understand wherefore they had gathered here and sat at the rich table. The talk ceased. They thought it was time to go home, but could not overcome the weariness which glued their muscles, and they kept on sitting there, yet apart and torn away from each other, like pale fires scattered over a dark field.

But the musicians were paid to play, and again they took their instruments, and again tunes full of studied mirth and studied sorrow began to flow and to rise. They unfolded the customary melody, but the guests hearkened in dull amazement. Already they knew not why it is necessary, and why it is well, that people should pluck strings, inflate their cheeks, blow in thin pipes, and produce a bizarre, many-voiced noise.

"What bad music!" said someone. The musicians took offense and left. Following them, the guests left one after another, for night was already come. And when placid darkness encircled them and they began to breathe with more ease, suddenly Lazarus' image loomed up before each one in formidable radiance: the blue face of a corpse, grave-clothes gorgeous and resplendent, a cold look, in the depths of which lay motionless an unknown horror. As though petrified, they were standing far apart, and darkness enveloped them, but in the darkness blazed brighter and brighter the supernatural vision of him who for three days had been under the enigmatical sway of death. For three days had he been dead: thrice had the sun risen and set, but he had been dead; children had played, streams murmured over pebbles, the wayfarer had lifted up hot dust in the highroad, but he had been dead. And now he is again among them, touches them, looks at them, and through the black disks of his pupils, as through darkened glass, stares the unknowable Yonder.

3.

No one was taking care of Lazarus, for no friends, no relatives were left to him, and the great desert, which encircled the holy city, came near the very threshold of his dwelling. And the desert entered his house, and stretched on his couch, like a wife, and extinguished the fires. No one was taking care of Lazarus. One after the other, his sisters—Mary and Martha—forsook him. For a long while Martha was loath to abandon him, for she knew not who would feed him and pity him. She wept and prayed. But one night, when the wind was roaming in the desert and with a hissing sound the cypresses were bending over the roof, she dressed noiselessly, and secretly left the house. Lazarus probably heard the door slam; it banged against the side-post under the gusts of the desert wind, but he did not rise to go out and look at her that was abandoning him. All the night long the cypresses hissed over his head and plaintively thumped the door, letting in the cold, greedy desert.

Like a leper he was shunned by everyone, and it was proposed to tie a bell to his neck, as is done with lepers, to warn people against sudden meetings. But someone remarked, growing frightfully pale, that it would be too horrible if by night the moaning of Lazarus' bell were suddenly heard under the windows, and so the project was abandoned.

And since he did not take care of himself, he would probably have starved to death, had not the neighbors brought him food in fear of something that they sensed but vaguely. The food was brought to him by children; they were not afraid of Lazarus, nor did they mock him with naive cruelty, as children are wont to do with the wretched and miserable. They were indifferent to him, and Lazarus answered them with the same coldness; he had no desire to caress the black little curls, and to look into their innocent shining eyes. Given to Time and to the desert, his house was crumbling down, and long since had his famishing goats wandered away to the neighboring pastures. His bridal garments became threadbare. Ever since that happy day when the musicians played, he had worn them unaware of the difference of the new and the worn. The bright colors grew dull and faded; vicious dogs and the sharp thorns of the desert turned the tender fabric into rags.

By day, when the merciless sun slew all things alive, and even scorpions sought shelter under stones and writhed there in a mad desire to sting, he sat motionless under the sun's rays, his blue face and the uncouth, bushy beard lifted up, bathing in the fiery flood.

When people still talked to him, he was once asked: "Poor Lazarus, does it please you to sit thus and to stare at the sun?"

And he had answered: "Yes, it does."

So strong, it seemed, was the cold of his three days' grave, so deep the darkness, that there was no heat on earth to warm Lazarus, nor a splendor that could brighten the darkness of his eyes. That is what came to the mind of those who spoke to Lazarus, and with a sigh they left him.

And when the scarlet, flattened globe would lower, Lazarus would set out for the desert and walk straight toward the sun, as if striving to reach it. He always walked straight toward the sun, and those who tried to follow him and to spy upon what he was doing at night in the desert, retained in their memory the black silhouette of a tall stout man against the red background of an enormous flattened disk. Night pursued them with her horrors, and so they did not learn of Lazarus' doings in the desert, but the vision of the black on red was forever branded on their brains. Just as a beast with a splinter in its eye furiously rubs its muzzle with its paws, so they too foolishly rubbed their eyes, but what Lazarus had given was indelible, and Death alone could efface it.

But there were people who lived far away, who never saw Lazarus and knew of him only by report. With daring curiosity, which is stronger than fear and feeds-upon it, with hidden mockery, they would come to Lazarus who was sitting in the sun and enter into conversation with him. By this time Lazarus' appearance had changed for the better and was not so terrible. The first minute they snapped their fingers and thought of how stupid the inhabitants of the holy city were; but when the short talk was over and they started homeward, their looks were such that the inhabitants of the holy city recognized them at once and said: "Look, there is one more fool on whom Lazarus has set his eye;" and they shook their heads regretfully, and lifted up their arms.

There came brave, intrepid warriors, with tinkling weapons; happy youths came with laughter and song; busy tradesmen, jingling their money, ran in for a moment, and haughty priests leaned their crosiers against Lazarus' door, and they were all strangely changed, as they came back. The same terrible shadow swooped down upon their souls and gave a new appearance to the old familiar world.

Those who still had the desire to speak, expressed their feelings thus:

"All things tangible and visible grew hollow, light and transparent, similar to lightsome shadows in the darkness of night;

"For that great darkness, which holds the whole cosmos, was dispersed neither by the sun nor by the moon and the stars, but like an immense black shroud enveloped the earth and like a mother embraced it;

"It penetrated all the bodies, iron and stone, and the particles of the bodies, having lost their ties, grew lonely; and it penetrated into the depth of the particles, and the particles of particles became lonely;

"For that great void, which encircles the cosmos, was not filled by things visible, neither by the sun, nor by the moon and the stars, but reigned unrestrained, penetrating everywhere, severing body from body, particle from particle;

"In the void, hollow trees spread hollow roots threatening a fantastic fall; temples, palaces, and houses loomed up and they were hollow; and in the void men moved about restlessly, but they were light and hollow like shadows;

"For time was no more, and the beginning of all things came near their end: the building was still being built, and builders were still hammering away, and its ruins were already seen and the void in its place; the man was still being born, but already funeral candles were burning at his head, and now they were extinguished, and there was the void in place of the man and of the funeral candles;

"And wrapped by void and darkness the man in despair trembled in the face of the horror of the infinite."

Thus spake the men who had still a desire to speak. But, surely, much more could those have told who wished not to speak, and died in silence.

4.

At that time there lived in Rome a renowned sculptor. In clay, marble and bronze he wrought bodies of gods and men, and such was their beauty that people called them immortal. But he himself was discontented and asserted that there was something even more beautiful, that he could not embody either in marble or in bronze. "I have not yet gathered the glimmers of the moon, nor have I my fill of sunshine," he was wont to say, "and there is no soul in my marble, no life in my beautiful bronze." And when on moonlight nights he slowly walked along the road, crossing the black shadows of cypresses, his white tunic glittering in the moonshine, those who met him would laugh in a friendly way and say:

"Are you going to gather moonshine, Aurelius? Why then did you not fetch baskets?"

And he would answer, laughing and pointing to his eyes:

"Here are the baskets wherein I gather the sheen of the moon and the glimmer of the sun."

And so it was: the moon glimmered in his eyes and the sun sparkled therein. But he could not translate them into marble, and therein lay the serene tragedy of his life. He was descended from an ancient patrician race, had a good wife and children, and suffered from no want.

When the obscure rumor about Lazarus reached him, he consulted his wife and friends and undertook the far journey to Judea to see him who had miraculously risen from the dead. He was somewhat weary in those days and he hoped that the road would sharpen his blunted senses.

What was said of Lazarus did not frighten him: he had pondered much over Death, did not like it, but he disliked also those who confused it with life. "In this life are life and beauty," thought he; "beyond is Death, and enigmatical; and there is no better thing for a man to do than to delight in life and in the beauty of all things living." He had even a vainglorious desire to convince Lazarus of the truth of his own view and restore his soul to life, as his body had been restored. This seemed so much easier because the rumors, shy and strange, did not render the whole truth about Lazarus and but vaguely warned against something frightful.

Lazarus had just risen from the stone in order to follow the sun which was setting in the desert, when a rich Roman, attended by an armed slave, approached him and addressed him in a sonorous voice: "Lazarus!"

Lazarus

And Lazarus beheld a superb face, lit with glory, and arrayed in fine clothes, and precious stones sparkling in the sun. The red light lent to the Roman's face and head the appearance of gleaming bronze: that also Lazarus noticed. He resumed obediently his place and lowered his weary eyes.

"Yes, you are ugly, my poor Lazarus," quietly said the Roman, playing with his golden chain; "you are even horrible, my poor friend; and Death was not lazy that day when you fell so heedlessly into his hands. But you are stout, and, as the great Caesar used to say, fat people are not ill-tempered; to tell the truth, I don't understand why men fear you. Permit me to spend the night in your house; the hour is late, and I have no shelter."

Never had anyone asked Lazarus' hospitality.

"I have no bed," said he.

"I am somewhat of a soldier and I can sleep sitting," the Roman answered. "We shall build a fire."

"I have no fire."

"Then we shall have our talk in the darkness, like two friends. I think you will find a bottle of wine."

"I have no wine."

The Roman laughed.

"Now I see why you are so somber and dislike your second life. No wine! Why, then we shall do without it: there are words that make the head go round better than the Falernian."[1]

---

1. Falernian was a strong white wine popular in the classical Roman period, produced from Aglianico grapes on the slopes of Mount Falernus (now Monte Massico) near the border of Latium and Campania. The wine

By a sign he dismissed the slave, and they remained alone. And again, the sculptor started speaking, but it was as if, together with the setting sun, life had left his words; and they grew pale and hollow, as if they staggered on unsteady feet, as if they slipped and fell down, drunk with the heavy lees of weariness and despair. And black chasms grew up between the words, like far-off hints of the great void and the great darkness.

"Now I am your guest, and you will not be unkind to me, Lazarus!" said he. "Hospitality is the duty even of those who for three days were dead. Three days, I was told, you rested in the grave. There it must be cold...and thence comes your ill habit of going without fire and wine. As to me, I like fire; it grows dark here so rapidly...The lines of your eyebrows and forehead are quite, quite interesting: they are like ruins of strange palaces, buried in ashes after an earthquake. But why do you wear such ugly and queer garments? I have seen bridegrooms in your country, and they wear such clothes—are they not funny?—and terrible?... But are you a bridegroom?"

The sun had already disappeared, a monstrous black shadow came running from the east, it was as if gigantic bare feet began rumbling on the sand, and the wind sent a cold wave along the backbone.

"In the darkness you seem still larger, Lazarus, as if you have grown stouter in these moments. Do you feed on darkness, Lazarus? I would fain have a little fire—at least a little fire, a little fire. I feel somewhat chilly, your nights are so barbarously cold. Were it not so dark,

______

was celebrated by the poets Catullus and Horace among many others.

I should say that you were looking at me, Lazarus. Yes, it seems to me you are looking…Why, you are looking at me, I feel it—but there you are smiling."

Night came, and filled the air with heavy blackness.

"How well it will be, when the sun will rise tomorrow anew…I am a great sculptor, you know; that is how my friends call me. I create. Yes, that is the word… but I need daylight. I give life to the cold marble, I melt sonorous bronze in fire, in bright hot fire…Why did you touch me with your hand?"

"Come," said Lazarus. "You are my guest."

They went to the house. And a long night enveloped the earth.

The slave, seeing that his master did not come, went to seek him, when the sun was already high in the sky. And he beheld his master side by side with Lazarus: in profound silence they were sitting right under the dazzling and scorching rays of the sun and looking upward. The slave began to weep and cried out: "My master, what has befallen you, master?"

The very same day the sculptor left for Rome. On the way Aurelius was pensive and taciturn, staring attentively at everything—the men, the ship, the sea, as if trying to retain something. On the high sea a storm burst upon them, and all through it Aurelius stayed on the deck and eagerly scanned the seas looming near and sinking with a dull boom.

At home his friends were frightened at the change which had taken place in Aurelius, but he calmed them, saying meaningly: "I have found it."

And without changing the dusty clothes he wore on his journey, he fell to work, and the marble obediently resounded under his sonorous hammer. Long and eagerly, he worked, admitting no one, until one morning he announced that the work was ready and ordered his friends to be summoned, severe critics and connoisseurs of art. And to meet them he put on bright and gorgeous garments, that glittered with yellow gold—and scarlet byssus.

"Here is my work," said he thoughtfully.

His friends glanced, and a shadow of profound sorrow covered their faces. It was something monstrous, deprived of all the lines and shapes familiar to the eye, but not without a hint at some new, strange image.

On a thin, crooked twig, or rather on an ugly likeness of a twig, rested askew a blind, ugly, shapeless, outspread mass of something utterly and inconceivably distorted, a mad heap of wild and bizarre fragments, all feebly and vainly striving to part from one another. And, as if by chance, beneath one of the wildly-rent salients a butterfly was chiseled with divine skill, all airy loveliness, delicacy, and beauty, with transparent wings, which seemed to tremble with an impotent desire to take flight.

"Wherefore this wonderful butterfly, Aurelius?" said somebody falteringly.

"I know not," was the sculptor's answer.

But it was necessary to tell the truth, and one of his friends who loved him best said firmly: "This is ugly, my poor friend. It must be destroyed. Give me the hammer."

And with two strokes he broke the monstrous mass into pieces, leaving only the infinitely delicate butterfly untouched.

From that time on Aurelius created nothing. With profound indifference he looked at marble and bronze, and on his former divine works, where everlasting beauty rested. With the purpose of arousing his former fervent passion for work and awakening his deadened soul, his friends took him to see other artists' beautiful works, but he remained indifferent as before, and the smile did not warm up his tightened lips. And only after listening to lengthy talks about beauty, he would retort wearily and indolently: "But all this is a lie."

By day, when the sun was shining, he went into his magnificent, skillfully built garden, and having found a place without shadow, he exposed his bare head to the glare and heat. Red and white butterflies fluttered around; from the crooked lips of a drunken satyr, water streamed down with a splash into a marble cistern, but he sat motionless and silent, like a pallid reflection of him who, in the far-off distance, at the very gates of the stony desert, sat under the fiery sun.

5.

And now it came to pass that the great, deified Augustus himself summoned Lazarus. The imperial messengers dressed him gorgeously, in solemn nuptial clothes, as if Time had legalized them, and he was to remain until his very death the bridegroom of an unknown bride. It was as if an old, rotting coffin had been gilded and furnished with new, gay tassels. And men, all in trim and bright attire, rode after him, as if in bridal procession indeed, and those foremost trumpeted loudly, bidding people to clear the way for the emperor's messengers. But Lazarus' way was deserted: his native land cursed the hateful name of him who had miraculously risen from the dead, and people scattered at the very news of his appalling approach. The solitary voice of the brass trumpets sounded in the motionless air, and the wilderness alone responded with its languid echo.

Then Lazarus went by sea. And his was the most magnificently arrayed and the most mournful ship that ever mirrored itself in the azure waves of the Mediterranean Sea. Many were the travelers aboard, but like a tomb was the ship, all silence and stillness, and the despairing water sobbed at the steep, proudly curved prow. All alone sat Lazarus exposing his head to the blaze of the sun, silently listening to the murmur and splash of the wavelets, and afar seamen and messengers were sitting, a vague group of weary shadows. Had the thunder burst and the wind attacked the red sails, the ships would probably have perished, for none of those aboard had either the will or the strength to struggle for life. With a supreme effort some mariners would reach the board and eagerly scan the blue, transparent deep, hoping to see a naiad's pink shoulder flash in the hollow of an azure wave, or a drunken gay centaur dash along and in frenzy splash the wave with his hoof. But the sea was like a wilderness, and the deep was dumb and deserted.

With utter indifference Lazarus set his feet on the street of the eternal city, as if all her wealth, all the magnificence of her palaces built by giants, all the resplendence, beauty, and music of her refined life were but the echo of the wind in the wilderness, the reflection of the desert quicksand. Chariots were dashing, and along the streets were moving crowds of strong, fair, proud builders of the eternal city and haughty participants in her life; a song sounded; fountains and women laughed a pearly laughter; drunken philosophers harangued, and the sober listened to them with a smile; hoofs struck the stone pavements. And surrounded by cheerful noise, a stout, heavy man was moving, a cold spot of silence and despair, and on his way, he sowed disgust, anger, and vague, gnawing weariness. Who dares to be sad in Rome? the citizens wondered indignantly, and frowned. In two days, the entire city already knew all about him who had miraculously risen from the dead, and shunned him shyly.

But some daring people there were, who wanted to test their strength, and Lazarus obeyed their imprudent summons. Kept busy by state affairs, the Emperor constantly delayed the reception, and seven days did he who had risen from the dead go about visiting others.

And Lazarus came to a cheerful Epicurean, and the host met him with laughter: "Drink, Lazarus, drink!" he shouted. "Would not Augustus laugh to see you drunk?"

And half-naked drunken women laughed, and rose petals fell on Lazarus' blue hands. But then the Epicurean looked into Lazarus' eyes, and his gayety ended forever. Drunkard remained he for the rest of his life; never did he drink, yet forever was he drunk. But instead of the gay revelry which wine brings with it, frightful dreams began to haunt him, the sole food of his stricken spirit. Day and night he lived in the poisonous vapors of his nightmares, and Death itself was not more frightful than its raving, monstrous forerunners.

And Lazarus came to a youth and his beloved, who loved each other and were most beautiful in their passions. Proudly and strongly embracing his love, the youth said with serene regret: "Look at us, Lazarus, and share our joy. Is there anything stronger than love?" And Lazarus looked. And for the rest of their life, they kept on loving each other, but their passion grew gloomy and joyless, like those funeral cypresses whose roots feed on the decay of the graves and whose black summits in a still evening hour seek in vain to reach the sky. Thrown by the unknown forces of life into each other's embraces, they mingled tears with kisses, voluptuous pleasures with pain, and they felt themselves doubly slaves, obedient slaves to life, and patient servants of the silent Nothingness. Ever united, ever severed, they blazed like sparks and like sparks lost themselves in the boundless Dark.

And Lazarus came to a haughty sage, and the sage said to him: "I know all the horrors you can reveal to me. Is there anything you can frighten me with?" But before long the sage felt that the knowledge of horror was far from being the horror itself, and that the vision of Death was not Death. And he felt that wisdom and folly are equal before the face of Infinity, for infinity knows them not. And it vanished, the dividing-line between knowledge and ignorance, truth and falsehood, top and bottom, and the shapeless thought hung suspended in the void. Then the sage clutched his gray head and cried out frantically: "I cannot think! I cannot think!"

Thus under the indifferent glance for him, who miraculously had risen from the dead, perished everything that asserts life, its significance and joys. And it was suggested that it was dangerous to let him see the emperor, that it was better to kill him, and having buried him secretly, to tell the emperor that he had disappeared no one knew whither. Already swords were being whetted and youths devoted to the public welfare prepared for the murder, when Augustus ordered Lazarus to be brought before him next morning, thus destroying the cruel plans.

If there was no way of getting rid of Lazarus, at least it was possible to soften the terrible impression his face produced. With this in view, skillful painters, barbers, and artists were summoned, and all night long they were busy over Lazarus' head. They cropped his beard, curled it, and gave it a tidy, agreeable appearance. By means of paints, they concealed the corpselike blueness of his hands and face. Repulsive were the wrinkles of suffering that furrowed his old face, and they were puttied, painted, and smoothed; then, over the smooth background, wrinkles of good-tempered laughter and pleasant, carefree mirth were skillfully painted with fine brushes.

Lazarus submitted indifferently to everything that was done to him. Soon he was turned into a becomingly stout, venerable old man, into a quiet and kind grandfather of numerous offspring. It seemed that the smile, with which only a while ago he was spinning funny yarns, was still lingering on his lips, and that in the corner of his eye serene tenderness was hiding, the companion of old age. But people did not dare change his nuptial garments, and they could not change his eyes, two dark and frightful glasses through which the unknowable Yonder looked at men.

6.

Lazarus was not moved by the magnificence of the imperial palace. It was as if he saw no difference between the crumbling house, closely pressed by the desert, and the stone palace, solid and fair, and indifferently he passed into it. The hard marble of the floors under his feet grew similar to the quicksand of the desert, and the multitude of richly dressed and haughty men became like void air under his glance. No one looked into his face, as Lazarus passed by, fearing to fall under the appalling influence of his eyes; but when the sound of his heavy footsteps had sufficiently died down, the courtiers raised their heads and with fearful curiosity examined the figure of a stout, tall, slightly bent old man, who was slowly penetrating into the very heart of the imperial palace. Were Death itself passing, it would be faced with no greater fear: for until then the dead alone knew Death, and those alive knew Life only—and there was no bridge between them. But this extraordinary man, although alive, knew Death, and enigmatical, appalling, was his cursed knowledge. "Woe," people thought; "he will take the life of our great, deified Augustus;" and then sent curses after Lazarus, who meanwhile kept on advancing into the interior of the palace.

Already did the Emperor know who Lazarus was, and prepared to meet him. But the monarch was a brave man, and felt his own tremendous, unconquerable power, and in his fatal duel with him who had miraculously risen from the dead he wanted not to invoke human help. And so, he met Lazarus face to face.

"Lift not your eyes upon me, Lazarus," he ordered. "I heard your face is like that of Medusa and turns into stone whomsoever you look at. Now, I wish to see you and talk with you, before I turn into stone," he added in a tone of kingly jesting, not devoid of fear.

Coming close to him, he carefully examined Lazarus' face and his strange festal garments. And although he had a keen eye, he was deceived by his appearance.

"So. You do not appear terrible, my venerable old man. But the worse for us, if horror assumes such a respectable and pleasant air. Now let us have a talk."

Augustus sat, and questioning Lazarus with his eye as much as with words, started the conversation:

"Why did you not greet me as you entered?"

Lazarus answered indifferently: "I knew not it was necessary."

"Are you a Christian?"

"No."

Augustus approvingly shook his head.

"That is good. I do not like Christians. They shake the tree of life before it is covered with fruit, and disperse its odorous bloom to the winds. But who are you?"

With a visible effort Lazarus answered: "I was dead."

"I had heard that. But who are you now?"

Lazarus was silent, but at last repeated in a tone of weary apathy: "I was dead."

"Listen to me, stranger," said the Emperor, distinctly and severely giving utterance to the thought that had come to him at the beginning, "my realm is the realm of Life, my people are of the living, not of the dead. You are here one too many. I know not who you are and what you saw there; but, if you lie, I hate your lies, and if you tell the truth, I hate your truth. In my bosom I feel the throb of life; I feel strength in my arm, and my proud thoughts, like eagles, pierce the space. And yonder in the shelter of my rule, under the protection of laws created by me, people live and toil and rejoice. Do you hear the battle-cry, the challenge men throw into the face of the future?"

Augustus, as if in prayer, stretched forth his arms and exclaimed solemnly: "Be blessed, O great and divine Life!"

Lazarus was silent, and with growing sternness the Emperor went on: "You are not wanted here, miserable remnant, snatched from under Death's teeth, you inspire weariness and disgust with life; like a caterpillar in the fields, you gloat on the rich ear of joy and belch out the drivel of despair and sorrow. Your truth is like a rusty sword in the hands of a nightly murderer, and as a murderer you shall be executed. But before that, let me look into your eyes. Perchance only cowards are afraid of them, but in the brave they awake the thirst for strife and victory; then you shall be rewarded, not executed…Now, look at me, Lazarus."

At first it appeared to the deified Augustus that a friend was looking at him, so soft, so tenderly fascinating was Lazarus' glance. It promised not horror, but sweet rest, and the Infinite seemed to him a tender mistress, a compassionate sister, a mother. But stronger and stronger grew its embraces, and already the mouth, greedy of hissing kisses, interfered with the monarch's breathing, and already to the surface of the soft tissues of the body came the iron of the bones and tightened its merciless circle, and unknown fangs, blunt and cold, touched his heart and sank into it with slow indolence.

"It pains," said the deified Augustus, growing pale. "But look at me, Lazarus, look."

It was as if some heavy gates, ever closed, were slowly moving apart, and through the growing interstice the appalling horror of the Infinite poured in slowly and steadily. Like two shadows entered the shoreless void and the unfathomable darkness; they extinguished the sun, ravished the earth from under the feet, and the roof from over the head. No more did the frozen heart ache.

"Look, look, Lazarus," ordered Augustus, tottering.

Time stood still, and the beginning of each thing grew frightfully near to its end. Augustus' throne, just erected, crumbled down, and the void was already in the place of the throne and of Augustus. Noiselessly did Rome crumble down, and a new city stood on its site and it too was swallowed by the void. Like fantastic giants, cities, states and countries fell down and vanished in the void darkness, and with uttermost indifference did the insatiable black womb of the Infinite swallow them.

"Halt!" ordered the Emperor.

In his voice sounded already a note of indifference, his hands dropped in languor, and in the vain struggle with the onrushing darkness his fiery eyes now blazed up, and now went out.

"My life you have taken from me, Lazarus," said he in a spiritless, feeble voice.

And these words of hopelessness saved him. He remembered his people, whose shield he was destined to be, and keen salutary pain pierced his deadened heart. "They are doomed to death," he thought wearily. "Serene shadows in the darkness of the Infinite," thought he, and horror grew upon him. "Frail vessels with living, seething blood, with a heart that knows sorrow and also great joy," said he in his heart, and tenderness pervaded it. Thus pondering and oscillating between the poles of Life and Death, he slowly came back to life, to find in its suffering and in its joys a shield against the darkness of the void and the horror of the Infinite.

"No, you have not murdered me, Lazarus," said he firmly, "but I will take your life. Begone."

That evening the deified Augustus partook of his meats and drinks with particular joy. Now and then his lifted hand remained suspended in the air, and a dull glimmer replaced the bright sheen of his fiery eye. It was the cold wave of Horror that surged at his feet. Defeated, but not undone, ever awaiting its hour, that Horror stood at the Emperor's bedside, like a black shadow all through his life, it swayed his nights, but yielded the days to the sorrows and joys of life. The following day, the hangman with a hot iron burned out Lazarus' eyes. Then he was sent home. The deified Augustus dared not kill him.

Lazarus returned to the desert, and the wilderness met him with hissing gusts of wind and the heat of the blazing sun. Again, he was sitting on a stone, his rough, bushy beard lifted up; and the two black holes in place of his eyes looked at the sky with an expression of dull terror.

Afar off the holy city stirred noisily and restlessly, but around him everything was deserted and dumb.

No one approached the place where lived he who had miraculously risen from the dead, and long since his neighbors had forsaken their houses. Driven by the hot iron into the depth of his skull, his cursed knowledge hid there in an ambush. As if leaping out from an ambush, it lunged its thousand invisible eyes into the man, and no one dared look at Lazarus.

And in the evening, when the sun, reddening and growing wider, would come nearer and nearer the western horizon, the blind Lazarus would slowly follow it. He would stumble against stones and fall, stout and weak as he was; would rise heavily to his feet and walk on again; and on the red screen of the sunset his black body and outspread hands would form a monstrous likeness of a cross.

And it came to pass that once he went out and did not come back. Thus seemingly ended the second life of him who for three days had been under the enigmatical sway of death, and rose miraculously from the dead.

On the River

by Guy de Maupassant

March 1931 (vol. 17, no. 2)
Translated from the French by Jonathan Sturges

I had rented, last summer, a little country house on the banks of the Seine a few miles from Paris, and I used to go down there every night to sleep. In a few days, I made the acquaintance of one of my neighbors, a man between thirty and forty, who was certainly the most curious type that I had ever met. He was an old rowing man, crazy about rowing, always near the water, always on the water, always in the water. He must have been born in a boat, and he would certainly die in a boat at last.

One night, while we were walking together along the Seine, I asked him to tell me some stories about his life upon the river; and at that the good man suddenly became animated, transfigured, eloquent, almost poetical! In his heart there was one great passion, devouring and irresistible—the river.

"Ah!" said he to me, "how many memories I have of that river which is flowing there beside us! You people who live in streets, you don't know what the river is. But just listen to a fisherman simply pronouncing the word. For him it is the thing mysterious, the thing profound, unknown, the country of mirage and of fantasmagoria, where one sees, at night, things which do not exist, where one hears strange noises, where one trembles causelessly, as though crossing a graveyard. And it is, indeed, the most sinister of graveyards—a graveyard where there are no tombstones.

"To the fisherman the land seems limited, but of dark nights, when there is no moon, the river seems limitless. Sailors have no such feeling for the sea. Hard she often is and wicked, the great Sea; but she cries, she shouts, she deals with you fairly, while the river is silent and treacherous. It never even mutters, it flows ever noiselessly, and this eternal flowing movement of water terrifies me far more than the high seas of ocean.

"Dreamers pretend that the Sea hides in her breast great blue regions where drowned men roll to and fro among the huge fish, in the midst of strange forests and in crystal grottoes. The river has only black depths, where one rots in the slime. For all that it is beautiful when it glitters in the rising sun or swashes softly along between its banks where the reeds murmur.

"The poet says of the ocean: 'Oh seas, you know sad stories! Deep seas, feared by kneeling mothers, you tell the stories to one another at flood tides! And that is why you have such despairing voices when at night you come toward us nearer and nearer.'

"Well, I think that the stories murmured by the slender reeds with their little soft voices must be yet more sinister than the gloomy dramas told by the howling of the high seas.

"But, since you ask for some of my recollections, I will tell you a curious adventure which I had here about ten years ago.

"I then lived, as I still do, in the house of the old lady Lafon, and one of my best chums, Louis Bernet, who has now given up for the Civil Service his oars, his low shoes, and his sleeveless jersey, lived in the village of C—, two leagues farther down. We dined together every day—sometimes at his place, sometimes at mine.

"One evening, as I was returning home alone and rather tired, wearily pulling my heavy boat, a twelve-footer, which I always used at night, I stopped a few seconds to take breath near the point where so many reeds grow, down that way, about two hundred meters before you come to the railroad bridge. It was a beautiful night; the moon was resplendent, the river glittered, the air was calm and soft. The tranquility of it all tempted me; I said to myself that to smoke a pipe just here would be extremely nice. Action followed upon the thought; I seized my anchor and threw it into the stream.

"The boat, which floated down again with the current, pulled the chain out to its full length, then stopped; and I seated myself in the stem on a sheepskin, as comfortable as possible. One heard no sound—no sound; only sometimes I thought I was aware of a low, almost insensible lapping of the water along the bank, and I made out some groups of reeds which, taller than their fellows, took on surprising shapes, and seemed from time to time to stir.

"The river was perfectly still, but I felt myself moved by the extraordinary silence which surrounded me. All the animals—the frogs and toads, those nocturnal singers of the marshes—were silent. Suddenly on my right, near me, a frog croaked; I started; it was silent; I heard nothing more, and I resolved to smoke a little by way of a distraction. But though I am, so to speak, a regular blackener of pipes, I could not smoke that night; after the second puff, I sickened of it, and I stopped. I began to hum a tune; the sound of my voice was painful to me; so I stretched myself out in the bottom of the boat and contemplated the sky."

"For some time, I remained quiet, but soon the slight movements of the boat began to make me uneasy. I thought that it was yawing tremendously, striking now this bank of the stream, and now that; then I thought that some Being or some invisible force was dragging it down gently to the bottom of the water, and then was lifting it up simply to let it fall again. I was tossed about as though in the midst of a storm; I heard noises all around me; with a sudden start I sat upright; the water sparkled; everything was calm.

On the River

"I saw that my nerves were unsettled, and I decided to go. I pulled in the chain; the boat moved; then I was conscious of resistance; I pulled harder; the anchor did not come up, it had caught on something at the bottom of the river and I could not lift it. I pulled again—in vain. With my oars I got the boat round up-stream in order to change the position of the anchor. It was no use; the anchor still held. I grew angry, and in a rage I shook the chain. Nothing moved. There was no hope of breaking the chain, or of getting it loose from my craft, because it was very heavy, and riveted at the bow into a bar of wood thicker than my arm; but since the weather continued fine, I reflected that I should not have to wait long before meeting some fisherman, who would come to my rescue. My mishap had calmed me; I sat down, and I was now able to smoke my pipe. I had a flask of brandy with me; I drank two or three glasses, and my situation made me laugh. It was very hot, so that, if needs must, I could pass the night under the stars without inconvenience.

"Suddenly a little knock sounded against the side. I started, and a cold perspiration froze me from head to foot. The noise came, no doubt, from some bit of wood drawn along by the current, but it was enough, and I felt myself again overpowered by a strange nervous agitation. I seized the chain, and I stiffened myself in a desperate effort. The anchor held. I sat down exhausted.

"But, little by little, the river had covered itself with a very thick white mist, which crept low over the water, so that, standing up, I could no longer see either the stream or my feet or my boat, and saw only the tips of the reeds, and then, beyond them, the plain, all pale in the moonlight, and with great black stains which rose toward heaven, and which were made by clumps of Italian poplars. I was as though wrapped to the waist in a cotton sheet of a strange whiteness, and there began to come to me weird imaginations. I imagined that someone was trying to climb into my boat, since I could no longer see it, and that the river, hidden by this opaque mist, must be full of strange creatures swimming about me. I experienced a horrible uneasiness, I had a tightening at the temples, my heart beat to suffocation; and, losing my head, I thought of escaping by swimming; then in an instant the very idea made me shiver with fright. I saw myself lost, drifting hither and thither in this impenetrable mist, struggling among the long grass and the reeds which I should not be able to avoid, with a rattle in my throat from fear, not seeing the shore, not finding my boat. And it seemed to me as though I felt myself being drawn by the feet down to the bottom of this black water.

"In fact, since I should have had to swim up-stream at least five hundred meters before finding a point clear of rushes and reeds, where I could get a footing, there were nine chances to one that, however good a swimmer I might be, I should lose my bearings in the fog and drown.

"I tried to reason with myself. I realized that my will was firmly enough resolved against fear; but there was something in me besides my will, and it was this which felt afraid. I asked myself what it could be that I dreaded; that part of me which was courageous railed at that part of me which was cowardly; and I never had comprehended so well before the opposition between those two beings which exist within us, the one willing, the other resisting, and each in turn getting the mastery.

"This stupid and inexplicable fear grew until it became terror. I remained motionless, my eyes wide open, with a strained and expectant ear. Expecting— what? I did not know save that it would be something terrible. I believe that if a fish, as often happens, had taken it into its head to jump out of the water, it would have needed only that to make me fall stark on my back into a faint.

"And yet, finally, by a violent effort, I very nearly recovered the reason which had been escaping me. I again took my brandy-flask, and out of it I drank great drafts. Then an idea struck me, and I began to shout with all my might, turning in succession toward all four quarters of the horizon. When my throat was complete-ly paralyzed, I listened. A dog howled, a long way off.

"Again I drank; and I lay down on my back in the bottom of the boat. So I remained for one hour, perhaps for two, sleepless, my eyes wide open, with nightmares all about me. I did not dare to sit up, and yet I had a wild desire to do so; I kept putting it off from minute to minute. I would say to myself: 'Come! get up!' and I was afraid to make a movement. At last, I raised myself with infinite precaution, as if life depended on my making not the slightest sound, and I peered over the edge of the boat.

"I was dazzled by the most marvelous, the most astonishing spectacle that it can be possible to see. It was one of those fantasmagoria from fairyland; it was one of those visions described by travelers returned out of far countries, and which we hear without believing.

"The mist, which two hours before was floating over the water, had gradually withdrawn and piled itself upon the banks. Leaving the river absolutely clear, it had formed, along each shore, long low hills about six or seven meters high, which glittered under the moon with the brilliancy of snow, so that one saw nothing except this river of fire coming down these two white mountains; and there, high above my head, a great, luminous moon, full and large, displayed herself upon a blue and milky sky.

"All the denizens of the water had awaked; the bull-frogs croaked furiously, while, from instant to instant, now on my right, now on my left, I heard those short, mournful, monotonous notes which the brassy voices of the marsh-frogs give forth to the stars. Strangely enough, I was no longer afraid; I was in the midst of such an extraordinary landscape that the most curious things could not have astonished me.

"How long the sight lasted I do not know, because at last I had grown drowsy. When I again opened my eyes, the moon had set, the heaven was full of clouds. The water lashed mournfully, the wind whispered, it grew cold, the darkness was profound.

"I drank all the brandy I had left; then I listened shiveringly to the rustling of the reeds and to the sinister noise of the river. I tried to see, but I could not make out the boat nor even my own hands, though I raised them close to my eyes.

"However, little by little the density of the blackness diminished. Suddenly I thought I felt a shadow slipping along nearby me; I uttered a cry; a voice replied—it was a fisherman. I hailed him; he approached, and I told him of my mishap. He pulled his boat alongside, and both together we heaved at the chain. The anchor did not budge. The day came on—somber, gray, rainy, cold—one of those days which bring always a sorrow and a misfortune. I made out another craft; we hailed it. The man aboard of it joined his efforts to ours: then, little by little, the anchor yielded. It came up, but slowly, slowly, and weighted down by something very heavy.

"At last, we perceived a black mass, and we pulled it alongside.

"It was the corpse of an old woman with a great stone round her neck."

Tales of
Madness

Epigraphe Pour un Livre Condamne

by Charles Baudelaire

March 1928 (vol. 11, no. 3)
Translated from the French by Clark Ashton Smith

Bucolic reader, reader wholly
Simple, sober and benign,
Cast down this volume saturnine
And orgiaque and melancholy.
If thou hast learned no lessonry
Of Satan, wileful dean and wise,
Herein were naught for thy surmise,
And madness were my words to thee.
But if thy vision, unbeguiled,
Can dive adown the gulfs of hell,
Read me, and learn to love me well;
Tormented soul, alone, exiled,
And fain of some lost realm divine,
Pity me…lest my curse be thine.

The White Dog

by Fyodor Sologub

February 1927 (vol. 7, no. 2)
Translated from the Russian by Anonymous

Everything was irksome for Alexandra Ivanovna in the workshop of this out-of-the way town. It was the shop in which she had served as apprentice and now for several years as seamstress.

Everything irritated Alexandra Ivanovna; she quarreled with everyone and abused the apprentices. Among others to suffer from her tantrums was Tanechka, the youngest of the seamstresses, who had only recently become an apprentice.

In the beginning, Tanechka submitted to her abuse in silence. In the end she revolted, and, addressing her assailant, said quite calmly and affably, so that everyone laughed, "Alexandra Ivanovna, you are a dog!"

Alexandra Ivanovna scowled.

"You are a dog yourself!" she exclaimed.

Tanechka was sitting sewing. She paused now and then from her work and said, calmly and deliberately, "You always whine…you certainly are a dog…You have a dog's snout…And a dog's ears…And a wagging tail… The mistress will soon drive you out of doors, because you are the most detestable of dogs—a poodle."

Tanechka was a young, plump, rosy-cheeked girl with a good-natured face which revealed a trace of cunning. She sat there demurely, barefooted, still dressed in her apprentice's clothes; her eyes were clear, and her brows were highly arched on her finely curved white forehead, framed by straight dark chestnut hair, which looked black at a distance. Tanechka's voice was clear, even, sweet, insinuating, and if one could have heard its sound only, and not given heed to the words, it would have given the impression that she was paying Alexandra Ivanovna compliments.

The other seamstresses laughed, the apprentices chuckled, they covered their faces with their black aprons and cast side glances at Alexandra Ivanovna, who was livid with rage.

"Wretch!" she exclaimed. "I will pull your ears for you! I won't leave a hair on your head!"

Tanechka replied in a gentle voice: "The paws are a bit short…The poodle bites as well as barks…It may be necessary to buy a muzzle."

Alexandra Ivanovna made a movement toward Tanechka. But before Tanechka had time to lay aside her work and get up, the mistress of the establishment entered.

"Alexandra Ivanovna," she said sternly, "what do you mean by making such a fuss?"

Alexandra Ivanovna, much agitated, replied, "Irina Petrovna, I wish you would forbid her to call me a dog!"

Tanechka in her turn complained: "She is always snarling at something or other."

But the mistress looked at her sternly and said, "Tanechka, I can see through you. Are you sure you didn't begin it? You needn't think that because you are a seamstress now you are an important person. If it weren't for your mother's sake—"

Tanechka grew red, but preserved her innocent and affable manner. She addressed her mistress in a subdued voice: "Forgive me, Irina Petrovna, I will not do it again. But it wasn't altogether my fault ..."

Alexandra Ivanovna returned home almost ill with rage. Tanechka had guessed her weakness. "A dog! Well, then, I am a dog." thought Alexandra Ivanovna, "but it is none of her affair! Have I looked to see whether she is a serpent or a fox? It is easy to find one out, but why make a fuss about it? Is a dog worse than any other animal?"

The clear summer night languished and sighed. A soft breeze from the adjacent fields occasionally blew down the peaceful streets. The moon rose clear and full, that very same moon which rose long ago at another place, over the broad desolate steppe, the home of the wild, of those who ran free and whined in their ancient earthly travail.

And now, as then, glowed eyes sick with longing; and her heart, still wild, not forgetting in town the great spaciousness of the steppe, felt oppressed; her throat was troubled with a tormenting desire to howl.

She was about to undress, but what was the use? She could not sleep, anyway. She went into the passage. The planks of the floor bent and creaked under her, and small shavings and sand which covered them tickled her feet not unpleasantly.

She went out on the doorstep. There sat the *babushka* Stepanida, a black figure in her black shawl, gaunt and shriveled. She sat with her head bent, and seemed to be warming herself in the rays of the cold moon.

Alexandra Ivanovna sat down beside her. She kept looking at the old woman sideways. The large curved nose of her companion seemed to her like the beak of an old bird.

"A crow?" Alexandra Ivanovna asked herself.

She smiled, forgetting for the moment her longing and her fears. Shrewd as the eyes of a dog, her own eyes lighted up with the joy of her discovery. In the pale green light of the moon the wrinkles of her faded face became altogether invisible, and she seemed once more young and merry and light-hearted, just as she was ten years ago, when the moon had not yet called upon her to bark and bay of nights before the windows of the dark bathhouse.

She moved closer to the old woman, and said affably, "*Babushka* Stepanida, there is something I have been wanting to ask you."

The old woman turned to her, her dark face furrowed with wrinkles, and asked in a sharp, oldish voice that sounded like a caw, "Well, my dear? Go ahead and ask."

Alexandra Ivanovna gave a repressed laugh; her thin shoulders suddenly trembled from a chill that ran down her spine.

She spoke very quietly: "*Babushka* Stepanida, it seems to me—tell me is it true?—I don't know exactly how to put it—but you, *babushka*, please don't take offense—it is not from malice that I—"

"Go on, my dear, say it," said the old woman, looking at Alexandra Ivanovna with glowing eyes.

"It seems to me, *babushka*—please, now, don't take offense—as if you, *babushka*, were a crow."

The old woman turned away. She nodded her head, and seemed like one who had recalled something. Her head, with its sharply outlined nose, bowed and nodded, and at last it seemed to Alexandra Ivanovna that the old woman was dozing. Dozing, and mumbling something under her nose—nodding and mumbling old forgotten words, old magic words.

An intense quiet reigned out of doors. It was neither light nor dark, and everything seemed bewitched with the inarticulate mumbling of old, forgotten words. Everything languished and seemed lost in apathy.

Again a longing oppressed her heart. And it was neither a dream nor an illusion. A thousand perfumes, imperceptible by day, became subtly distinguishable, and they recalled something ancient and primitive.

In a barely audible voice the old woman mumbled, "Yes, I am a crow. Only I have no wings. But there are times when I caw, and I caw, and tell of woe. And I am given to forebodings, my dear; each tame I have one I simply must caw. People are not particularly anxious to hear me. And when I see a doomed person, I have such a strong desire to caw."

The old woman suddenly made a sweeping movement with her arms, and in a shrill voice cried out twice: "Kar-r, Kar-r!"

Alexandra Ivanovna shuddered, and asked, "*Babushka*, at whom are you cawing?"

"At you, my dear," the old woman answered. "I am cawing at you."

It had become too painful to sit with the old woman any longer. Alexandra Ivanovna went to her own room. She sat down before the open window and listened to two voices at the gate.

"It simply won't stop whining!" said a low and harsh voice.

"And uncle, did you see?" asked an agreeable young tenor.

Alexandra Ivanovna recognized in this last the voice of the curly-headed, freckled-faced lad who lived in the same court.

A brief and depressing silence followed. Then she heard a hoarse and harsh voice say suddenly. "Yes, I saw. It's very large—and white. It lies near the bathhouse, and bays at the moon."

The voice gave her an image of the man, of his shovel-shaped beard, his low, furrowed forehead, his small, piggish eyes, and his spread-out fat legs.

"And why does it bay, uncle?" asked the agreeable voice.

And again, the hoarse voice did not reply at once.

"Certainly to no good purpose— and where it came from is more than I can say."

"Do you think, uncle, it may be a werewolf?" asked the agreeable voice.

"I should not advise you to investigate," replied the hoarse voice.

She could not quite understand what these words implied, nor did she wish to think of them. She did not feel inclined to listen further. What was the sound and significance of human words to her? The moon looked straight into her face and persistently called her and tormented her. Her heart was restless with a dark longing, and she could not sit still.

A lexandra Ivanovna quickly undressed herself. Naked, all white, she silently stole through the passage; she then opened the outer door (there was no one on the step or outside) and ran quickly across the court and the vegetable garden, and reached the bathhouse. The sharp contact of her body with the cold air and her feet with the cold ground gave her pleasure. But soon her body was warm.

She lay down in the grass, on her stomach. Then, raising herself on her elbows, she lifted her face toward the pale, brooding moon, and gave a long, drawn-out whine.

"Listen, uncle, it is whining," said the curly-haired lad at the gate. The agreeable tenor voice trembled perceptibly.

"Whining again, the accurst one!" said the hoarse, harsh voice slowly.

They rose from the bench. The gate latch clicked. They went silently across the courtyard and the vegetable garden, the two of them. The older man, black-bearded and powerful, walked in front, a gun in his hand. The curly-headed lad followed tremblingly, and looked constantly behind.

Near the bathhouse, in the grass, lay a huge white dog, whining piteously. Its head, black on the crown, was raised to the moon, which pursued its way in the cold sky; its hind legs were strangely thrown backward, while the front ones, firm and straight, pressed hard against the ground.

In the pale green and unreal light of the moon it seemed enormous. So huge a dog was surely never seen on earth. It was thick and fat. The black spot, which began at the head and stretched in uneven strands down the entire spine, seemed like a woman's loosened hair. No tail was visible; presumably it was turned under. The fur on the body was so short that in the distance the dog seemed wholly naked, and its hide shone dimly in the moonlight, so that altogether if resembled the body of a nude woman, who lay in the grass and bayed at the moon.

The man with the black beard took aim. The curly-haired lad crossed himself and mumbled something.

The discharge of a rifle sounded in the night air. The dog gave a groan, jumped up on its hind legs, became a naked woman, who, her body covered with blood, started to run, all the while groaning, weeping and raising cries of distress.

The black-bearded one and the curly-haired one threw themselves in the grass, and began to moan in wild terror.

On a Train with a Madman

by Pan-Appan

July 1935 (vol. 26, no. 1)
Adapted from the German by Roy Temple House

Hallucinations and illusions, said Judge Hochdoerfer thoughtfully, in the sense of pure imaginings caused by a tight collar or an excited brain which manufactures something out of nothing, are much less frequent than most people suppose. A mirage is not something imagined, but something misplaced. No one can be certain that knowledge of the future is scientifically impossible. Even our scientists know very little as to what space and time really are. But it is certain that our faculties of apprehension are much less circumscribed than many of us suspect.

I want to tell you of something that happened to me when I was still a young fellow in Germany. I must admit, as an item of legitimate evidence in the case, that I had been drinking, but I must testify, too, that in those days a moderate amount of liquor only sharpened my wits instead of dulling them.

I was a recent graduate of one of the smaller German universities, and I had stopped off in the little college town for a moist and joyous reunion with old college mates. I had crawled sulkily into a third-class compartment of the train, and sat brooding list-lessly at the window as the panting iron horse pulled us jerkily and noisily from the scene of my student frolics toward the scene of my dull daily labors.

I was so absorbed in the painful business of con-trasting the jovial past with the lack-luster present, that I scarcely realized that the train had stopped. Suddenly it dawned on me that I had company in my compartment, which I had thus far occupied all alone. The old fellow, who had clambered with visible haste into the smallish box which is a European railway com-partment, was so strange and almost uncanny in both looks and manner that he was not long in shaking me out of my meditative mood. In spite of the unusually warm weather, his coat collar was turned up around his ears, and he had pulled his broad-brimmed hat down over his face so that very little of it was visible but the tip of his nose, a long corkscrew affair which peeped out of his defensive armament like the muzzle of a cannon from a beleaguered fortress.

Just as the train was leaving the station, I noticed that the crowd on the platform had grown agitated and excited. There were calls and cries, but as we had begun to move, I could not catch a hint of what it was all about. There was fear and perplexity on many faces, as if some danger was imminent. As I leaned out of the window, I saw a row of protruding heads all along the train. Everybody was puzzled and alarmed. Back on the platform, we could see the station-master, the center of an excited group, waving his signal-flag wildly.

Whatever it was all about, the train moved on with steadily increasing speed, and the frightened many-headed turtle drew in its heads one after another.

At last, I gave up trying to fathom the mystery and pulled in my noodle with the others. Warm as it was, the air was pulling through the compartment uncomfortably, and I started to close the window a few inches. But the leather strap by which I was drawing it up slipped out of my hands, and the window dropped again with a bang.

The sight of my new companion sent the cold shivers down my back. The old man had left his corner diagonally across from me and was sitting directly opposite me, his knees almost touching mine. His look and manner had changed completely. He had uncovered his face, and his head was no longer drawn down between his shoulders, but stood up like the head of a bird, on a long neck which was almost bare of flesh but was fuzzy with ragged long hairs. His face was nothing but skin, muscle and tendon, so that every change of expression, every diabolical distortion, came out in all its ghastly nakedness. The eyes were horrible. They lay so deep in their sockets that they were scarcely visible, but the savage glitter in them made me think of some beast of prey. They wandered over my person in a sort of cruel ecstasy and bored a path into my inmost being as if they were trying to penetrate every secret of my soul and set a-quiver every fiber of my nervous system.

I stared at this frightful caricature of a man with a sort of fascinated helplessness, while he gazed back at me with a cynical smile in which I could read his consciousness of power and his determination to torture his victim to the full. But there was something else in his gaze, a mysterious something which was not merely curiosity, something like fanaticism, like a mission and a purpose.

"Pardon me, sir," as if from a great distance, a squeaky eunuch-voice reached my ear. The polite phrase, however, was not spoken in a tone of courteous caution, but with an air of command. "Pardon me, sir, if I look at you a little harder than one stranger would usually be expected to look at another."

I did not answer his courteous phrase. I think I should have found it impossible to speak a word at that moment.

I tried to rise from my seat. My mind was not clear; I was only half conscious. My body was dulled and stiff. But I was tormented with an agony of apprehension. My throat was burning. My tongue felt as if it were swelling bigger and bigger and filling my mouth so full that my jaw dropped wider and wider open. I knew dimly that I was sitting like an imbecile with gaping mouth and a vacant, fixed stare. Still, I said nothing. I don't think the creature was waiting for an answer or expecting one. He was just taking his time, calmly, gorgeously.

I suppose there was an expression of surprize even in my stupid eyes, and I think my head jerked, although every muscle in my body seemed paralyzed.

"I am sure you have heard of me."

My brain was functioning after a fashion, and I was trying in vain to recall a modern bearer of the uncanny name my new acquaintance had just spoken. But the doctor went on calmly, in a moment:

"Yes, you have heard of me, and you know of my phenomenal cures, which have put suffering humanity deeply in my debt."

All at once I did remember the whole story. My brain seemed suddenly to awaken to something like normal activity, and I recalled what I had read in the newspaper that very morning. It had even been mentioned in our alumni group at breakfast.

The paper had told the story of a small-town physician who had enjoyed an excellent reputation, especially for his surgical work, but who had lived and worked till he had passed middle life without becoming known to any degree beyond the narrow field of his labors.

His opportunity had come when a foreign potentate who was traveling through the country was stopped at the doctor's little city by an attack of illness. It was the recurrence of a hereditary disease which famous physicians all over the world had diagnosed as incurable, so that its return in an acute form would no doubt prove fatal. The ailment had come back with dangerous intensity, and His Highness' suite had already, by code telegram, prepared the responsible authorities in his home country for the eventuality of his being brought home in a serious condition, if he came home at all. Someone reported that a physician in the town was an unusually skillful surgeon, and more as a matter of humanitarian form than because anyone expected anything of him, the local sawbones was sent for. He was confident and was allowed to try his hand. Behind closed and locked doors, with all curtains drawn, His Highness was treated. No one knew anything of the diagnosis or the treatment. But the outcome was that the country surgeon cured his patient. After a week of treatment—a week during which the doctor and the regal patient were alone together, for no physician of the suite, no minister, no confidential secretary, came near the bedside—His Highness was visibly out of danger; and the medical men of the royal retinue shook their heads in apprehension and hinted at dangerous charlatanry or even at black magic. These palace M.D.'s were for the time being in complete disgrace, and His Highness had no eyes for anyone but his savior. The village doctor was made Physician in Ordinary to His Highness, with a salary beside which his modest income up to that date seemed a ridiculous pittance, and with such fame and fortune in prospect as turned his head completely.

The fortunate outcome of his audacious experiment convinced the poor fellow that he had found the grand panacea for all human ills, the *remedium optimum* of the old alchemists, the infallible Philosopher's Stone. And it was not long till he left his brilliant court position for an insane asylum, where he planned the craziest cures for all types of human ailments, announcing proudly that there was no disease which he could not master and that he was on the way to the perfection of a treatment which would end the reign of the King of Terrors himself.

This unfortunate maniac had escaped from his sanitarium two or three days before the day of my trip, and with the unbelievable ingenuity which frequently develops in the mentally unbalanced, he had thus far eluded his pursuers.

And this old man shut up in the same box with me was that dangerous maniac! I had no doubt of it.

My mind was working a little more freely now, and I began to plan how I might reach the bell-cord and stop the train. But I was still unable to move my limbs, and I was becoming conscious that a sweetish narcotic perfume was filling the air. I struggled against its effects, and I wondered, in my puzzled and strange condition, why I did not lose consciousness entirely. I saw everything about me, I heard every sound, I knew what was happening, even though dimly. But I could not move, I could not resist, I could not even protest by word or gesture.

"There is no disease," the ghastly creature went on proudly after a long pause, "that I can't conquer. I can heal them, I can cure them, I can floor them, I can down them, I can send them about their business every time."

He was growing excited, he punctuated his phrases with strange titterings, and his long, sharp finger-nails cut the air like knives as he gesticulated more and more wildly. His skinny hands were like the claws of some unclean and enormous bird of prey.

I calculated that it would be a good hour before we could reach the next station, and that long before that I should have fallen a prey to this terrible creature. But I sat idle and motionless, like a helpless bird which a beady-eyed reptile has fascinated and whose life-span depends entirely on the reptile's sovereign will.

"Now, my dear friend," the madman went on with a grin, but at the same time with an air of officious solicitude, "I know that I shall be able to free you from your trouble."

There was a touch of irony in his manner, yet he spoke with intent, confident seriousness. I could feel my pupils grow larger. But I could not move. The man had opened a case of surgical instruments, and the light glittered on an array of knives, hooks, needles and strangely formed murderous contraptions such as I had never seen before.

"Your trouble would soon have reached the chronic stage and would have been very difficult to handle."

He stopped, took out a terrible tiny scalpel and began to whet it on his thumb-nail, blinking impertinently at my trembling legs as he did so.

"Lie down on the bench!"

This rude command brought a red flush of indignation to my pale cheeks. Yet I had no choice but to obey, not simply because I was afraid of the fellow—although I was never so deathly afraid of anything in my life—but because I no longer had any command over my own members. So I slipped down on my stomach on the bench. But he squealed at me indignantly—he seemed to take the position I was trying to assume as a deadly insult:

"Not with your backside up like that! Face up, I tell you! I must get at your face!"

And when I was slow and clumsy in carrying out his order, he seized me by the shoulder, threw my head back with a jerk, and gazed greedily into my eyes, which suddenly began to water and turn convulsively inward. It was a terrible moment.

"A very interesting case!" he exclaimed with a grin. "A spontaneous complex divergence of the ocular field. You should have come to me long ago. This dangerous strabismus—" And he held a little mirror in front of my eyes.

It was true. I was cross-eyed. I was so impossibly and idiotically cross-eyed that it was incomprehensible to me that I had never noticed it before. I had never had the slightest suspicion that my eyes were not perfectly straight and parallel.

"Don't be alarmed!" he said soothingly, but with that ghoulish sarcasm in his tone again. "The operation will scarcely cause any pain at all."

At that moment I felt a very disagreeable pressure against the pit of my stomach, a pressure that drove the breath almost completely out of me. Some invisible power—for my cataleptic condition made it impossible for me to turn my eyes at the bidding of my will—held me in my uncomfortable and perilous position. I tried to realize that my last moment had come. But though I had no power to move my frozen muscles, which had surrendered abjectly to the will of another, though my body lay there waiting supinely for my fate, my mind had not surrendered. Something began repeating inside me, with desperate insistence — "The train MUST stop—the train MUST stop—"

My eyelids were propped open and I could no more have closed them than I could have lifted the car. I lay there gazing in agony at the shining blade which was approaching the corner of my eye.

"They will be working together in just a moment now. It is a case of double strabismus. Both eyes turn in. The operation is a little complicated. I shall have to cut the muscles and take both eyeballs out, but I will put them back in a moment just as they were, or rather, just as they ought to have been and weren't."

Good heavens! He was going to blind me completely, and bleed me to death in the process! The awful imminence of my fate all at once gave me the strength to resist. With a fierce yell I leaped to my feet and pushed the creature back.

The effect of my declaration of independence was astonishing. The old man seemed to shrink into himself, much as I had seen him first, and then—he melted into the air and disappeared. It seemed as if a kind of gray veil floated off out of the window.

I looked about me in complete bewilderment. The cold sweat was dripping from my forehead.

The compartment was empty. The train had stopped, out in the open country. I heard the confused sound of many voices arguing, crying, commanding, down on the track below me. Still in a daze, I leaned out of the window.

A group of men were struggling with an individual who seemed to be possessed with the desperate strength of a giant. His hat had fallen from his head. It was the long-nosed, skinny bird-head of my late companion. With a dozen hands gripping him firmly, the madman suddenly ceased struggling and squealing.

I heard an agonizing groan. It came from the train, from the next compartment to mine. I opened my door, stepped out on the running-board which extended along the side of the car, and entered the next compartment.

On one of the benches, a man lay on his back. His face was covered with a cloth. With a beating heart I drew the cloth away. Two suffering eyes stared up at me from a face which had been cruelly slashed with some sharp instrument—two eyes that turned inward toward the bleeding nose. The poor fellow had the worst case of cross-eyes I ever saw in my life!

I have never fully understood what had happened. The man in the next compartment was not seriously injured, but it seemed impossible to arouse him entirely from a sort of frightened lethargy. After his face had been dressed by a surgeon, he did, in my hearing, stammer a disjointed story about a man who had entered his compartment at the last station, remarked on the unfortunate condition of his eyes, produced a set of instruments, ordered him to lie down on the seat, enforcing his will by some strange hypnotic power—all of this strange and puzzling to the poor fellow's other hearers, but familiar and intelligible to me. Just at the moment when the madman was about to attack his victim's eyes with his deadly little knife (I think I understood from the frightened fellow's stammering and bewildered story), the old man staggered back as if someone had pushed him violently, made a few vicious passes at the prostrate sufferer's face and nose with his weapon—then, the train having come to a stop, he flung his great handkerchief over the still petrified face, crying:

"There, you can wipe your bloody nose with that!"

Then he had flung the compartment door open and jumped out.

I learned more of the story from others.

The engine-driver had obeyed a signal to stop the train. Train employees and passengers had seen a wild creature leap out of a compartment and storm up and down the parallel track, declaiming that he had been in the act of performing a difficult and helpful surgical operation on a suffering fellow-man, and that while so doing he had been feloniously and brutally assaulted by someone on that train. He was the greatest doctor in all the world, he announced in a piercing squeal, a doctor who could raise the dead if need be, and he was determined to have condign punishment visited on the miscreant who had interfered with his noble work, if he found it necessary to punish him himself with the resources of edged tools, poisons, and deadly gases which his science placed at his disposal. This blood-curdling eloquence had frightened various old women and little children into hysterics, but the raving creature had been speedily tied up and silenced.

That, gentlemen, is all I know.

Who stopped the train, you ask? Well, I thought for a time that the mad doctor had pulled the cord himself, in his determination to secure the punishment of his wicked assailant—who must have been I myself, as far as I can figure the bewildering thing out. But as I put all the evidence together, I arrived at a different conclusion.

I remembered that while I still lay on the bench on my back, and seemed to see the horrible glittering eyes boring into mine and the bright little knife coming relentlessly nearer and nearer my face, I was conscious that the train was slowing up. I remembered how earnestly, how determinedly, how commandingly, something inside me had insisted that the train must stop. And, gentlemen, as sure as I sit here, I believe that *I myself, lying stark and helpless on that seat, without the power to move a muscle, by the sheer force of my desperate, insistent desire, I stopped that train.*

A Masterpiece of Crime

by Jean Richepin

March, 1936 (vol. 27, no. 3)

Translated from the French by H. Twitchell

His baptismal name was Oscar; his family name, Lapissotte; both commonplace. He was poor, without talent, and he believed himself to be a genius. His first act on entering upon a literary career was to adopt a pseudonym; his second to adopt another. In ten years, he managed to employ every sort of nom-de-plume that his active fancy could suggest. All this was done to excite the curiosity of his contemporaries, but this curiosity scarcely ever made the least effort to discover the secrets of his secluded life. Under all these borrowed names, noble and plebeian, romantic and ordinary, he still remained unknown, the poorest and most obscure of literary men.

With patience exhausted, pride humbled, and a life spoiled by vain and futile hopes, there seemed no better way than to end it by a suicide or a crime. Oscar Lapissotte was not brave enough to choose death. Besides, his pretensions to intellectual superiority led him to feel a sort of pleasure in the thought of committing some grand crime. He said to himself that, so far, his genius had taken a false turn, as it had applied itself to dreams of art when it was really destined for the violence of action. And, too, crime would bring him a fortune, and wealth would bring appreciation of those talents which his poverty had served to hide from the sordid world. Artistically and morally, he proved to himself that he must commit a crime. He did commit a crime and for the first time in his life he created a masterpiece.

2.

At one time Oscar Lapissotte had lived on the sixth floor of a house in the Rue Saint-Denis. Scarcely noticed among the many other tenants and known only by one of his numerous pseudonyms, he had been the lover of a goodnatured, gossiping creature who told him all her small affairs. She was employed by a rich old widow who was an invalid.

One evening, about ten years after this, when leaving one of his friends who was an inmate of a hospital for a time, he chanced, in making his way out, to pass through a ward where he saw a woman whom he at once recognized as his old sweetheart. She was evidently dying. She told him that she had not been with her mistress for three weeks and that her place had been filled. Her mistress was too feeble to visit her and she was very wretched.

"I understand that," said Oscar. "You wish to see her, do you not?"

"Oh! that is not what worries me. It is because I am afraid, if I die here, Madame may read the letters I left at her house and will despise me after I am dead."

"Why should she despise you?"

"Listen, I will tell you the whole truth. You have been my lover; but that was a long time ago and it is all past. I can confide to you the fact that I have had others. You did not care for me long. You are an artist, a man of the world. I was agreeable to you for a time and that was all. But I met at this house a man of my own class in life, a coachman. If Madame had known it, it would have been my ruin. I did so many wicked things for him. I do not want her to know what I have done."

"My dear woman," said Oscar, brusquely, "explain more fully, you speak too fast. You must make everything quite plain if you wish me to aid you."

At this moment, Oscar Lapissotte had no idea of committing a crime. He simply followed the instinct of a man of letters and scented a plot for a story.

"Well," replied the woman, "I will try to explain. I fell suddenly ill with an attack of apoplexy, in the street, and they brought me here where Madame has left me because I was too ill to be moved. I wrote to her and she answered, but sent her servant to see me in her place. But neither to Madame nor to the servant have I spoken of that which torments me. I have a packet of letters from the coachman. In those letters are mentioned certain things: some thefts, which he told me to commit; and then he wrote afterward, thanking me for what I had done. For I stole; yes, I stole for him, stole from my mistress! I ought to have burned the letters, but in them there were always endearing terms and promises of marriage; so I have kept them. One day the scoundrel threatened to take them away from me in order to compromise me. I had refused him money and he made me understand that once master of those papers, he would make me do as he wished. I have been horribly afraid, but still I would not destroy the letters. For greater security, I asked Madame for the privilege of placing some important family documents in one of her secretaries. She gave me a desk with a key. I know, of course, that I need only say to her now that I need the papers, but I mistrust the maid who would bring them. From some words which she let fall I suspect that she loves the coachman. He is a cunning fellow, and if he plays the lover to her, it is only to gain possession of the letters whose hiding-place he knows. Now you understand my trouble. Oh, if you would be so good as to help me! I do not deserve it, it is true; but it would be so kind of you to render me this service."

"What service?"

"To bring me those letters."

"But how can I get them?"

"It is all very simple. This evening, about ten o'clock, Madame will take chloral to make her sleep, and she sleeps very soundly. After that, the servant is not there at that hour, for she goes away every evening at seven o'clock, after dinner. You may be sure that she has never told the maid that she takes chloral, for fear that she might be robbed. She has told no one but me, in whom she had perfect confidence, poor woman. Well, you can enter then; she will never hear you and you can bring me my letters when you come away. You know there are two entrances to the house. If you go in by the stairway for the concierge, no one will see you. Oh, tell me that you will do this for me!"

"But—the secretary—how can I open it or the door of the apartment?"

"I have two keys to the secretary. I had another one made, to my shame, in order to rob my good mistress. Here it is, with that of my own drawer. Here also is the key of the kitchen door at the top of the concierge's stairs. I give them to you. I do not know why, but I have faith in you, and I am sure that you will do this for me, so that I may die in peace."

Oscar Lapissotte took the keys. His eyes were fixed and staring; a strange pallor swept across his face; his thin and wrinkled cheeks twitched nervously. For suddenly, the possibility of the great crime had appeared to him. This woman dead, the thing was easy enough to execute.

"Oh, I am stifling!" said the sick woman whose long talk had exhausted her. "Give me a drink; give me water!"

The place was only half-lighted by the night lamp. All the patients in the surrounding beds were asleep.

Oscar raised the head of the dying woman; drew the pillow from under, and placed it over her mouth, where he held it with a grasp of iron for at least ten minutes. He had the frightful courage to count the moments, watch in hand. When he uncovered the face, the woman was dead. She had not made a movement, nor uttered a cry. She seemed to have succumbed at once. He replaced the pillow under her head, straightened the covering under the chin, and the body lay as if sleeping.

The bed was near the door; so the assassin escaped without difficulty. He slipped silently through the corridors and found himself outside without having been seen by anyone.

It was now twenty minutes past nine. Without losing a moment, eager for the execution of his crime, he made his way swiftly toward the Rue Saint-Denis. He entered the house before ten o'clock. On the way he had matured his plans. He went first to the stable, where he thought to find some belongings of the coachman. He took from there a cravat, tore from it a small piece, and put this in his pocket. Then he mounted the stairway. The room was on the first floor and he ran no risk of being seen.

He opened the door noiselessly, found himself in the bedchamber, and with one strong grasp strangled the old woman who slept there so soundly. Again, he showed the same sang-froid, and did not relax his grip upon the lean old throat for a quarter of an hour.

Then he opened the desk. In the large drawer in the center, there were deeds and notes and other papers. In the left-hand drawer were some bank-notes, in the one at the right some gold coins. He left the deeds and papers, but made a bundle of the bank-notes and gold pieces and thrust them into his pockets. Then he turned his attention to the letters. He found them easily, in the corner, just where the maid had told him.

He burned them in the fireplace, taking care, however, to leave intact those pieces that would most surely compromise the maid and the coachman. A few well-chosen ones sufficed to reveal the whole history of theft. He placed these near the chimney corner, so arranged as to make it appear that the letters had been burned in haste and that the criminal had departed before they were completely consumed.

He placed the piece of cravat, rumpled and torn, in the hands of the dead woman. Then he passed swiftly through the hall to the street, where he assumed the loitering gait of a boulevardier.

Decidedly, Oscar Lapissotte was not mistaken in thinking himself a man of genius: he had the genius for crime and had worked with the hand of a master.

3.

A crime is not a masterpiece unless the author of it remains unpunished. And the impunity is not really complete unless justice condemns an innocent person. Oscar Lapissotte had everything perfect and complete. Justice did not hesitate for an instant to find the assassin. He was, without a doubt, the coachman. Were not the fragments of letters infallible proof? Who but the coachman, a lover of the maid, could know so well the circumstances favorable to the commission of such a crime? Who else could have had the keys? Had he not begun by stealing from his mistress, with the connivance of the maid? Was it not quite reasonable to believe that he had finally taken the leap which separates the thief from the murderer? Besides, the piece of cravat was an accuser not to be refuted. And to add to his misfortunes, the coachman had bad antecedents. As a last and overwhelming proof, the man could not tell what he had been doing at that fatal hour. He denied, protested and affirmed his innocence again and again, but all was against him; nothing appeared in his favor.

He was judged, condemned to death and executed. Judges, jury, the lawyers, the newspapers, the public, all agreed that he died justly. There remained only one thing which puzzled them all, and that was that it could not be discovered what he had done with the money. It was believed that the scoundrel had concealed it in some safe place, but no one doubted that he had stolen it. If ever a criminal was proved guilty, it was this one.

4.

They say that the consciousness of a good action performed gives profound peace. But there are few people who have the courage to admit that a wicked act which escapes punishment also brings its happiness. Barbey d'Aurevilly, in his admirable *Diaboliques*, has not been afraid to write a story entitled "Happiness in Crime", and he is right; for there are rascals who are happy.

Oscar Lapissotte could enjoy to the utmost the double murder and could taste its fruits in absolute serenity. He experienced neither remorse nor terror. The only feeling he knew was one of immense pride. It was the pride of an artist, which made him forget every moral consideration; it was the perfection of his work, and the consciousness that he had shown himself to be really great, and this furnished him means to slake his ever-growing thirst for fame and glory.

He profited by his new fortune and forced his way through the portals of journals and magazines; he was able to feast the critic; but he could not compel the attention of the public. His verse, his prose, his dramas, all failed to possess any power of pleasing the people. Literary men knew a little of Anatole Desroses, the man of letters who had more money than talent; but all were agreed in denying him the least spark of real talent, or genius. He was daily convinced of his own inability and mediocrity.

"And yet," he said to himself sometimes with a brightening of the eye, "and yet, if I wished! If I should tell them of my masterpiece! For I have created a masterpiece! It may be that Anatole Desroses is a fool, but Oscar Lapissotte is a man of genius. It is a pity that a deed so well planned, so powerfully conceived, so vigorously executed, so completely successful, should remain unknown. Oh, that day I had the true, the real inspiration which leads to perfection. Abbe Prevost has scribbled a hundred romances, but only one

Manon Lescaut. Bernardin de Saint-Pierre left only *Paul and Virginia.* There are many geniuses who produce only one great work. But indeed, what a work! That remains like a monument in literature. And I am of that family of geniuses. I have produced but one good thing. Why have I lived it instead of writing it? If I had written it, I should be famous. I should have not only a story to show, but all the world would read it, for it would be unique of its kind. I have produced a masterpiece of crime."

This idea became at length a mania with him. For years he cherished it. He let it consume him; at first the regret that he had not had the dream instead of the act, then the desire to relate the fact as a dream. What haunted him was not the demon of perversity, the singular power which urges men of the Edgar Allan Poe type to cry their secret aloud; it was the need of fame, the desire for glory. His fixed idea pursued him with a thousand specious reasonings.

"Why should you not write the truth? What do you fear? Anatole Desroses is safe from justice. The crime is old. It is forgotten by all the world. The author of it is known, he is dead and buried. You will have the reputation of having artistically arranged an old law case. You will reveal in it all the obscure thoughts, all the rancorous hatreds that have urged the murderer to the commission of the crime; all the faculties employed to commit it; all the circumstances that the marvelous inventor we call chance has furnished you. You are alone in the secret of the deed and no one will guess that you are the real author of it. They will see in the story only the effort of an extraordinary imagination. And then you will be the man you wish to be: the great author who reveals himself late, but with a masterstroke. You will enjoy your crime as never a criminal has enjoyed one before. You will have gained by it not only fortune, but fame also. And who knows? After this first success, when you have a name, the public will read again your other works, and will see without a doubt what an unjust opinion they have had of you. On the road to fame, it is only the first step which costs. Recall a little of that courage that you had one particular day in your life. See how well it succeeded. It cannot fail to succeed now. You have known once how to seize opportunity by the forelock. Do so again. Shall you allow yourself to shrink from it? You know well that the deed was grand, do you not? Well, then, tell it without fear, without hesitation, proudly, in all its majestic honor. Be boldly courageous, renounce the pseudonym and sign your own name. It is not Jacques de la Mole, Antoine Guirland, nor even Anatole Desroses. It is not the host of men without talent that you wish to render illustrious; it is yourself, it is Oscar Lapissotte!"

So one evening, Oscar Lapissotte seated himself before a pile of white paper, his head on fire, his hand burning, like a great poet who feels himself about to create some grand work, and he wrote the true history of his crime. He told of the miserable struggles of Oscar Lapissotte, his Bohemian life, his multiplied failures, his proud mediocrity, his rancorous hatreds, the ever-haunting thoughts of suicide and crime, the revolt of a heart that fancy had deceived and that wished to avenge itself on the reality, the whole a romance in metaphysics. Then in a sober fashion and with frightful clearness, he described the scene at the hospital, the scene in the Rue Saint-Denis, the death of the innocent coachman, the triumph of the real murderer. With a subtlety of details curious and almost satanic, he analyzed the causes which had decided the author to publish his crime, and he finished by the apotheosis of Oscar Lapissotte, who put his signature at the end of this confession.

5.

"The Masterpiece of Crime" appeared in the *Revue des Deux Mondes*[1] and had prodigious success. One can gain some idea of it by reading a few of the following extracts from some of the articles which greeted its appearance: "Everyone knows that the nom-de-plume of Oscar Lapissotte conceals an author who delights in this sort of disguise, Monsieur Anatole Desroses. After having, for a long time, wasted his talents in light journalistic work, Monsieur Anatole Desroses has just given us his true measure. The story is drawn from a judicial trage-dy which occurred about ten years ago in the Rue Saint-Denis. But the imagination of the romancer has known how to transform a vulgar assassination into a wonderfully complex and interesting story. Poor

---

1. A monthly magazine of culture and public affairs, established in Paris in 1829 and still printed today.

Gaboriau[2] himself would not have thought of the strange complications that Monsieur Anatole Desroses has invented. We shall give part of the 'Masterpiece of Crime' in our next Sunday's Issue." (*Figaro*.)

"Masterpiece, indeed, this 'Masterpiece of Crime'! This pen has the sharpness of a sword and the keenness of a scalpel. It spares nothing, it lays bare the darkest thoughts of the mind, the inmost feelings of the soul. One sees here clearly, too clearly indeed, all, everything. It is a sulfurous clearness accorded to the eye of the evil one himself; it is the finger of the evil one, this finger of Monsieur Anatole Desroses, which drags away the covering of crime and shows the human heart in all its nakedness. He pleases, this Monsieur Anatole Desroses, like a vice, a forbidden pleasure." (*Constitutionelle*.)

In short, there was a concert of plaudits, some generous, some envious, some foolish, from the Prudhommes[3] and other lights of journalism.

6.

Yet in all these articles, in the most flattering even, two things were always found which irritated Oscar Lapissotte. The first was that they persisted in taking his true name for a

2. Émile Gaboriau (1832–1873) was a French writer, best known as a pioneer of detective fiction.

3. A reference to the historian, journalist, and publisher Louis-Marie Prudhomme (1752–1830). A royalist critic of the French Revolution and Napoleon, Prudhomme complied an index of all known victims of the Reign of Terror, among other works.

nom-de-plume and in calling him Anatole Desroses. The second was the fact that they spoke too much of his imagination and seemed wholly incredulous as to the probability of his story being a true one. These two desiderata tormented him to such a degree that he forgot in them all the happiness of his budding glory. Artists are made thus, so that even when the public and the critics lull them to slumber on a bed of roses, they suffer if one leaf is crumpled.

So, one day, when someone congratulated the great author who had written *the Masterpiece of Crime*, and highly flattered him, the great author answered, stepping quite close to him:

"Oh, Monsieur, you would felicitate me in quite another strain if you knew the real truth of the affair. My novel is not a romance; it really has happened. The crime has been committed just as I have related it. And it is I who committed it. I called myself by my true name, Oscar Lapissotte." He said this quite coldly, with a grand air of conviction, speaking every word slowly and distinctly as if he wished to be believed.

"Ah, charming, charming!" exclaimed the flatterer. "The pleasantry is rather lugubrious, however. It is like the best of Baudelaire."

The following day all the journals repeated the anecdote. They found it delicious, this attempt at mystification by which Anatole Desroses wished to make himself pass for an assassin. Decidedly he was original and quite worthy of living in Paris.

Oscar Lapissotte became furious. In making this confession, he had acted, to a degree, mechanically. But now he really wished to be believed by someone. He repeated his confession to all his friends whom he met on the boulevard. The first day it seemed rather droll. The second day his friends found it monotonous. The third day he was thought decidedly tiresome. At the end of the week, he was frankly adjudged an imbecile. He was unable to live up to the reputation of a great author, everyone said. His warmest partisans began to torment him by telling him strange and incredible stories. This descent from the heights of fame exasperated him.

"Oh, it is too much!" he said. "No one will give credence to that which is the exact truth; no one will believe that I have not only written, but executed, a Masterpiece of Crime! Well, I shall have a clear conscience in the matter. Tomorrow, all Paris shall know who Oscar Lapissotte is!"

7.

He sought out the judge who had presided when the case from the Rue Saint-Denis was tried. "Monsieur," said he, "I have come to give myself into custody. I am Oscar Lapissotte."

"It is unnecessary to continue, Monsieur," replied the judge. "I have read your novel, and I extend you my congratulations. I know also the eccentricity with which you have amused yourself for the past week. Another than myself might perhaps be annoyed that you should carry your pleasantry to this extreme. But I love the fine arts and all literary productions, and I shall pardon your sprightly farce since it gives me the pleasure of knowing you."

"But, Monsieur," said Oscar, impatient under these polite phrases, "it is no farce! I swear to you that I am Oscar Lapissotte; that I have committed this crime and that I am going to prove it to you."

"Well, Monsieur," replied the judge, "you will see how accommodating I am. For the curiosity of the thing, I am going to lend myself to this farce. I confess to you that I enjoy in advance the pleasure of seeing how a mind as subtle as your own can adapt itself to the task of proving to me this absurdity."

"The absurdity! But what I related is the absolute truth. The coachman was not guilty. It is I who have—"

"I believe you have said all that, Monsieur, in your novel which I have read. But, if it pleases you to tell it to me yourself, I shall take great pleasure in listening to your story, though it will prove nothing at all, except that which is already proved: that you have an imagination singularly rich and strange."

"I have had only imagination enough to commit this crime."

"Not to commit it, but to write it, dear sir, to write it. Stop one moment and let me tell you my opinion of it. You have had almost too much imagination; you have passed the limits permitted to the fancy of the author; you have invented certain circumstances that are not to be considered as possible, or probable, at least."

"But when I tell you—"

"Allow me; I beg your pardon, but you must admit that I possess some judgment in criminal matters. Well, I assure you that the circumstances of your crime are not naturally arranged. The meeting with the maid in the hospital is too unlikely, and then there are other improbabilities.

As a work of art, your novel is charming, original, well-planned, what you call strong; and I admit that you are perfectly right, you authors, to travesty reality in this way. But your famous crime in itself is impossible. My dear Monsieur Desroses, I am sorry to give you the least annoyance; but if I admire you as a man of letters, I cannot accept you seriously as a criminal."

"It is that which you must do now," shouted Oscar Lapissotte, rushing upon the magistrate. He was frothing at the lips, his eyes were bloodshot, his whole body was bursting with rage. He would have strangled the judge had not his cries brought help. The judge's assistants overcame the furious man, and bound him.

Five days later he was taken to Charenton[4] as a hopeless maniac.

"See to what literary ambition may lead!" said the newspapers the following day. "Anatole Desroses has produced, just once, a great work. He has been so wrought up by it that he has ended by believing that his dream was reality. It is the old fable of Pygmalion and his statue."

---

4.   Charenton was a lunatic asylum, founded in 1645 by Brothers of Charity in Charenton-Saint-Maurice, a suburb of Paris. Among its famous inmates were Paul Verlaine and the Marquis de Sade.

8.

The most frightful part of it all was that Oscar Lapissotte was not a madman. He had all his reason and was only the more tortured by it.

"Now all misfortunes are mine," he said. "They will believe neither in my name nor in my crime. When I am dead, I shall pass simply for Anatole Desroses, a scribbler who had the genius to create only one fine work; and they will know as a fictitious personage this Oscar Lapissotte, this being that I am, the man of action, decision, the hero of ferocity, the living negation of remorse. Oh, let them guillotine me but let them know the truth! Were it for one moment only, before thrusting my neck under the ax; were it for one second even while the knife fell; were it only for the length of a flash of lightning, that I might have the certainty of my glory and the vision of my immortality!"

These exaltations were treated with cold water. At last, by living with one fixed idea and in the company of madmen, he actually became mad. And when he had reached this point he was discharged as cured!

Oscar Lapissotte finished by believing that he was really Anatole Desroses, and that he had never been an assassin. He died with the conviction that he had dreamed his crime and not committed it!

Tales of Revenge

The Song of the Brothers of Mercy

by Friedrich Schiller

December 1926 (vol. 8, no. 6)

Translated from the German by Francis Hard,
pseudonym of Farnsworth Wright

With rapid pace on strideth Death;
No breathing spell to man is given:
Midway the course Death stops his breath,
And sends him to his God unshriven;
And whether he's prepared or no,
Each man before his Judge must go.

The Queen of Spades

by Alexander Pushkin

August 1927 (vol. 10, no. 2)

Translated from the Russian by Unknown

There was a card party at the rooms of Narumoff of the Horse Guards. The long winter night passed away imperceptibly, and it was five o'clock in the morning before the company sat down to supper. Those who had won ate with a good appetite, the others sat staring absently at their empty plates. When the champagne appeared, however, the conversation became animated.

"And how did you fare, Surin?" asked the host.

"Oh, I lost, as usual. I must confess that I am unlucky: I play *mirandole*,[1] I always keep cool, I never allow anything to put me out, and yet I always lose!"

---

1. A term in the French card game of faro, meaning to play one card at a time and to not double one's bets. In the game, a banker plays against any number of players, with winning and losing determined by the matching of cards turned up by the banker to those already exposed. Developed in

"And you did not once allow yourself to be tempted to back the red? Your firmness astonishes me."

"But what do you think of Hermann?" said one of the guests, pointing to a young engineer. "He has never had a card in his hand in his life, he has never in his life laid a wager, and yet he sits here till five in the morning watching our play."

"Play interests me very much," said Hermann, "but I am not in the position to sacrifice the necessary in the hope of winning the superfluous."

"Hermann is a German: he is economical—that is all!" observed Tomsky. "But if there is one person that I can not understand, it is my grandmother, the Countess Anna Feodorovna."

"How so?" inquired the guests.

"I can not understand," continued Tomsky, "how it is that my grandmother does not punt."

"What is there remarkable about an old lady of eighty not punting?" asked Narumoff.

"Then you do not know why?"

"No, I haven't the faintest idea."

"Oh, then listen! About sixty years ago my grandmother went to Paris, where she created quite a sensation. People used to run after her to catch a glimpse of the 'Muscovite Venus.' Richelieu made love to her, and my grandmother maintains that he almost blew out his brains in consequence of her cruelty. At that time ladies used to play at faro. On one occasion at the court, she lost a large sum to the Duke of Orleans. On returning

France during the late 17th century, faro was popular with gamblers worldwide until the First World War.

home, my grandmother removed the patches from her face, took off her hoops, informed my grandfather of her loss at the gaming table, and ordered him to pay the money. My deceased grandfather, as far as I remember, was a sort of house-steward to my grandmother. He dreaded her like fire; but, on hearing of such a heavy loss, he almost went out of his mind; he calculated the various sums she had lost, and pointed out to her that in six months she had spent half a million francs, that neither their Moscow nor Saratoff estates were in Paris, and finally refused point-blank to pay the debt. My grandmother gave him a box on the ear and slept by herself as a sign of her displeasure. The next day she sent for her husband, hoping that this domestic punishment had produced an effect upon him, but she found him inflexible. For the first time in her life, she entered into reasonings and explanations with him, thinking to be able to convince him by pointing out to him that there are debts and debts, and that there is a great difference between a prince and a coachmaker. But it was all in vain: my grandfather remained obdurate.

"But the matter did not rest there. My grandmother did not know what to do. She had shortly before become acquainted with a very remarkable man. You have heard of Count St. Germain, about whom so many marvelous stories are told. You know that he represented himself as the Wandering Jew, as the discoverer of the elixir of life, of the philosopher's stone, and so forth. Some laughed at him as a charlatan; but St. Germain was a very fascinating person, much sought after in the best circles. My grandmother knew that he had large sums of money at his disposal, and she wrote a letter asking him to come to her without delay. The queer old man immediately waited upon her and found her overwhelmed with grief. She described to him in the blackest colors the barbarity of her husband, and ended by declaring that her whole hope depended upon his friendship.

"St. Germain reflected.

"'I could advance you the sum you want,' said he, 'but I know that you would not rest easy until you had paid me back, and I should not like to bring fresh troubles upon you. But there is another way of getting out of your difficulty: you can win back your money.'

"'But, my dear count,' replied my grandmother, 'I tell you that I haven't any money left.'

"'Money is not necessary,' replied St. Germain: 'listen to me.'

"Then he revealed to her a secret, for which each of us would give a good deal."

The young officers listened with increased attention. Tomsky lit his pipe, puffed away for a moment and then continued:

"That same evening my grandmother went to Versailles to the *jeu de la reine*.[2] The Duke of Orleans kept the bank; my grandmother excused herself in

---

2. "The game of the queen" a term for gambling events held on a daily basis by the French royal court during the 17th and 18th centuries. These ranged from intimate gatherings to large tournaments. The queen typically hosted gambling in the Peace Salon, at the southern end of the Hall of Mirrors, while at Versailles.

an off-hand manner for not having yet paid her debt, by inventing some little story, and then began to play against him. She chose three cards and played them one after the other: all three won *sonika*—that is, in the quickest possible time—and my grandmother recovered every farthing that she had lost."

"Mere chance!" said one of the guests.

"A tale!" observed Hermann.

"Perhaps they were marked cards!" said a third.

"I do not think so," replied Tomsky gravely.

"What!" said Narumoff; "you have a grandmother who knows how to hit upon three lucky cards in succession, and you have not succeeded in getting the secret from her?"

"That's the deuce of it," replied Tomsky: "she had four sons, one of whom was my father; all four were determined gamblers, and yet not to one of them did she ever reveal her secret. But this is what I heard from my uncle, Count Ivan Ilyich, and he assured me, on his honor, that it was true. The late Chaplitzky—the same who died in poverty after having squandered millions—once lost, in his youth, about three hundred thousand rubles. He was in despair. My grandmother, who was always very severe upon the extravagance of young men, took pity, however, upon Chaplitzky. She gave him three cards, telling him to play them one after the other, at the same time exacting from him a solemn promise that he would never play at cards again as long as he lived. Chaplitzky then went to his victorious opponent, and they began a fresh game. On the first card he staked fifty thousand rubles and won *sonika*; he doubled the stake and won again, till at last, by pursuing the same tactics, he won back more than he had lost.

"But it is time to go to bed: it is a quarter to six already."

And indeed it was already beginning to dawn: the young men emptied their glasses and then took leave of each other.

2.

The old countess was seated in her dressing room before her looking glass. Three waiting maids stood around her. One held a small pot of rouge, another a box of hair-pins, and the third a tall cap with bright red ribbons. The countess had no longer the slightest pretensions to beauty, but she still preserved the habits of her youth, dressed in strict accordance with the fashion of seventy years before, and made as long and as careful a toilette as she would have done sixty years previously. Near the window, at an embroidery frame, sat a young lady, her ward.

"Good morning, grandmamma," said a young officer, entering the room. "Bonjour, Mademoiselle Lisa. Grandmamma, I want to ask you something."

"What is it, Paul?"

"I want you to let me introduce one of my friends to you, and to allow me to bring him to the ball on Friday."

"Bring him directly to the ball and introduce him to me there. Were you at B—'s yesterday?"

"Yes; everything went off very pleasantly, and dancing was kept up until five o'clock. How charming Yeletzkaya was!"

"But, my dear, what is there charming about her? Isn't she like her grandmother, the Princess Daria Petrovna? By the way, she must be very old, the Princess Daria Petrovna."

"How do you mean, old?" cried Tomsky thoughtlessly; "she died seven years ago."

The young lady raised her head and made a sign to the young officer. He then remembered that the old countess was never to be informed of the death of any of her contemporaries, and he bit his lips. But she heard the news with indifference.

"Dead!" said she; "and I did not know it. We were appointed maids of honor at the same time, and when we were presented to the Empress…"

And the countess for the hundredth time related to her grandson one of her anecdotes.

"Come, Paul," said she, when she had finished her story, "help me to get up. Lizanka, where is my snuffbox?"

And the countess with her three maids went behind a screen to finish her toilette. Tomsky was left alone with the young lady.

"Who is the gentleman you wish to introduce to the countess?" asked Lizaveta Ivanovna in a whisper.

"Narumoff. Do you know him?"

"No. Is he a soldier or a civilian?"

"A soldier."

"Is he in the Engineers?"

"No, in the Cavalry. What made you think he was in the Engineers?"

The young lady smiled, but made no reply.

"Paul," cried the countess from behind the screen, "send me some new novel, only pray don't let it be one of the present-day style."

"What do you mean, grandmother?"

"That is, a novel in which the hero strangles neither his father nor his mother, and in which there are no drowned bodies. I have a great horror of drowned persons."

"There are no such novels nowadays. Would you like a Russian one?"

"Are there any Russian novels? Pray send me one!"

"Good-bye, grandmother: I am in a hurry... Good-bye, Lizaveta Ivanovna."

And Tomsky left the boudoir.

Lizaveta Ivanovna was left alone: she laid aside her work and began to look out the window. A few minutes afterward, at a corner house on the other side of the street, a young officer appeared. A deep blush covered her cheeks; she took up her work again and bent her head down over the frame. At the same moment the countess returned.

"Order the carriage, Lizaveta," said she; "we will go for a drive."

Lizaveta arose from the frame and began to arrange her work.

"What is the matter with you, my child, are you deaf?" cried the countess. "Order the carriage to be made ready at once."

"I will do so this moment," replied the young lady, hastening into the anteroom.

A servant entered and gave the countess some books from Prince Paul Alexandrovich.

"Tell him that I am much obliged to him," said the countess. "Lizaveta ! Where are you running to?"

"I am going to dress."

"There is plenty of time, my dear, sit down here and read to me."

Her companion took the book and read a few lines.

"Louder," said the countess. "What is the matter with you, my child? Have you lost your voice? Wait—give me that footstool—a little nearer—that will do."

Lizaveta read two more pages. The countess yawned.

"Put the book down," said she; "what a lot of nonsense! Send it back to Prince Paul with my thanks. But where is the carriage?"

"The carriage is ready," said Lizaveta, looking out into the street.

"How is it you are not dressed?" asked the countess. "I must always wait for you. It is intolerable."

Liza hastened to her room. She had not been there two minutes, before the countess began to ring with all her might. The three waiting maids came running in at one door and the valet at another.

"How is it that you can not hear me when I ring for you?" said the countess. "Tell Lizaveta Ivanovna I am waiting for her."

Lizaveta returned with her hat and cloak on.

"At last you are here!" said the countess. "But why such an elaborate toilette? Whom do you intend to captivate? What sort of weather is it? It seems rather windy."

"No, your Ladyship, it is very calm," replied the valet.

"You never think of what you are talking about. Open the window. So it is: windy and bitterly cold. Unharness the horses. Lizaveta, we won't go out—there was no need for you to deck yourself like that."

"What a life is mine!" thought Lizaveta Ivanovna.

And, in truth, Lizaveta Ivanovna was a very unfortunate creature. The old countess had by no means a bad heart, but she was capricious, like a woman who had been spoilt by the world, as well as being avaricious and egotistical, like all old people who have seen their best days, and whose thoughts are with the past and not the present. She participated in all the vanities of the great world, went to balls, where she sat in a corner, painted and dressed in old-fashioned style, like a deformed but indispensable ornament of the ballroom; all the guests on entering approached her and made a profound bow, as if in accordance with a set ceremony, but after that nobody took further notice of her.

Her numerous domestics, growing fat and old in her antechamber and servants' hall, did just as they liked, and vied with each other in robbing the aged countess in the most barefaced manner. Lizaveta Ivanovna was the martyr of the household. She made tea, and was reproached for using too much sugar; she read novels aloud to the countess, and the faults of the author were visited upon her head; she accompanied the countess in her walks, and was held answerable for the weather or the state of the pavement. A salary was attached to the post, but she very rarely received it, although she was expected to dress like everybody else, that is to say, like very few indeed. In society she played the most pitiable role. Everybody knew her, and nobody paid her any attention. At balls she danced only when a partner was wanted, the ladies would only take hold of her arm when it was necessary to lead her out of the room to attend to their dresses. She was very self-conscious, and felt her position keenly, and she looked about her with impatience for a deliverer to come to her rescue; but the young men, calculating in their giddiness, honored her with but very little attention, although Lizaveta Ivanovna was a hundred times prettier than the bare-faced and cold-hearted marriageable girls around whom they hovered. Many a time did she quietly slink away from the glittering but wearisome drawing room, to go and cry in her own poor little room, in which stood a screen, a chest of drawers, a looking-glass and a painted bedstead, and where a tallow candle burnt feebly in a copper candlestick.

One morning—this was about two days after the evening party described at the beginning of this story, and a week previous to the scene at which we have just assisted—Lizaveta Ivanovna was seated near the window at her embroidery frame, when, happening to look out into the street, she caught sight of a young engineer officer, standing motionless with his eyes fixed upon her window. She lowered her head and went on again with her work. About five minutes afterward she looked out again—the young officer was still standing in the same place. Not being in the habit of coquetting with passing officers, she did not continue to gaze out into the street, but went on sewing for a couple of hours, without raising her head. Dinner was announced. She rose up and began to put her embroidery away, but glancing casually out of the window, she perceived the officer again. This seemed to her very strange. After dinner she went to the window with a certain feeling of uneasiness, but the officer was no longer there—and she thought no more about him.

A couple of days afterward, just as she was stepping into the carriage with the countess, she saw him again. He was standing close behind the door, with his face half-concealed by his fur collar, but his dark eyes sparkled beneath his cap. Lizaveta felt alarmed, and she trembled as she seated herself in the carriage.

On returning home, she hastened to the window—the officer was standing in his accustomed place, with his eyes fixed upon her. She drew back, a prey to curiosity and agitated by a feeling that was quite new to her.

From that time forward not a day passed without the young officer making his appearance under the window at the customary hour, and between him and her there was established a sort of mute acquaintance. Sitting in her place at work, she used to feel his approach; and raising her head, she would look at him longer and longer each day. The young man seemed to be very grateful to her: a sudden flush covered his pale cheek each time their glances met. After about a week she commenced to smile at him.

When Tomsky asked permission of his grandmother the countess to present one of his friends to her, the young girl's heart beat violently. But hearing that Narumoff was not an engineer, she regretted that by her thoughtless question she had betrayed her secret to the volatile Tomsky.

Hermann was the son of a German who had become a naturalized Russian, and from whom he had inherited a small capital. Being firmly convinced of the necessity of preserving his independence, Hermann did not touch his private income, but lived on his pay, without allowing himself the slightest luxury. And though he was a gamester at heart, he never touched a card, for he considered his position did not allow him, as he said, "to risk the necessary in the hope of winning the superfluous," yet he would sit for nights together at the card table and follow the game with feverish anxiety.

The story of the three cards had produced a powerful impression upon his imagination, and all night long he could think of nothing else. "If," he thought to himself the following evening, as he walked along the streets of St. Petersburg, "if the old countess would but reveal her secret to me! If she would only tell me the names of the three winning cards! Why should I not try my fortune? I must get introduced to her and win her favor—become her lover. But all that will take time, and she is eighty-seven years old: she might be dead in a week, in a couple of days even. But the story itself: can it really be true? No! Economy, temperance and industry: those are my three winning cards; by means of them I shall be able to double my capital—increase it sevenfold, and procure for myself ease and independence."

Musing in this manner, he walked on until he found himself in one of the principal streets of St. Petersburg, in front of a house of antiquated architecture. The street was blocked with equipages; carriages one after the other drew up in front of the brilliantly illuminated doorway. At one moment there stepped out onto the pavement the well-shaped little foot of some young beauty, at another the heavy boot of a cavalry officer, and then the silk stockings and shoes of a member of the diplomatic world. Furs and cloaks passed in rapid succession before the gigantic porter at the entrance.

Hermann stopped. "Whose house is this?" he asked of the watchman at the corner.

"The Countess Anna Feodorovna's," replied the watchman.

Hermann started. The strange story of the three cards again presented itself to his imagination. He began walking up and down before the house, thinking of its owner and her strange secret. Returning late to his modest lodging, he could not go to sleep for a long time, and when at last he did doze off, he could dream of nothing but cards, green tables, piles of bank-notes and heaps of ducats. He played one card after the other, winning uninterruptedly, and then he gathered up the gold and filled his pockets with the notes. When he woke up late the next morning, he sighed over the loss of his imaginary wealth, and then sallying out into the town, he found himself once more in front of the countess' residence. He looked up at the windows. At one of these he saw a head with luxuriant black hair, which was bent down probably over some book or an embroidery frame. The head was raised. Hermann saw a fresh complexion and a pair of dark eyes. That moment decided his fate.

3.

Lizaveta Ivanovna had scarcely taken off her hat and cloak before the countess sent for her and again told her to get the carriage ready. The vehicle drew up before the door, and they prepared to take their seats. Just at the moment when two footmen were assisting the old lady to enter the carriage, Lizaveta saw her engineer standing close beside the wheel; he grasped her hand; alarm caused her to lose her presence of mind, and the young man disappeared—but not before he had left a letter between her fingers. She concealed it in her glove, and during the whole of the drive she neither saw nor heard anything.

It was the custom of the countess to be constantly asking such questions as: "Who was that person that met us just now? What is the name of this bridge? What is written on that signboard?" On this occasion, however, Lizaveta returned such vague and absurd answers that the countess became angry with her.

"What is the matter with you, my dear?" she exclaimed. "Have you taken leave of your senses, or what is it? Do you not hear me or understand what I say? Heaven be thanked, I am still in my right mind and speak plainly enough!"

Lizaveta Ivanovna did not hear her. On returning home she ran to her room and drew the letter out of her glove. It contained a declaration of love; it was tender, respectful, and copied word for word from a German novel. But Lizaveta did not know anything of the German language, and she was quite delighted.

For all that, the letter caused her to feel exceedingly uneasy. For the first time in her life she was entering into secret and confidential relations with a young man. His boldness alarmed her. She reproached herself for her imprudent behavior, and knew not what to do. Should she cease to sit at the window and, by assuming an appearance of indifference toward him, put a check upon the young officer's desire for further acquaintance with her? Should she send his letter back to him, or should she answer him in a cold and decided manner? At length she resolved to reply to him.

She sat down at her little writing table, took pen and paper, and began to think.. Several times she began the letter and then tore it up, for the way she had expressed herself seemed either too inviting or too coldly decisive. At last she succeeded in writing a few lines with which she felt satisfied.

"I am convinced," she wrote, "that your intentions are honorable, and that you do not wish to offend me by any imprudent behavior, but our acquaintance must not begin in such a manner. I return your letter, and I hope that I shall never have any cause to complain of this undeserved slight."

The next day, as soon as Hermann made his appearance, Lizaveta rose from her embroidery, went into the drawing room, opened the ventilator and threw the letter into the street, trusting that the young officer would have the perception to pick it up.

Hermann hastened forward, picked it up and then repaired to a confectioner's shop. Breaking the seal of the envelope, he found inside it his own letter and Lizaveta's reply. He had expected this, and he returned home, his mind deeply occupied.

Three days afterward, a bright eyed young girl from a milliner's establishment brought Lizaveta a letter. Lizaveta opened it with great uneasiness, fearing that it was a demand for money, when suddenly she recognized Hermann's handwriting.

"You have made a mistake," she said: "this letter is not for me"

"Oh, yes, it is for you," replied the girl, smiling very knowingly. "Have the goodness to read it."

Lizaveta glanced at the letter. Hermann requested an interview.

"It can not be," she cried, alarmed at the audacious request, and the manner in which it was made. "This letter is certainly not for me."

And she tore it into fragments.

"If the letter was not for you, why have you torn it up?" said the girl. "I should have given it back to the person who sent it."

"Be good enough, my dear," said Lizaveta, disconcerted by this remark, "not to bring me any more letters, and tell the person who sent you that he ought to be ashamed."

But Hermann was not the man to be thus put off. Every day Lizaveta received from him a letter, sent now in this way, now in that. They were no longer translated from the German. Hermann wrote them under the inspiration of passion, and spoke in his own language, and they bore full testimony to the inflexibility of his desire and the disordered condition of his uncontrollable imagination. Lizaveta no longer thought of sending them back to him: she became intoxicated with them and began to reply to them, and little by little her answers became longer and more affectionate.

At last she threw out of the window to him the following letter: "This evening there is going to be a ball at the embassy. The countess will be there. We shall remain until two o'clock. You have now an opportunity of seeing me alone. As soon as the countess is gone, the servants will very probably go out, and there will be nobody left but the Swiss, and he usually goes to sleep in his lodge. Come about half-past eleven. Walk straight upstairs. If you meet anybody in the anteroom, ask if the countess is at home. You will be told 'No,' in which case there will be nothing left for you to do but to go away again. But it is most probable that you will meet nobody. The maid-servants will all be together in one room. On leaving the anteroom, turn to the left, and walk straight on until you reach the countess' bedroom. In the bedroom, behind a screen, you will find two doors: the one on the right leads to a cabinet, which the countess never enters; the one on the left leads to a corridor, at the end of which is a little winding staircase; this leads to my room."

Hermann trembled like a tiger, as he waited for the appointed time to arrive. At ten o'clock in the evening he was already in front of the countess' house. The weather was terrible; the wind blew with great violence; the sleety snow fell in large flakes; the lamps emitted a feeble light, the streets were deserted; from time to time a sledge, drawn by a sorry-looking hack, passed by, on the lookout for a belated passenger. Hermann was enveloped in a thick overcoat, and felt neither wind nor snow.

At last the countess' carriage drew up. Hermann saw two footmen carry out in their arms the bent form of the old lady, wrapped in sable fur, and immediately behind her, clad in a warm mantle, and with her head ornamented with a wreath of fresh flowers, followed Lizaveta. The door was closed. The carriage rolled away heavily through the yielding snow. The porter shut the street door; the windows became dark.

Hermann began walking up and down near the deserted house; at length he stopped under a lamp and glanced at his watch: it was twenty minutes past eleven.

At half-past eleven precisely, he ascended the steps of the house, and made his way into the brightly illuminated vestibule. He hastily ascended the staircase, opened the door of the anteroom and saw a footman sitting asleep in an antique chair by the side of a lamp. With a light, firm step Hermann passed by him. The drawing room and dining room were in darkness, but a feeble reflection penetrated thither from the lamp in the anteroom.

Hermann reached the countess' bedroom. Before a shrine, which was full of old images, a golden lamp was burning. Faded stuffed chairs and divans with soft cushions stood in melancholy symmetry around the room, the walls of which were hung with China silk. On one side of the room hung two portraits painted in Paris by Madame Lebrun.[3] In the corners stood porcelain shepherds and shepherdesses, dining room clocks, bandboxes, roulettes, fans and the various playthings for the amusement of ladies that

---

3. Élisabeth Louise Vigée Le Brun (1755–1842), often referred to simply as Madame Le Brun, was a French painter who specialized in portraiture. Marie-Antoinette was a major patron, and Le Brun painted over 30 portraits of the Queen and her family.

were in vogue at the end of the last century, when Montgolfier's balloons and Mesmer's magnetism were the rage. Hermann stepped behind the screen. At the back of it stood a little iron bedstead; on the right was the door which led to the cabinet; on the left, the other which led to the corridor. He opened the latter, and saw the little winding staircase which led to the room of the poor companion. But he retraced his steps and entered the dark cabinet.

The time passed slowly. All was still. The clock in the drawing room struck twelve; the strokes echoed through the room one after the other, and everything was quiet again. Hermann stood leaning against the cold stove. He was calm; his heart beat regularly, like that of a man resolved upon a dangerous but inevitable undertaking. One o'clock in the morning struck; then two; and he heard the distant noise of carriage-wheels. An involuntary agitation took possession of him. The carriage drew near and stopped. He heard the sound of the carriage-steps being let down. All was bustling within the house. The servants were running hither and thither, there was a confusion of voices, and the rooms were lit up. Three antiquated chambermaids entered the bedroom, and they were shortly afterward followed by the countess, who, more dead than alive, sank into a Voltaire armchair. Hermann peeped through a chink. Lizaveta Ivanovna passed close by him, and he heard her hurried steps as she hastened up the little spiral staircase. For a moment his heart was assailed by something like a pricking of conscience, but the emotion was only transitory, and his heart became petrified as before.

The countess began to undress before her looking-glass. Her rose-bedecked cap was taken off, and then her powdered wig was removed from off her white and closely-cut hair. Hairpins fell in showers around her. Her yellow satin dress, brocaded with silver, fell down at her swollen feet.

Hermann was a witness of the repugnant mysteries of her toilette; at last the countess was in her night-cap and dressing gown, and in this costume, more suitable to her age, she appeared less hideous and deformed.

Like most old people, the countess suffered from sleeplessness. Having undressed, she seated herself at the window in a Voltaire armchair and dismissed her maids. The candles were taken away, and once more the room was left with only one lamp burning in it. The countess sat there looking quite yellow, mumbling with her flaccid lips and swaying to and fro. Her dull eyes expressed complete vacancy of mind, and, looking at her, one would have thought that the rocking of her body was not a voluntary action of her own, but was produced by the action of some concealed galvanic mechanism.

Suddenly the deathlike face assumed an inexplicable expression. The lips ceased to tremble, the eyes became animated: before the countess stood an unknown man.

"Do not be alarmed, for heaven's sake, do not be alarmed!" said he in a low but distinct voice. "I have no intention of doing you any harm, I have only come to ask a favor of you."

The old woman looked at him in silence, as if she had not heard what he had said. Hermann thought that she was deaf, and, bending down toward her ear, he repeated what he had said. The aged countess remained silent as before.

"You can insure the happiness of my life," continued Hermann, "and it will cost you nothing. I know that you can name three cards in order—"

Hermann stopped. The countess appeared now to understand what he wanted; she seemed as if seeking for words to reply.

"It was a joke," she replied at last. "I assure you it was only a joke."

"There is no joking about the matter," replied Hermann angrily. "Remember Chaplitzky, whom you helped to win."

The countess became visibly uneasy. Her features expressed strong emotion, but they quickly resumed their former immobility.

"Can you not name me these three winning cards?" continued Hermann.

The countess remained silent; Hermann continued: "For whom are you preserving your secret? For your grandsons? They are rich enough without it; they do not know the worth of money. Your cards would be of no use to a spendthrift. He who can not preserve his paternal inheritance will die in want, even though he had a demon at his service. I am not a man of that sort; I know the value of money. Your three cards will not be thrown away upon me. Come!"

He paused and tremblingly awaited her reply. The countess remained silent; Hermann fell upon his knees.

"If your heart has ever known the feeling of love," said he, "if you remember its rapture, if you have ever smiled at the cry of your new-born child, if any human feeling has ever entered into your breast, I entreat you by the feelings of a wife, a lover, a mother, by all that is most sacred in life, not to reject my prayer. Reveal to me your secret. Of what use is it to you? Maybe it is connected with some terrible sin, with the loss of eternal salvation, with some bargain with the devil. Reflect: you are old; you have not long to live; I am ready to take your sins upon my soul. Only reveal to me your secret. Remember that the happiness of a man is in your hands, that not only I, but my children, and grandchildren, will bless your memory and reverence you as a saint."

The old countess answered not a word.

Hermann rose to his feet.

"You old hag," he exclaimed, grinding his teeth, "then I will make you answer!"

With these words he drew a pistol from his pocket.

At the sight of the pistol, the countess for the second time exhibited strong emotion. She shook her head and raised her hands as if to protect herself from the shot; then she fell backward and remained motionless.

"Come, an end to this childish nonsense!" said Hermann, taking hold of her hand. "I ask you for the last time: will you tell me the names of your three cards, or will you not?"

The countess made no reply. Hermann perceived that she was dead!

4.

Lizaveta Ivanovna was sitting in her room, still in her ball dress, lost in deep thought. On returning home, she had hastily dismissed the chambermaid, who very reluctantly came forward to assist her, saying that she would undress herself, and with a trembling heart had gone up to her own room, expecting to find Hermann there, but yet hoping not to find him. At the first glance she convinced herself that he was not there, and she thanked her fate for having prevented him keeping the appointment. She sat down without undressing, and began to recall to mind all the circumstances which in so short a time had carried her so far. It was not three weeks since the time when she first saw the young officer from the window, and yet she was already in correspondence with him, and he had succeeded in inducing her to grant him a nocturnal interview! She knew his name only through his having written it at the bottom of some of his letters; she had never spoken to him, had never heard his voice, and had never heard him spoken of until that evening. But, strange to say, that very evening at the ball, Tomsky, being piqued with the young Princess Pauline N—, who, contrary to her usual custom, did not flirt with him, wished to revenge himself by assuming an air of indifference: he therefore engaged Lizaveta Ivanovna and danced an endless mazurka with her. During the whole of the time he kept teasing her about her partiality for engineer officers; he assured her that he knew far more than she imagined, and some of his jests were so happily aimed, that Lizaveta thought several times that her secret was known to him.

"From whom have you learnt all this?" she asked, smiling.

"From a friend of a person very well known to you," replied Tomsky; "from a very distinguished man."

"And who is this distinguished man?"

"His name is Hermann."

Lizaveta made no reply; but her hands and feet lost all sense of feeling.

"This Hermann," continued Tomsky, "is a man of romantic personality. He has the profile of a Napoleon, and the soul of a Mephistopheles. I believe that he has at least three crimes upon his conscience...How pale you have become!"

"I have a headache. But what did this Hermann— or whatever his name is—tell you?"

"Hermann is very much dissatisfied with his friend: he says that in his place he would act very differently. I even think that Hermann himself has designs upon you; at least, he listens very attentively to all that his friend has to say about you."

"And where has he seen me?"

"In church, perhaps; or on the parade—God alone knows where. It may have been in your room, while you were asleep, for there is nothing that he—"

Three ladies approaching him interrupted the conversation, which had become so tantalizingly interesting to Lizaveta.

The lady chosen by Tomsky was the Princess Pauline herself. She succeeded in effecting a reconciliation with him during the numerous turns of the dance, after which he conducted her to her chair. On returning to his place, Tomsky thought no more of either Hermann or Lizaveta. She longed to renew the interrupted conversation, but the mazurka came to an end, and shortly afterward the old countess took her departure.

Tomsky's words were nothing more than the customary small talk of the dance, but they sank deep into the soul of the young dreamer. The portrait, sketched by Tomsky, coincided with the picture she had formed within her own mind, and thanks to the latest romances, the ordinary countenance of her admirer became invested with attributes capable of alarming her and fascinating her imagination at the same time. She was now sitting with her bare arms crossed and with her head, still adorned with flowers, sunk upon her uncovered bosom. Suddenly the door opened and Hermann entered. She shuddered.

"Where were you?" she asked in a terrified whisper.

"In the old countess' bedroom," replied Hermann: "I have just left her. The countess is dead."

"My God! What do you say?"

"And I am afraid," added Hermann, "that I am the cause of her death."

Lizaveta looked at him, and Tomsky's words found an echo in her soul: "This man has at least three crimes upon his conscience!" Hermann sat down by the window and related all that had happened.

Lizaveta listened to him in terror. So all those passionate letters, those ardent desires, this bold obstinate pursuit—all this was not love! Money—that was what his soul yearned for! She could not satisfy his desire and make him happy! The poor girl had been nothing but the blind tool of a robber, of the murderer of her aged benefactress! She wept bitter tears of agonized repentance. Hermann gazed at her in silence: his heart, too, was a prey to violent emotion, but neither the tears of the poor girl, nor the wonderful charm of her beauty, enhanced by her grief, could produce any impression upon his hardened soul. He felt no pricking of conscience at the thought of the dead old woman. One thing only grieved him: the irreparable loss of the secret from which he had expected to obtain great wealth.

"You are a monster!" said Lizaveta at last.

"I did not wish for her death," replied Hermann. "My pistol was not loaded."

Both remained silent.

The day began to dawn. Lizaveta extinguished her candle: a pale light illumined her room. She wiped her tear-stained eyes and raised them toward Hermann: he was sitting near the window, with his arms crossed and with a fierce frown upon his forehead. In this attitude he bore a striking resemblance to the portrait of Napoleon. This resemblance struck Lizaveta even.

"How shall I get you out of the house ?" said she at last. "I thought of conducting you down the secret staircase, but in that case it would be necessary to go through the countess' bedroom, and I am afraid."

"Tell me how to find this secret staircase—I will go alone."

Lizaveta arose, took from her drawer a key, handed it to Hermann and gave him the necessary instructions. Hermann pressed her cold, limp hand, kissed her bowed head, and left the room.

He descended the winding staircase, and once more entered the countess' bedroom. The dead old lady sat as if petrified; her face expressed profound tranquility. Hermann stopped before her, and gazed long and earnestly at her, as if he wished to convince himself of the terrible reality; at last he entered the cabinet, felt behind the tapestry for the door, and then began to descend the dark staircase, filled with strange emotions. "Down this very staircase," thought he, "perhaps coming from the very same room, and at this very same hour sixty years ago, there may have glided, in an embroidered coat, with his hair dressed *à l'oiseau royal*[4] and pressing to his heart his three-cornered hat, some young gallant, who has long been moldering in the grave, but the heart of his aged mistress has only today ceased to beat."

---

4. "The royal bird" an elaborate unisex hairstyle of the 18th century, involving a tall wig of curled hair.

At the bottom of the staircase Hermann found a door, which he opened with the key, and then traversed a corridor which conducted him into the street.

5.

Three days after the fatal night, at nine o'clock in the morning, Hermann repaired to the Convent of —, where the last honors were to be paid to the mortal remains of the old countess. Although feeling no remorse, he could not altogether stifle the voice of conscience, which said to him: "You are the murderer of the old woman!" In spite of his entertaining very little religious belief, he was exceedingly superstitious; and believing that the dead countess might exercise an evil influence on his life, he resolved to be present at her obsequies in order to implore her pardon.

The church was full. It was with difficulty that Hermann made his way through the crowd of people. The coffin was placed upon a rich catafalque beneath a velvet baldachin. The deceased countess lay within it, with her hands crossed upon her breast, with a lace cap upon her head and dressed in a white satin robe. Around the catafalque stood the members of her household: the servants in black caftans, with armorial ribbons upon their shoulders, and candles in their hands; the relatives—children, grandchildren and great-grandchildren—in deep mourning.

Nobody wept; tears would have been an affectation. The countess was so old that her death could have surprized nobody, and her relatives had long looked upon her as being out of the world. A famous preacher pronounced the funeral sermon. In simple and touching words he described the peaceful passing away of the righteous, who had passed long years in calm preparation for a Christian end. "The angel of death found her," said the orator, "engaged in pious meditation and waiting for the midnight bridegroom."

The service concluded amidst profound silence. The relatives went forward first to take farewell of the corpse. Then followed the numerous guests, who had come to render the last homage to her who for so many years had been a participator in their frivolous amusements. After these followed the members of the countess' household. The last of these was an old woman of the same age as the deceased. Two young women led her forward by the hand. She had not strength enough to bow down to the ground—she merely shed a few tears and kissed the cold hand of her mistress.

Hermann now resolved to approach the coffin., He knelt down upon the cold stones and remained in that position for some minutes; at last he arose, as pale as the deceased countess herself; he ascended the steps of the catafalque and bent over the corpse.

…At that moment it seemed to him that the dead woman darted a mocking look at him and winked with one eye. Hermann started back, took a false step and fell to the ground. Several persons hurried forward and raised him up. At the same moment Lizaveta Ivanovna was borne fainting into the porch of the church. This episode disturbed for some minutes the solemnity of the gloomy ceremony. Among the congregation arose a deep murmur, and a tall, thin chamberlain, a near relative of the deceased, whispered in the ear of an Englishman who was standing near him, that the young officer was a natural son of the countess, to which the Englishman replied: "Oh!"

During the whole of that day, Hermann was strangely excited. Repairing to an out-of-the-way restaurant to dine, he drank a great deal of wine, contrary to his usual custom, in the hope of deadening his inward agitation. But the wine only served to excite his imagination still more. On returning home, he threw himself upon his bed without undressing, and fell into a deep sleep.

When he awoke, it was already night, and the moon was shining into the room. He looked at his watch: it was a quarter to three. Sleep had left him; he sat down upon his bed and thought of the funeral of the old countess.

At that moment somebody in the street looked in at his window, and immediately passed on again. Hermann paid no attention to this incident. A few minutes afterward he heard the door of his anteroom open. Hermann thought that it was his orderly, drunk as usual, returning from some nocturnal expedition, but presently he heard footsteps that were unknown to him: somebody was walking softly over the floor in slippers. The door opened, and a woman dressed in white entered the room. Hermann mistook her for his old nurse, and wondered what could bring her there at that hour of the night. But the white woman glided rapidly across the room and stood before him—and Hermann recognized the countess!

"I have come to you against my wish," she said in a firm voice: "but I have been ordered to grant your request. Three, seven, ace, will win for you if played in succession, but only on these conditions: that you do not play more than one card in twenty-four hours, and that you never play again during the rest of your life. I forgive you my death, on condition that you marry my companion, Lizaveta Ivanovna."

With these words she turned round very quietly, walked with a shuffling gait toward the door and disappeared. Hermann heard the street door open and shut, and again he saw someone look in at him through the window.

For a long time Hermann could not recover himself. He then rose up and entered the next room. His orderly was lying asleep upon the floor, and he had much difficulty in waking him. The orderly was drunk as usual, and no information could be obtained from him. The street door was locked. Hermann returned to his room, lit his candle, and wrote down all the details of his vision.

6.

Two fixed ideas can no more exist together in the moral world than two bodies can occupy one and the same place in the physical world. "Three, seven, ace" soon drove out of Hermann's mind the thought of the dead countess. "Three, seven, ace" were perpetually running through his head and continually being repeated by his lips. If he saw a young girl, he would say: "How slender she is! Quite like the three of hearts." If anybody asked: "What is the time?" he would reply: "Five minutes to 7." Every stout man that he saw reminded him of the ace. "Three, seven, ace" haunted him in his sleep, and assumed all possible shapes. The threes bloomed before him in the forms of magnificent flowers, the sevens were represented by Gothic portals, and the aces became transformed into gigantic spiders. One thought alone occupied his whole mind—to make a profitable use of the secret which he had purchased so dearly. He thought of applying for a furlough so as to travel abroad. He wanted to go to Paris and tempt fortune in some of the public gambling houses that abounded there. Chance spared him all this trouble.

There was in Moscow a society of rich gamesters, presided over by the celebrated Chekalinsky, who had passed all his life at the card-table and had amassed millions, accepting bills of exchange for his winnings and paying his losses in ready money. His long experience obtained for him the confidence of his companions, and his open house, his famous cook, and his agreeable and fascinating manners gained for him the respect of the public. He came to St. Petersburg. The young men of the capital flocked to his rooms, forgetting balls for cards, and preferring the emotions of faro to the seductions of flirting. Narumoff conducted Hermann to Chekalinsky's residence.

They passed through a suite of magnificent rooms, filled with attentive domestics. The place was crowded. Generals and privy councilors were playing at whist; young men were lolling carelessly upon the velvet-covered sofas, eating ices and smoking pipes. In the drawing room, at the head of a long table, around which were assembled about a score of players, sat the master of the house keeping the bank. He was a man of about sixty years of age, of very dignified appearance; his head was covered with silvery-white hair; his full, florid countenance expressed good-nature, and his eyes twinkled with a perpetual smile. Narumoff introduced Hermann to him. Chekalinsky shook him by the hand in a friendly manner, requested him not to stand on ceremony, and then went on dealing.

The game occupied some time. On the table lay more than thirty cards. Chekalinsky paused after each throw, in order to give the players time to arrange their cards and note down their losses, listened politely to their requests, and put straight the corners of cards that some player's hand had chanced to bend. At last the game was finished. Chekalinsky shuffled the cards and prepared to deal again.

"Will you allow me to take a card?" said Hermann, stretching out his hand from behind a stout gentleman who was punting.

Chekalinsky smiled and bowed silently, as a sign of acquiescence. Narumoff laughingly congratulated Hermann on his abjuration of that abstention from cards which he had practised for so long a period, and wished him a lucky beginning.

"Stake!" said Hermann, writing some figures with chalk on the back of his card.

"How much?" asked the banker, contracting the muscles of his eyes; "excuse me, I can not see quite clearly."

"Forty-seven thousand rubles," replied Hermann.

At these words every head in the room turned suddenly round, and all eyes were fixed upon Hermann.

"He has taken leave of his senses!" thought Narumoff.

"Allow me to inform you," said Chekalinsky, with his eternal smile, "that you are playing very high; nobody here has ever staked more than two hundred and seventy-five rubles at once."

"Very well," replied Hermann; "but do you accept my card or not?"

Chekalinsky bowed in token of consent.

"I only wish to observe," said he, "that although I have the greatest confidence in my friends, I can only play against ready money. For my own part, I am quite convinced that your word is sufficient, but for the sake of the order of the game, and to facilitate the reckoning up, I must ask you to put the money on your card."

Hermann drew from his pocket a bank-note and handed it to Chekalinsky, who, after examining it in a cursory manner, placed it on Hermann's card.

He began to deal. On the right a nine turned up, and on the left a three.

"I have won!" said Hermann, showing his card.

A murmur of astonishment arose among the players. Chekalinsky frowned, but the smile quickly returned to his face. "Do you wish me to settle with you?" he said to Hermann.

"If you please," replied the latter.

Chekalinsky drew from his pocket a number of bank-notes and paid at once. Hermann took up his money and left the table. Narumoff could not recover from his astonishment. Hermann drank a glass of lemonade and returned home.

The next evening he again repaired to Chekalinsky's. The host was dealing. Hermann walked up to the table; the punters immediately made room for him. Chekalinsky greeted him with a gracious bow.

Hermann waited for the next deal, took a card and placed upon it his forty-seven thousand rubles, together with his winnings of the previous evening.

Chekalinsky began to deal. A knave turned up on the right, a seven on the left.

Hermann showed his seven.

There was a general exclamation. Chekalinsky was evidently ill at ease, but he counted out the ninety-four thousand rubles and handed them over to Hermann, who pocketed them in the coolest manner possible and immediately left the house.

The next evening Hermann appeared again at the table. Everyone was expecting him. The generals and privy councilors left their whist to watch such extraordinary play. The young officers quitted their sofas, and even the servants crowded into the room.

All pressed round Hermann. The other players left off punting, impatient to see how it would end. Hermann stood at the table and prepared to play alone against the pale but still smiling Chekalinsky. Each opened a pack of cards. Chekalinsky shuffled. Hermann took a card and covered it with a pile of bank-notes. It was like a duel. Deep silence reigned around.

Chekalinsky began to deal; his hands trembled. On the right a queen turned up, and on the left an ace.

"Ace has won!" cried Hermann, showing his card.

"Your queen has lost," said Chekalinsky, politely.

Hermann started; instead of an ace, there lay before him the queen of spades! He could not believe his eyes, nor could he understand how he had made such a mistake.

At that moment it seemed to him that the queen of spades smiled ironically and winked her eye at him. He was struck by her remarkable resemblance…

"The old countess!" he exclaimed, seized with terror.

Chekalinsky gathered up his winnings. For some time, Hermann remained perfectly motionless. When at last he left the table, there was a general commotion in the room.

"Splendidly punted!" said the players. Chekalinsky shuffled the cards afresh, and the game went on as usual.

Hermann went out of his mind, and is now confined in room Number 17 of the Obukhoff Hospital. He never answers any questions, but he constantly mutters with unusual rapidity: "Three, seven, ace!" "Three, seven, queen!"

Lizaveta Ivanovna has married a very amiable young man, a son of the former steward of the old countess. He is in the service of the government, and receives a good income. Lizaveta is also supporting a poor relative. Tomsky has been promoted to the rank of captain, and has become the husband of the Princess Pauline.

The Severed Hand

by Wilhelm Hauff

October 1925 (vol. 6, n. 4)
Adapted from the German by Anonymous

I was born in Constantinople; my father was a dragoman at the Porte[1], and he also carried on a fairly lucrative business in sweet-scented perfumes and silk goods. He gave me a good education; he partly instructed me himself, and also he had me instructed by one of our priests. He at first intended that I should succeed him in business, but as I showed greater aptitude in my studies than he had expected, he destined me, on the advice of his friends, to be a doctor; for if a doctor has learned a little more than the ordinary charlatan, he can make his fortune in Constantinople. Many Frenchmen frequented our house, and one of

---

1. A dragoman is a guide or interpreter, especially in Arabic, Persian, and Turkish speaking countries. The Porte refers to the Ottoman central government, a synecdoche originating from the various gates and entrances to official buildings, such as the Sublime Porte at the Topkapi Palace in Istanbul.

them persuaded my father to allow me to travel to the city of Paris in his native land, where such learning could be best acquired, and free of charge. He wished to take me with him gratuitously on his journey home. My father, who had also traveled in his youth, agreed, and the Frank told me to hold myself in readiness three months thence.

I was beside myself with joy at the idea of seeing foreign countries, and eagerly awaited the moment when we should embark. The Frank at last concluded his business and prepared himself for the journey. On the evening before our departure my father led me into his little bedroom.

There I saw splendid clothes and weapons lying on the table. My gaze was chiefly attracted to an immense heap of gold, for I had never before seen so much collected together.

My father embraced me and said: "Behold, my son, I have procured clothes for your journey. These weapons are yours; they are the same which my grandfather hung around me when I went abroad. I know that you can use them aright, but make use of them only when you are attacked; on such occasions, however, defend yourself bravely. My property is not large; behold, I have divided it into three parts: one part for you, another for my support and spare money, but the third is to me a sacred and untouched property—it is for you in the hour of need." Thus spake my old father, tears standing in his eyes, perhaps from some foreboding, for I never saw him again.

The journey passed off very well; we soon reached the land of the Franks, and six days later we arrived in the large city of Paris. There my Frankish friend hired a room for me, and advised me to spend wisely my money, which amounted in all to two thousand dollars. I lived three years in this city, and learned what is necessary for a skillful physician to know. I should not, however, be stating the truth if I said that I liked being there, for the customs of this nation displeased me; besides, I had only a few chosen friends there, and these were noble young men.

The longing for home at last possessed me mightily; during the whole of that time, I had not heard anything from my father, and I therefore seized a favorable opportunity of returning home. An embassy from France left for Turkey. I acted as surgeon to the suite of the ambassador and arrived happily in Stamboul.[2]

My father's house was locked, and the neighbors, who were surprized at seeing me, told me my father had died two months ago. The priest who had instructed me in my youth brought the key; alone and desolate I entered the empty house. Everything was just as my father had left it, except that the gold which I was to inherit was gone. I questioned the priest about it, and he said, bowing: "Your father died a saint, for he has bequeathed his gold to the Church." This was, and remained, inexplicable to me. However, what could I

---

2. A variant form of Istanbul. Attested, like the standard name itself, from early on in the Middle Ages. In the 19th and early 20th centuries, Western European and American sources often used Constantinople to refer to the metropolis as a whole, but Stamboul to refer to the central area located on the historic peninsula, i.e. Byzantine-era Constantinople inside the walls.

do? I had no witness against the priest, and had to be content that he had not considered the house and the goods of my father as a bequest.

This was the first misfortune that I encountered. Henceforth nothing but ill-luck attended me. My reputation as a doctor would not spread at all, because I was ashamed to act the charlatan; and I felt everywhere the want of the recommendation of my father, who would have introduced me to the richest and most distinguished persons, but who now no longer thought of the poor Zaleukos! My father's goods also had no sale, for his customers had deserted him after his death, and new ones are only to be got slowly.

Thus, when I was one day meditating sadly over my position, it occurred to me that I had often seen in France men of my nation traveling through the country exhibiting their goods in the markets of the towns. I remembered that the people liked to buy of them, because they came from abroad, and that such a business would be most lucrative. Immediately I resolved what to do. I disposed of my father's house, gave part of the money to a trusty friend to keep for me, and with the rest I bought what are very rare in France: shawls, silk goods, ointments and oils; then I took a berth on board a ship, and thus entered upon my second journey to the land of the Franks.

It seemed as if fortune had favored me again as soon as I had turned my back upon the Castles of the Dardanelles. Our journey was short and successful. I traveled through the large and small towns of the Franks, and found everywhere willing buyers of my goods. My friend in Stamboul always sent me fresh stores, and my wealth increased day by day. When at last I had saved so much that I thought I might venture on a greater undertaking, I traveled with my goods to Italy. I also employed my knowledge of physic, which brought me not a little money. On reaching a town, I had it published that a Greek physician had arrived, who had already healed many; and my balsam and medicine gained me many a sequin.[3] Thus at length I reached the city of Florence in Italy.

I resolved to remain in this city for some time, partly because I liked it so well, partly also because I wished to recruit myself from the exertions of my travels. I hired a vaulted shop, in that part of the town called Santa Croce, and not far from this a couple of well-appointed rooms at an inn, leading out upon a balcony. I immediately had my bills circulated, which announced me to be both physician and merchant. Scarcely had I opened my shop when I was besieged by buyers, and in spite of my high prices I sold more than anyone else, because I was obliging and friendly toward my customers.

Thus I had already lived four days happily in Florence, when one evening, as I was about to close my vaulted room, and was examining once more the contents of my ointment boxes, as I was in the habit of doing, I found in one of the small boxes a piece of paper, which I did not remember to have put in it.

---

3. The sequin (Italian: *zecchino*) was a gold coin minted by the Republic of Venice from the 13th century onwards. The design remained unchanged for over 500 years, until the takeover of Venice by Napoleon in 1797. No other coin design has been produced over such a long historical period.

The Severed Hand

I unfolded the paper, and found in it an invitation to be on the bridge which is called Ponte Vecchio that night exactly at midnight. For a long time, I sat and wondered as to who it might be who had invited me there; and not knowing a single soul in Florence, I thought perhaps I should be secretly conducted to a patient—a thing which had often occurred before. I therefore determined to proceed thither, but took care to gird on the sword which my father had once presented to me.

When it was close upon midnight I set out on my journey, and soon reached the Ponte Vecchio. I found the bridge deserted, and determined to await the appearance of him who had called me. It was a cold night; the moon shone brightly, and I looked down upon the waves of the Arno, which sparkled in the moonlight. It was striking twelve o'clock from all the churches of the city, when I looked up and saw a tall man standing before me completely covered in a scarlet cloak, one end of which hid his face.

At first I was somewhat frightened, because he had made his appearance so suddenly; but shortly afterward I was myself again and said: "If it is you who ordered me here, what do you want?" The man in scarlet turned round and said in an undertone: "Follow!" At this, however, I felt a little timid about going alone with this stranger. I stood still and said: "Not so, sir; kindly first tell me where; you might also let me see your countenance a little, so that I may convince myself you mean me no harm." The red one, however, seemed to pay no attention to this. "If you are unwilling, Zaleukos, remain," he replied, and continued his way. I grew angry. "Do you think," I exclaimed, "a man like me allows himself to be made a fool of, to be forced to wait on this cold night for nothing?"

In three bounds I had reached him, seized him by the cloak, and cried still louder, whilst laying hold of my saber with the other hand. His cloak remained in my hand, but the stranger had disappeared round the nearest corner.

I became calmer by degrees. I had the cloak, at any rate, and it was this which would give me the key to this remarkable adventure. I put it on and continued on my way home. When I was at a distance of about a hundred paces from it, someone brushed very closely by me and whispered in the language of the Franks: "Take care, Count; nothing can be done tonight." Before I had time to turn round, this somebody had passed, and I merely saw a shadow hovering along the houses. I perceived that these words did not concern me, but rather the cloak; yet it gave me no explanation concerning the affair.

On the following morning I considered what was to be done. At first I had intended to have the cloak cried in the streets, as if I had found it. But then the stranger might send for it by a third person, and thus no light would be thrown upon the matter. Whilst I was thus thinking, I examined the cloak more closely. It was made of thick Genoese velvet scarlet in color, edged with astrakhan fur and richly embroidered with gold. The magnificent appearance of the fur put a thought in my mind which I resolved to carry out.

The Severed Hand

I carried it into my shop and exposed it for sale, but placed such a high price upon it that I was sure nobody would buy it. My object in this was to scrutinize everybody sharply who asked for the fur cloak; for the figure of the stranger, which I had seen but superficially, though with some certainty, after the loss of the cloak, I should recognize amongst a thousand.

There were many would-be purchasers for the cloak, the extraordinary beauty of which attracted everybody; but none resembled the stranger in the slightest degree, and nobody was willing to pay such a high price as two hundred sequins for it. What astonished me was that when I asked if there was not such a cloak in Florence, everybody answered, "No," and all assured me that they never had seen so precious and tasteful a piece of work.

Evening was drawing near, when at last a young man appeared, who had already been to my place, and had already offered me a great deal for the cloak. He threw a purse with sequins upon the table, and exclaimed: "Of a truth, Zaleukos, I must have your cloak, even if I should turn into a beggar over it!" He immediately began to count out his pieces of gold. I was in a dangerous position: I had exposed the cloak only to attract the attention of my stranger, and now a young fool came to pay an immense price for it. However, what could I do? I yielded; for on the other hand I was delighted at the idea of being so handsomely recompensed for my nocturnal adventure.

The young man put the cloak around him and went away, but on reaching the threshold he returned; unfastening a piece of paper which had been tied to the cloak, and throwing it toward me, he exclaimed: "Here, Zaleukos, hangs something which I dare say does not belong to the cloak." I picked up the piece of paper carelessly, but behold, on it these words were written: "Bring the cloak at the appointed hour tonight to the Ponte Vecchio, and four hundred sequins are yours." I stood thunderstruck. Thus I had lost my fortune and completely missed my aim! Yet I did not think long. I picked up the two hundred sequins, jumped after the one who had bought the cloak, and said: "Dear friend, take hack your sequins and give me the cloak; I can not possibly part with it." He first regarded the matter as a joke; but when he saw that I was in earnest, he became angry at my demand, called me a fool, and finally it came to blows.

I was fortunate enough, to wrench the cloak away from him in the scuffle, and was about to run away with it, when the young man called the police to his assistance, and we both appeared before the judge. The latter was much surprized at the accusation, and adjudicated the cloak in favor of my adversary. I offered the young man twenty, fifty, eighty, even a hundred sequins in addition to his two hundred, if he would part with the cloak. What my entreaties could not do, my gold did. He accepted it. I went away with the cloak triumphantly, and had to appear to the whole city of Florence as a madman. I did not care, however, about the opinion of the people, for I knew that I had profited after all by the bargain.

Impatiently I awaited the night. At the same hour as before I went with the cloak under my arm toward the Ponte Vecchio. With the last stroke of twelve the figure appeared out of the darkness and came toward me. It was unmistakably the man whom I had seen the day before. "Have you the cloak?" he asked me. "Yes, sir," I replied; "but it cost me a hundred sequins ready money. "I know it," replied the other. "Look: here are four hundred." He went with me toward the wide balustrade of the bridge, and counted out the money. There were four hundred; they sparkled magnificently in the moonlight; their glitter rejoiced my heart. Alas! I did not anticipate that this would be its last joy. I put the money in my pocket, and was desirous of looking thoroughly at my kind and unknown benefactor; but he wore a mask, through which dark eyes stared at me frightfully. "I thank you, sir, for your kindness," I said to him; "what else do you require of me? I tell you beforehand it must be an honorable transaction."

"There is no occasion for alarm," he replied, whilst winding the cloak around his shoulders; "I require your assistance as surgeon, not for one alive, but dead."

"What do you mean?" I exclaimed, full of astonishment.

"I arrived with my sister from abroad," he said, and beckoned me at the same time to follow him. "I lived here with her at the house of a friend. My sister died yesterday suddenly of a disease, and my relatives wish to bury her tomorrow. According to an old custom of our family, all are to be buried in the tomb of our ancestors; many, notwithstanding, who died in foreign countries are buried there and embalmed. I do not begrudge my relatives her body, but for my father I want at least the head of his daughter, in order that he may see her once more."

This custom of severing the heads of beloved relatives appeared to me somewhat dreadful, yet I did not dare object to it lest I should offend the stranger. I told him that I was acquainted with the embalming of the dead, and begged him to conduct me to the deceased. Yet I could not help asking why all this must be done mysteriously and at night. He answered me that his relatives, who considered his intention horrible, objected to it by daylight; if the head were severed, then they could say no more about it; although he might have brought me the head to embalm, yet a natural feeling had prevented him from severing it himself.

In the meantime, we had reached a large, splendid house. My companion pointed it out to me as the end of our nocturnal walk. We passed the principal entrance of the house, entered a little door, which the stranger carefully locked behind him, and now ascended in the dark a narrow spiral staircase. It led toward a dimly lighted passage, out of which we entered a room lighted by a lamp fastened to the ceiling.

In this room was a bed, on which the corpse lay. The stranger turned aside his face, evidently endeavoring to hide his tears. He pointed toward the bed, telling me to do my business well and quickly, and left the room.

I took my instruments, which as surgeon I always carried about with me, and approached the bed. Only the head of the corpse was visible, and it was so beautiful that I experienced involuntarily the deepest sympathy. Dark hair hung down in long plaits, the features were pale, the eyes closed. I took my sharpest knife, and with one stroke cut the throat. But oh horror! the dead opened her eyes, but immediately closed them again, and with a deep sigh she now seemed to breathe her last. At the same moment a stream of hot blood shot toward me from the wound. I was convinced that the poor creature had been killed by me. I had no doubt that she was dead, for there was no recovery from this wound. I stood for several minutes in painful anguish at what had happened. Had the man of the red cloak deceived me, or had his sister merely been apparently dead? The latter seemed to me more likely. But I dared not tell the brother of the deceased that perhaps a less deliberate cut might have awakened her without killing her; therefore I wished to sever the head completely; but once more the dying woman groaned, stretched herself out in painful movements, and died.

Fright overpowered me, and, shuddering, I hastened out of the room. But outside in the passage it was dark, for the light was out. I felt my way haphazard along the wall in the dark and descended the stairway. I found the door ajar, and breathed more freely on reaching the street. Urged on by terror, I rushed toward my dwelling place, and buried myself in the cushions of my bed, trying to forget the terrible thing I had done.

But sleep deserted me, and only the morning admonished me again to take courage. It seemed to me probable that the man who had induced me to commit this nefarious deed might not denounce me. I immediately resolved to set to work in my vaulted room, and, if possible, to assume an indifferent look. But alas! an additional circumstance increased my anxiety still more. My cap and my girdle, as well as my instruments, were wanting, and I was uncertain whether I had left them in the room of the murdered girl or whether I had lost them in my flight. The former seemed indeed the more likely, and thus I could easily be discovered as the murderer.

At the accustomed hour I opened my vaulted room. My neighbor came in, as was his wont every morning, for he was a talkative man. "Well," he said, "what do you say about the terrible affair which occurred during the night?" I pretended not to know anything. "What, do you not know what is known all over the town? Are you not aware that the loveliest flower in Florence, Bianca, the governor's daughter, was murdered last night? I saw her only yesterday driving through the streets in so cheerful a manner with her intended one, for today the marriage was to have taken place." I felt each word of my neighbor like a sword-thrust. Many a time my torment was renewed, for every one of my customers told me of the affair, each one more ghastly than the one before, and yet nobody could relate anything more terrible than that which I had seen.

About midday a police officer entered my shop. "Signor Zaleukos," he said, producing the things which I had missed, "do these things belong to you?" I determined not to aggravate the affair by telling a lie, and acknowledged myself as the owner of the things. The police officer asked me to follow him, and led me toward a large building which I soon recognized as the prison. There he showed me into a room.

My situation was terrible, as I thought of it in solitude. The frightful idea of having committed a murder, unintentionally, constantly presented itself to my mind. I also could not conceal from myself that the glitter of the gold had captivated my feelings, otherwise I should not have fallen blindly into the trap.

Two hours after my arrest I was led out of my cell. I descended several steps until at last I reached a great hall. Around a long table draped in black were seated twelve men, mostly old men. There were benches along the sides of the hall, filled with the most distinguished personages of Florence. The galleries, which were above, were thickly crowded with spectators. When I had stepped toward the table covered with black cloth, a man with a gloomy and sad countenance arose; it was the governor. He told the assembly that he, as the father of the murdered girl, could not sentence, and that he resigned his place on this occasion to the eldest of the senators. The eldest of the senators was at least ninety years old. He stood in a bent attitude, and his temples were covered with thin white hair, but his eyes were as yet very fiery, and his voice powerful and weighty. He commenced by asking me whether I confessed to the murder. I requested him to allow me to speak, and related undauntedly and with a clear voice what I had done.

I noticed that the governor, during my recital, at one time turned pale, and at another time red. When I had finished, he rose angrily. "What, wretch!" he exclaimed; "do you even dare to impute to another person the crime which you have committed from greediness?" The senator reprimanded him for his interruption, since he had voluntarily renounced his right; besides, it was not clear that I did the deed from greediness, for, according to his own statement, nothing had been stolen from the victim. He even went farther. He told the governor that he must give an account of the early life of his daughter, for then only would it be possible to decide whether I had spoken the truth or not. At the same time, he adjourned the court for the day, in order, as he said, to consult the papers of the deceased, which the governor would give him.

I was taken back to my prison, where I spent a wretched day, always fervently wishing that a link might be discovered between the deceased and the man of the red cloak. Full of hope, I entered the Court of Justice the next day. Several letters were lying on the table. The old senator asked me whether they were in my handwriting. I looked at them and noticed that they must have been written by the same hand as the other two papers which I had received. I communicated this to the senators, but no attention was paid to my statement, and they told me that I might have written both, for the signature of the letters was undoubtedly a Z, the first letter of my name. The letters contained threats against the deceased, and warnings against the marriage she was about to contract.

The governor seemed to have given extraordinary information concerning me, for I was treated with more suspicion and rigor on this day. To justify myself, I referred to my papers, which must be in my room, but was told they had been looked for without success. Thus at the conclusion of this sitting all hope vanished, and on my being brought into court the third day, judgment was pronounced on me. I was convicted of willful murder, and condemned to death.

On the evening of this terrible day which had decided my fate, I was sitting in my lonely cell; my hopes were gone, my thoughts steadfastly fixed upon death, when the door of my prison opened, and in came a man, who for a long time looked at me silently. "Is it thus I find you again, Zaleukos?" he said. I had not recognized him by the dim light of my lamp, but the sound of his voice roused in me old remembrances. It was Valetti, one of those few friends whose acquaintance I had made in Paris when I was studying there. He said he had accidentally come to Florence, where his father, who was a distinguished man, lived. He had heard about my affair, and had come to hear from my own lips how I could have committed such a crime.

I related to him the whole affair. He seemed much surprized at it, and adjured me, as my only friend, to tell him all, so that I should not leave the world with a lie behind me. I confirmed my assertions with an oath that I spoke the truth, and that I was not guilty of anything, except that the glitter of the gold had dazzled me and that I had not perceived the improbability of the stranger's story. "Did you know Bianca?" Valetti asked me. I assured him that I had never seen her. Valetti now related to me that a profound mystery rested on the affair, that the governor had very much accelerated my condemnation, and now a report was spread that I had known Bianca for a long time and had murdered her out of revenge for her marriage with someone else. I told him that all this coincided exactly with the man of the red cloak, but that I was unable to prove his participation in the affair. Valetti embraced me weeping, and promised me to do all he could to save my life.

I had little hope, though I knew that Valetti was a clever man, well versed in the law, and that he would do all in his power to save my life. For two long days I was in uncertainty; at last Valetti appeared. "I bring consolation, though painful," he said. "You will live and be free with the loss of one hand." Affected, I thanked my friend for saving my life. He told me that the governor had been inexorable in regard to having the affair investigated a second time, but that he had at last agreed, in order not to seem unjust, that if a similar case could be found in the law books of the history of Florence, my punishment should be the same as the one recorded in these books. Valetti and his father had searched in the old books day and night, and at last found a case quite similar to mine. The sentence was: that his left hand be cut off, his property confiscated, and he himself banished forever. This was my punishment also, and he asked me to prepare for the painful hour which awaited me. I will not describe to you that terrible hour, when I laid my hand upon the block in the public market place and my own blood shot over me in broad streams.

V aletti took me to his house until I had recovered; he then most generously supplied me with money for traveling, for all I had acquired with so much difficulty had fallen a prey to the law. I left Florence for Sicily and embarked on the first ship that I found for Constantinople: My hope was fixed upon the sum which I had entrusted to my friend. I also requested to be allowed to live with him. But great was my astonishment when he asked me why I did not wish to live in my own house. He told me that some unknown man had bought a house in the Greek quarter in my name, and this very man had also told the neighbors of my early arrival. I immediately proceeded thither, accompanied by my friend, and was received by all my old acquaintances joyfully. An old merchant gave me a letter, which the man who bought the house for me had left behind. I read as follows: "Zaleukos! Two hands are prepared to work incessantly, in order that you may not feel the loss of one of yours. The house which you see and all its contents are yours, and every year you will receive enough to be counted amongst the rich of your people. Forgive him who is unhappier than yourself!"

I could guess who had written the letter, and in answer to my question the merchant told me it had been a man whom he took for a Frank, and who had worn a scarlet cloak. I knew enough to understand that the stranger was, after all, not entirely devoid of noble intentions. In my new house I found everything arranged in the best style, also a vaulted room stored with goods, more splendid than I had ever had.

Ten years have passed since. I still continue my commercial travels, more from old custom than necessity, yet I have never again seen that country where I became so unfortunate. Every year since, I have received a thousand gold-pieces; and although I rejoice to know that unfortunate man to be so noble, yet he cannot relieve me of the sorrow of my soul, for the terrible picture of the murdered Bianca is continually on my mind.

The Mystery
of the
Four Husbands

by Gaston Leroux

December 1929 (vol. 14, no. 6)

Translated from the French
by Mildred Gleason Prochet

T he old sea-dogs who spent their evenings seated on the terrace of the inn which overlooked the sea had never seen Zinzin arrive in such a condition before. His eyes wore popping from his head, and he was as pale as death. As soon as he had had time to drop into a chair, they pressed anxiously around him.

"What is the matter. Zinzin? What is the matter, old fellow?" Captain Michel asked.

Zinzin made a sign that he was still unable to speak, but at last he wiped his forehead.

"I have just come from the police commissioner," he began, "and he gave me a most horrible bit of news."

"Tell us about it before it becomes old stuff," Gaubert exclaimed. "The story is sure to change with time."

"Oh, this doesn't date from yesterday," Zinzin murmured with a sinister laugh.

"Then why so much excitement today?"

"I'll tell you why shortly." the other replied dismally. "I was mixed up in it when I was very young. It narrowly missed making me a land-lubber forever with a little garden plot over me! On my word! It's not the fault of the damned wedding story if I'm not fertilizing a crop of dandelions today. It caused a lot of stir in its time. They even took the case up to the court of assizes!"

"Stories of marriages exist by the legion," grouchy old Chaulieu remarked. "I know ten myself."

"I only know one," Zinzin replied with a groan, "but I warn you that it is more horrible than all ten of Chaulieu's put together!"

He sighed heavily again and lighted his pipe. "I never told you anything about it before," he spat out, "because it seemed such an utterly fantastic affair, but today I must talk! Good God! Good God!"

"Well, what is it? What is it, Zinzin?"

"It is a horrible story." Zinzin choked.

"Perhaps." Chaulieu added quietly and skeptically.

Zinzin cast him a murderous look. "In all my life I have only been in love once," he went on, "and it was that time. It never happened again because I never met another such girl. Her name was Olympe, and there were a dozen of us who wanted to marry her."

The Mystery of the Four Husbands

"And here the impossible begins," sneered Chaulieu.

"Twelve, I tell you! I'll give you their names in a moment, and that doesn't include those who did not openly propose. There wasn't a man in the whole country who would not have wanted to. She wasn't rich, but she came of good family—and beautiful! At the time of which I speak she was just seventeen years old. Her section of the country was noted for its beautiful women—a big pleasant suburb worth visiting if only to watch the girls come home from church on Sundays.

"Well! In all the town there was not one girl fit to tie her shoes, and that meant a lot…Listen, if you have ever gone to Cagnes,[1] perhaps you have seen Renoir's portraits of young girls…Those pictures are pure fantasy—pictures of flowers and sunlight, not humans. Well. Olympe was like that: a ray of sun and the petals of a rose. A dream! But a dream with eyes and a mouth!… enormous childish eyes with supernatural purity in their gaze, and the mouth of a woman! The mouth alone was of flesh and blood! Olympe was like an angel come down to earth to kiss!

"We were all crazy about her. She lived alone with her grandmother, who had taken her from school at the death of her parents and entrusted her to the safe care of the servant Palmire who was the girl's willing slave. Olympe was still much of a child, often playing with the country urchins, returning home

---

1. A small city on the French Riviera, between Nice and Antibes. Renoir settled in the area in 1908 and died there in 1919. His home and studio have been converted into a museum.

with armfuls of wild flowers, baskets filled with wild strawberries. She would run behind the flocks with the sheep-dogs when she crossed them on the road, and often scandalized the old women by returning home at night astride a goat!

"In nice weather the old people would sit outside their doors on little wooden benches and wait for her to come. She had a wonderful imagination and told them stories which she made up as she went along. The grandmother, who in her day had been the beautiful Madame Gratien, lived in a big old house on the Place de l'Abbaye. The gardens were closed in by walls and at the back looked out on the open country. She knew all the elite of the neighborhood and had maintained connections in the city.

"The behavior of her granddaughter had amused her in the beginning but at last it began to preoccupy her. Olympe seemed very thoughtless for her age… What would happen when she was alone in the world? Madame Gratien suddenly decided to marry her off as soon as possible.

"She had already received several offers for the hand of her granddaughter, and when it was known that she no longer discouraged suitors, they besieged her on all sides. This flood of admirers was a new game for Olympe. Finally one Sunday we were all gathered in the living-room, when the grandmother gave Olympe a little talking-to. She told her that she was beginning to be very tired and weary with life and that she would like to see Olympe settled down before she died. Olympe greeted this announcement with tears. We thought that the prospect of the old lady's death saddened her, but Olympe explained it differently. 'As though it were gay to marry!' she said when we tried to cheer her up.

"We burst out laughing at that and all swore that her husband would be perfectly willing to be her slave.

"'First of all, I do not want to leave Grandmother,' she said, 'nor Palmire…And secondly I want to live in our old house.'

"'Agreed, agreed,' we answered in chorus.

"'And now,' said good Madame Gratien, 'which one are you going to choose ?'

"'Oh, we'll talk of that later,' said Olympe. 'This is no way to marry people off. You're really not serious about it, Grandmother!'

"'For six months you've said the same thing: that you'd talk it over later. Now, it's become a joke. You know that I have always done everything you wanted before…Come; if you were obliged to choose one of these gentlemen, which would you take?'

"Olympe suddenly became serious, and we watched her anxiously…In spite of our apparent acceptance of the whole thing as a joke, we were dead serious…

"She stood up, walked around us, and sized us up from head to foot with such funny expressions that we were more than a little embarrassed. If I live to be a thousand, I'll never forget that scene! What an examination! To be truthful, we hardly dared breathe.

"She made us stand, lined us up, placing us, changing us—advancing a man to the head of the line and then, after looking him straight in the eyes, sending him back to third or fourth position. The grandmother encouraged us from time to time with a 'Hold yourselves well, gentlemen!…Hold yourselves well! …Be serious.'

"It was funny when one thinks that we were not all young men either! I well remember the arrival of the town registrar, respectable Monsieur Pacifire, who for two years had openly bid for Olympe's hand. He came late and naturally did not know what it was all about.

"She met him at the door and placed him, dumbfounded, at the end of the line. He had the last number! You can imagine how we laughed. But you can bet that when he knew what it was all about, he did not laugh at all!

"'At last! It is done!' she announced. 'If I marry I'll take Monsieur Delphin first, then Monsieur Hubert, then Monsieur Sabin, then my little Zinzin (as you see, I was number four), then Monsieur Jacobini…' and she went on down the whole twelve of us…I'll enumerate them: 1st Monsieur Delphin, a nice fellow with a great future ahead of him, son of the town pharmacist; he had taken his degree in science, was working for a fellowship in chemistry and was very well spoken of at the university. 2nd Monsieur Hubert, still young, about twenty-five, head forest warden. 3rd Dr. Felix Sabin, just out of college, and as merry as a lark…I think he had settled himself in the country with the idea of getting into politics. 4th yours truly, who had already taken to the sea but who would have given it all up to stay with Olympe. 5th Lieutenant Jacobini, son of a colonel in the guards, a distinguished, smart fellow who had just come back from a mission in South Africa where he had made something of a name for himself. 6th the son of a big land-owner with lots of money. 7th a young lawyer. 8th the son of a solicitor. 9th an old notary. 10th a traveling salesman. 11th the assistant of the district attorney. 12th Monsieur Pacifire, the registrar…yes, that makes twelve. We were only twelve that day!

"**S**ix months later, Olympe married number one, young Delphin. We all went to the wedding—but not to have a good time. I tried to reason against it, but I would have given anything to be in Delphin's shoes. The following year, however, I no longer envied him. He was dead!

"No one knows exactly what he died of. They say that he was poisoned by some laboratory work, but nothing was sure. The physician who attended him, Dr. Sabin, shook his head when he was questioned. I think that in reality he thought of only one thing: in short, that he had now become number two and that if anything were to happen to the forest warden who preceded him, he might yet hope for a chance!

"It seemed impossible, but Olympe had become even lovelier since her marriage. Now, when she passed in her widow's weeds,[2] she was something to kneel

---

2. The term "widow's weeds" refers to the clothing worn by female widows during the 19th century, typically a heavy black dress and black veil, part of the elaborate mourning rituals of the era.

before and worship. But she did not mourn her dead husband for long. In fact, if one can believe old Palmire, Monsieur Delphin was not excessively gay and for a young husband spent too much time in his laboratories, leaving his young wife for entire days while he searched for heaven knows what in the bottoms of his test-tubes.

"Monsieur Hubert's turn was bound to arrive, and he did not lose time in pressing his suit and in promising her all the gayeties that she had missed since her first marriage. He was a jolly fellow, that Hubert, fond of good food, an excellent drinker and hunter as was fitting with a man of his position and name.

"Big celebrations and big parties now took place at Olympe's. She began to ride horseback and there was not another like her for fifty miles around. It was a sight to see her hunt the deer and wild boar. Nothing frightened her. We had trouble to keep up with her, and afterward she presided over the banquet with a sparkle and an ardor that gave us all fever.

"She was more courted than ever, but she made fun of us, and kept her loveliest and gayest smiles for Dr. Sabin. 'He is number three,' she exclaimed, laughing. 'Everyone in turn!'

"'Hey !' Hubert interrupted. 'I never felt better in my life!'

"'And I take care of him,' replied the doctor. 'He is the one man whom I'm not permitted to kill. Thank the fortune, Hubert, which prohibits me from choosing my victims!'

"This was all very nice, but it seemed to me that Dr. Sabin made too much use of his position of family doctor in order to be familiar with Olympe. They were often seen alone in the park back of the house, or even going for a little outing in the forest when Hubert, called away on business or some bachelor party in the neighboring town, left Olympe for a few hours. She had become the general topic of conversation in the village. She scandalized the habitues of the five o'clock teas at Madame Tabureau's, the mayor's wife, or at Madame Blancmougin's, the wife of the solicitor whose son had received number eight in the general classing. Madame Blancmougin never ceased congratulating herself on her son's lucky escape.

"In fact, after the death of old Madame Gratien, which had occurred in the meantime, Olympe no longer kept her desires within any limits and she frightened many people by the liberty of those desires. Hubert made no attempt to restrain her. He was amused and flattered by the number of victims won by those innocent blue eyes and that bright mouth which seemed to be always asking for a kiss.

"He was a good liver, that Hubert, but not a real lover. 'My!' Palmire would whisper to those who liked to be informed of all that went on in the house, 'he certainly loves his food more than his bed. If Madame were not so honest, that fact might give him a bad jolt!'

"And so saying, she shook her head on seeing Olympe and Dr. Sabin come in from one of the lessons in driving. Those driving-lessons had started a lot of gossip which was cut short by a new misfortune in Place de l'Abbaye.

"Delphin had installed a laboratory in an isolated building in a far corner of the grounds and this Hubert had made into a sort of hunting-pavilion. He had furnished it with his guns, his knives, his rifles, his pistols, and had also stored his ammunition there. It was like a little armory, with the exception of the walls, which were decorated with the usual trophies. It was a pleasant little spot, covered with climbing vines and flowers, and there was a fine view of the fields and country beyond. He often had lunch served there in order to be alone with his wife or friends away from the ears of the servants.

"It was there that Hubert was found one afternoon in August with a pistol in his hands and a bullet through his heart.

"Suicide or accident? Several even murmured the word: crime!…but it was said so low that no one heard them.

"You can imagine what a stir it caused. An inquest was held. The assistant district attorney, who was number eleven, managed the affair. It was Dr. Sabin, number three, who was called to give his opinion on the nature of the death. He pronounced it accident. The inquest hesitated a long time between accident and suicide, but they finally concluded with the theory of the accident.

"'My goodness!' Palmire sighed when she was besieged by many wanting to know what Madame had to say about the death of her husband. 'What should she say? She knew nothing about it, of course. She had lunched in the little pavilion with Monsieur…They both had seemed very gay. She left him at about 2:30 in order to dress, for she was going to town with Dr. Sabin. About three o 'clock the gardener heard a shot and ran to the pavilion. He found Monsieur stretched out dead. And now you know as much as we do. Why should he have committed suicide? Life was beautiful and so was Olympe. He had everything to make him happy. And now Olympe is crying her eyes out, which is a stupid thing to do. No one is responsible for an accident, and it was his fault for not being more careful!'

"So spoke Palmire. The next year Olympe married Dr. Sabin."

"I expected it," interrupted Chaulieu; "if your blue-eyed angel with the passionate mouth had to give herself to all twelve of those gentlemen we haven't finished and it's not going to be a funny tale."

"I didn't promise you a funny story. I told you that it was horrible. Olympe did not give herself to all twelve, since I was number four and I'm still alive. Nevertheless, I excuse Chaulieu for his remark because in the village they began to say: 'They'll all go. She's capable of it.'

"'And why not? If it pleases Olympe?' Palmire replied whenever she heard something of that kind. And she added, scratching her long chin, 'She would be wrong in hesitating over it as far as the worth of those men is concerned!'

"It was a terrible thing that she said, in the ignorance of a servant ready to perjure her soul for her mistress.

"Dr. Sabin was certainly a courageous fellow to marry into a household which seemed destined to misfortune. Some good old woman of the kind particularly skillful in slipping in a malicious remark between a frown and a smile, remarked, however, 'Oh, nothing will happen to him. He knows what he is doing!'

"The town was abuzz with horrible remarks. Poor doctor! He did not deserve what was said, since he, too, died, exactly three months to the day after his wedding. He lasted even a shorter time than the others."

"Good Lord!" Gaubert whistled.

"And so it came your turn," said Captain Michel.

"It's beginning to be very amusing," remarked Chaulieu.

But they all stopped joking. Zinzin had become terribly pale and his hand trembled as he put down his glass. He looked with wild eyes at a man who was approaching the table.

"Hello," exclaimed the captain, "here's the police commissioner's orderly."

It was he in fact, and he bent over and whispered in Zinzin's ear:

"We've just had a telephone message. She has been dead ten years. You don't need to worry any longer." And with that he departed.

As for Zinzin, he staggered into the captain's arms and had to be taken home.

"Let's hope he doesn't kick off before the end of his story," said Gaubert gently.

Chaulieu shrugged his shoulders. "Bah," he said, "he is working for a climactic effect."

Nevertheless, we did not know the end of the story until eight days later. Zinzin certainly had been very ill. This time we listened without interrupting him.

It was my turn then, number four's turn. But I was still ignorant of the fact. I was sailing in the Baltic Sea when the thing happened, and I did not learn it until my return ashore. I threw myself on a train for home and on the way met Lieutenant Jacobini, number five, who had himself returned only a short while ago.

"Our trip was not a merry one. I confess that in spite of the certainty I now had of being able to marry Olympe and in spite of the hope Lieutenant Jacobini had of soon being able to cheer up my widow, this double prospect did not fill us with merriment. The house on Place de l'Abbaye seemed less like a place of joy to us now and more like a tomb!

"The first thing I asked Jacobini, after he had told me the sinister news, was naturally if he could give me a few details on the doctor's death. How had he died? He answered gloomily that he hadn't the faintest idea and that no one else had either; but that he more than anyone wanted to get to the bottom of it. That was the reason for his return.

"'And you?' he asked me.

"'Oh,' I answered, 'as for me, you can understand that I am interested in the matter at least as much as you are.'

"'Yes,' he replied without the slightest sarcasm, 'I understand that…It is an even more urgent matter for you.'

"'But,' I went on, 'they must have called his death by some name!'

"'Not any more of a name than they gave the death of Olympe's first husband. They claimed that Delphin was poisoned by some laboratory experiment, but the thing was never proved. And as far as Dr. Sabin is concerned it can't be that.'

"'All these deaths are certainly very strange! Tell me, Jacobini, aren't the police interested in this?'

"'Yes. Our assistant district attorney, number eleven, has ordered an investigation. I ought to add that Olympe was the first to ask it…They made an autopsy on the body…'

"'And?'

"'And found nothing… But that doesn't prove a thing,' he added in a tone which struck me.

"'What do you mean? Have you a suspicion?'

"'In such matters,' replied Jacobini. 'it is not permissible to have suspicions. One must be certain or keep still.' And he kept still.

"But all this did not tend to quiet my anxiety.

"'Then he died in his bed? Was he ill?'

"'No! Olympe found him about five o'clock in the afternoon in his room, stretched out on the floor with a table and chair overturned, his mouth still foaming and his face distorted from horror…It was proved that he had been in the room alone from three o'clock on and that the house was completely deserted, as the servants had gone to a near-by fair.'

"'And—Madame Sabin?'

"'She had lunched with him in the little pavilion at the end of the garden and had remained there to embroider with Palmire.'

"'Then what was the conclusion of the inquest?'

"'That Dr. Sabin died from an attack of epilepsy.'

"'Was he subject to it?'

"'No, but it seems that that does not always follow.'

"We were silent a long time. Then I sighed.

"'We ought to be sincerely sorry for Olympe,' I said, 'because otherwise it would be too horrible.'

"'Yes,' he replied after thinking a moment, 'you are right! It would be too horrible…She must be pitied. Besides, Palmire says that she is completely crushed. No one ever sees her now. She never goes out. According to gossip she wants to enter a convent… It is natural enough that after three unfortunate marriages like these she should be sick of matrimony— and—and I congratulate you,' he added with a strange laugh. Then he went on quickly, because he was an extremely polite fellow: 'I hope I haven't pained you in saying that?'

"'I don't know,' I answered.

"We arrived an hour later. We hadn't forewarned anyone and it was already late at night. We had decided to go directly to the Hotel de Bourgogne, and I was surprised to find the solicitor's son, number eight, waiting for us on the platform. I remember his name now; he was called Juste. There is nothing to say about him except that he was an honest fellow, and that Dr. Sabin had often treated him for rheumatism.

"'I knew that you had landed,' he said to me, 'and that you were taking this train. What hotel are you going to?'

"'To the Bourgogne with Lieutenant Jacobini.'

"Juste had been so preoccupied with me that he hadn't noticed my companion. He shook him warmly by the hand and said that he would go with us."

"**I** was growing more puzzled every moment. At the hotel he followed me to my room and gave me a packet for which he asked a receipt.

"'This was entrusted to my honor,' he said, 'with the mission of giving into your own hands.'

"I examined the sealed envelope quickly and recognized the writing immediately. My name was written on the outside with the addition: 'To be delivered after my death.'

"'Yes,' the other replied, 'I have accomplished my mission and I am only accountable to him; but since I haven't the faintest idea of what is contained in that letter, I want a receipt, to be on the safe side.'

"I gave him his receipt.

"'In giving you this letter,' I asked, 'Dr. Sabin said nothing special?'

"'Not a thing,' he replied. 'He told me nothing, absolutely nothing.'

"Upon which he shook my hand and took leave of me a bit hurriedly. He seemed free of a great weight. I opened the letter feverishly.

"Ten minutes later someone knocked at Jacobini's door. He was just about to get into bed and called out, asking who was there. As no one answered him, he went to the door and opened it impatiently. A ghost with a letter in its hands entered his room. This ghost was I and I hadn't strength enough even to speak. He sat me down, took the letter from my hands, locked the door and read.

"I will never forget him as he stood there, bent over the lamp. The letter which had plunged me into a sort of prostration had an entirely different effect on him. Everything about him seemed to tighten up, while with me there had been a complete loosening of my will-power. He frowned heavily, his eyebrows were knitted, his chin grew more prominent, and a dangerous flame like the cold steel flash of a sword lit the eyes intent on reading the document, a document which had been written by the trembling hand of a man who knew himself condemned to death."

"This is what Dr. Sabin had written. The original has long been in the police files but this is a copy:

Tales of Revenge

Dear Zinzin:

Before marrying Olympe I want you to read this: It is a man who is about to die who is writing you. I have been horribly poisoned. No one knows it except the guilty one or guilty ones and me. I have not complained, for I have got only what I deserved. Thanks to strong drugs I have been able at times to overcome the pain which is destroying me and still to appear human. Thus I have been able to see Juste without giving anything away to him, nor will you tell him anything unless he, too, should want to marry Olympe—in which case you will show him this letter. But I hope that this will be the end of the matter and that after my death no one will wish to take my place, our place, the place of the three men who have entered this house full of health and life and who have disappeared from it, carrying with them the enigma of their triple misfortune.

As far as possible keep scandal from Olympe. I have loved her too much. I still love her, perhaps. No scandal, therefore, unless it be absolutely necessary. And besides, I am certain of nothing. In such a case, proof of the guilt is necessary, and I have none. I might be able to accuse her with a chance of not making a mistake, but I haven't the right; and I will tell you why. You know that after Hubert's death I returned a verdict of suicide. But Humbert did not commit suicide. Hubert was murdered!

The Mystery of the Four Husbands

And 1 knew the truth at my first sight of the body by the position of the pistol in his hand. The weapon had been placed in his hand, after his death! I won't go into details, but I could have proved it very easily. I had been called immediately after the discovery of the body in the hope that perhaps life still stirred within him, but it was all over. Next to the corpse stood Olympe in tears. Before looking at the woman I had seen the pistol and had already reached a conclusion. Then I looked at the woman. You may have suspected the affectionate ties that bound us already. Besides, Olympe made no effort to hide the truth, and I had spoken to her about it more than once. Looking at her, it seemed to me that her eyes wavered after catching mine and they left me the impression of an ardent and silent plea. Even today I am sure that I was not mistaken and I feel a chill of horror. That woman killed Hubert in order to be mine! It was horrible, but I adored her, and not only did I not denounce her, but without her noticing and for pity of her I slipped the pistol into the correct position. I made the matter easy for the hoard of experts. You see, Zinzin, old man, I'm not hiding anything from you. You understand now why I haven't the right to accuse this woman. My cowardice has made me her accomplice.

I think we loved each other like the damned, trying to forget in the embrace of love a lost paradise. Between us there never came a thought of Hubert or of Delphin. One would have said that

*Olympe had never known those two men. But I,
I was curious to know how Delphin had died and I
began a cunning investigation which one day they
must have noticed. From that day on, I am sure,
my death was decided.*

*Certain contradictory remarks made by
Palmire concerning Delphin's experiments and
the rather mysterious circumstances of his death
led me to certain clues in which I found the almost
certainty of Olympe's guilt in the poisoning of
Delphin with Palmire as an accomplice. I had not
said anything yet to Olympe, who did not seem to
suspect my thoughts. I attempted to keep as hidden
as possible the hideous suspicions. But one day I
felt that I had been struck! A high fever, a strange
uneasiness and dull pains warned, me that I had
been poisoned. I still said nothing because I wanted
to know—to know. And I believed that I had done
the necessary things to save me in time from a
drug which was already attacking the sources of
life—and which I could not rid myself of.*

*How did they go about it?...To make sure that
it was she, I ate nothing except what she gave me,
and we drank from the same glass. Yes, but we did
not eat from the same plate! Ah, what horror!...
And this is where the matter rests today as I write
you this letter...I have just had an attack which I
have concealed from her. Is she really ignorant of it?
Or does she find pleasure in it? Lord God! And yet
my face has changed in these last weeks and several
times I have pushed her from my arms. Still she*

seems to have noticed nothing. Oh, the monster! The two monsters! Yes, two, because I have discovered Palmire spying on me and the two of them are always together. Nevertheless, Olympe said to me yesterday: "It's funny how men change after a few weeks of marriage! After a short while they are unrecognizable. They are no longer interesting!"

Zinzin, you will have this letter and I am going to talk to her. But I won't be telling her anything she doesn't already know. She must believe by now that I know by whose hands her first two husbands were killed; but I must tell her that I know that she is killing the third and that she must stop there!

Ah, Olympe, our Olympe!…If you knew, Zinzin, you would understand—and you would pardon me…Perhaps, after all, she is not guilty—perhaps Palmire is responsible, perhaps · Palmire did it all alone. Ah, my God, if that could be true!…This is an idea which has come to me a little late—too late!…Think it over, Zinzin. I am past thinking now. I suffer too much…And yet I do not like to die without knowing. If she could only prove to me that it is Palmire who did it done! I love her still, Zinzin!

"After this last line the writing was so disordered and jumbled that it was difficult to read, and the signature which followed seemed to express the supreme effort of a man from whom life is escaping. And yet Dr. Sabin could not have died that day. Probably by the feverish use of some medicine he was able to suspend his destiny. We know that the unfortunate man did not die until after lunch the next day…

"I made the copy which you have just read," Zinzin continued, "that same night, because Lieutenant Jacobini demanded the original. He had the right to it, since he was going to take my place! I said all the things that you or anyone would say in such horrible circumstances; but I realized that his mind was made up and that there was nothing more to do. Of course, it was no longer a question of love for Olympe.

"He had made a vow, a vow to punish her for her crimes. He would force her to confess, make her give herself up, and then we would see!…

"He did not tell me what we would see, but it was easy enough to understand on catching sight of his fierce, terrible look when he spoke.

"'Dr. Sabin got his just deserts,' he said to me, 'and I do not pity him; but that poor Hubert was my friend, and Delphin I loved as a younger brother and I may be responsible for his death. Therefore, I, Jacobini, am going to avenge them.'

"To accomplish that he decided to marry Olympe.

"'And if she doesn't want to marry?' I asked him.

"He laughed a horrible laugh. 'A woman like her will not refuse a man like me!'"

"He was right. Olympe married number five and I was best man for Jacobini. He insisted upon it. During the ceremony he stood with his arms crossed at the foot of the chancel beside his kneeling bride and looked already like a statue of vengeance. Olympe was no longer the girl we had all known and loved. There was something strangely funereal in her beauty and it seemed already to be bending under the hand of death. She looked like the figures in marble one sees on tombstones. I never expected to see her again, for the next day I set out to sea.

"At every port I threw myself on the newspapers; I opened my mail with trembling, feverish hands. No news reached me of the hideous tragedy that I felt must have been happening at home during my absence. When, three months later, I returned, my first question was…yes, you have guessed it…

"'Is nothing changed around here?'

"'Goodness, no.'

"'And how are the Jacobinis?'

"'The Jacobinis are fine,' I was told.

"The next day Jacobini came to call on me. He knew that I had just returned. He looked exceedingly well and had prolonged his furlough, since Olympe refused to leave the house even though he hated it. 'At heart I can't blame her,' he explained. 'She believes that if she leaves the house and this town where she spent such a happy youth it will look as though the evil tongues which claim she had a hand in the death of her three husbands have some cause for their suspicions.'

"I looked at Jacobini, but he met my gaze clearly.

"'I understand your astonishment,' he said, 'but Olympe is not to be suspected.'

"'So much the better, so much the better. Let's drop the subject, then.'

"'Zinzin!'

"'Yes, Jacobini!'

"'I have come to talk to you and you must listen to me. The first thing I did on returning to the house after the wedding was to show her Dr. Sabin's letter. Olympe cried, but did not seem in the least astonished.

"' "I had a suspicion of that," she confessed to me. "Everybody thinks I am a monster. I wonder that you wanted to many me."

"' "I will tell you why in due time," I replied, "but for the moment we are concerned with Dr. Sabin 's letter."

"' "What can I say?" she continued bitterly. "I am no more guilty of Hubert's death, of which they suspect me, than I am of my first husband's. Sabin loved me madly, and there were moments when his love was strangely like hatred. He let drop words from time to time that made me understand his horrible thought… and he started an abominable investigation. He questioned Palmire, who repeated everything to me. I tried to quiet him. Above all I wanted to avoid any scandal. I told myself that his state of mind would pass with time and that as I had nothing to hide, he would end by understanding that we were all the victims of a horrible fate. Then suddenly he believed himself poisoned. He did not tell me in the beginning. I myself did not mention the word 'poison', so that nothing definite should happen between us. I did not want to be forced to call in the police or to send him from the house, but as he continued to suffer I suggested that he consult a doctor. He did nothing. The day of his death he was under the influence of a strong drug that made him delirious. He insisted on coming to the table, and as I knew what he suspected I made a point of drinking only what he drank and of eating from the same plate. At the dessert he threw himself at my feet and begged my pardon for having suspected me. He said he knew now that he was being poisoned by 'that horrible Palmire'. And he begged me to aid him in fastening the guilt on her. As I tried naturally to defend her, he left me abruptly and locked himself in his room. You know the rest. It was I who asked for an autopsy.'"

"Lieutenant Jacobini stopped.

"'And that convinced you of her innocence?' I asked.

"'No,' he answered. 'If Olympe expected something of the nature of Sabin's letter, I was ready for an explanation such as she gave me with a few tears thrown into the bargain. My next remark to my bride of an hour was very abrupt. "And what about the tali-tali, Olympe? What have you done with it?' I asked.

"'She started and turned a deathly white. "Oh," she moaned, "so you think that I poisoned him with tali-tali?" [3]

---

3. [author's footnote] The tali-tali of which Lieutenant Jacobini speaks here is certainly a close relative of the poison described in Andre Demaison's work. In the *Diato* is written: "A man was hovering over the cauldron in which boiled the roots and bark of the sacred tree. At its name the children were terrified and the adults lost their mind; but the sorcerer, who was now pouring rice into the horrible soup, had declared that the poison could only harm those who sucked the marrow from the bones of their own kind..." And this is the picture of those put to the test: "The unfortunates fell to the ground, letting out hoarse and horrible cries of pain. The bodies curled into a ball like partridges wounded by the hunter's bullet, or ducks with their necks cut before life is lost with the flow of blood." The tali-tali of which Lieutenant Jacobini speaks produces fulminating effects if taken in a large

"'I took her by the wrist and it as like holding a hand of marble. "Listen, Olympe: Hubert died of an accident. I'll grant that and it doesn't matter to me; but Delphin was my friend and he and Dr. Sabin died the same death. They were both poisoned by the tali-tali which leaves no trace. It was I who gave the poison to Delphin that he might analyze it and find an antidote if possible. I brought it back with me on my last return from Africa and I want to know what has become of it. It is a terrible poison which the wizards down there give to the unfortunates who are suspected of having brought the anger of bad spirits on the village. Its victims are legion…I am responsible for what it has done in France…What have you done with the tali-tali, Olympe?"

"'Olympe looked up at me with frozen eyes. She was no longer crying. "There is no more tali-tali," she answered.

"" "Since when?" I asked brutally, trying to gain control over her obstinate mind, which was clearly fighting against me now.

"" "Since I asked Delphin to destroy it. That was a gift, sir, which you should never have made, not that I believe that he died of it, but because it would have been your fault if he had killed me with it. Was it the poison that was closed in the belly of a mahogany fetish covered with bizarre signs and curious designs burned into the wood?"

---

dose. In other cases, the poisoning may be slow. Sometimes It takes twenty-four hours for it to manifest itself in all its force. The victim, as happened to Dr. Sabin, seems to have fallen from an epileptic fit.

"' "That was it, Olympe. There is no possible error. You know the tali-tali well."

"' "Yes, Delphin used this poison and the barks of the tree which you brought him to make some experiments which interested me, much more than the rest of his work, as a matter of fact. His test-tubes and apparatus amused me in the beginning, but one tires of everything. I soon noticed, however, that Delphin was not well, and I blamed his languor on the bad air of the laboratory. I asked him to give up his work for a little while. He would not, so I asked him at least to do me the favor of destroying the tali-tali. He answered that there was nothing to fear because the tali-tali were only fatal to those who drank it and that he was certainly not crazy enough to drink the liquid, which he had already tried out on chickens and rabbits. He was amused at my childishness, but I gave him no peace until he had destroyed the tali-tali in front of me and Palmire. Tired of fighting with me about it he threw the fetish and the poison into the fire and it was burned up in a moment."

"' "How did the poison act in the fire?"

"' "First there was a long green flame like a sky-rocket and that was followed by a suffocating vapor which we ran from. As for the fetish itself, it was nothing more than an ember which flashed a last grimace before falling into ashes. That is all, sir, and I have nothing else to tell you, but if it was to hear this that you married me you might as well have dispensed with the ceremony. I would have given you the information just the same, and perhaps I would have loved you afterward. But now please leave this house and never let me see you again." '

"When Jacobini reached this point, he stopped and rolled himself a cigarette.

"'And then?' I asked.

"'Then I left her to question Palmire. I forced her to tell of the tali-tali also. I attacked her from all sides. She's an ignorant peasant and she could not have invented the chemical effects which she had seen in the fire. All she said agreed to the letter with what Olympe had told me. I asked her all kinds of questions which Olympe could not have foreseen. I went on into other matters and at the end of my investigation I went back to Olympe and threw myself on my knees before her. She pardoned me, Zinzin, because besides being honest she is also very good.'

"'Possible,' I said, 'but she is not proud!'

"A s you can well imagine, I did not go to call on them, but I saw Jacobini eight days later. An awful anguish was visible on his pale, restless face.

"'Zinzin,' he said to me in a hoarse voice, 'I think I'm infected with it, too. But perhaps it is only an idea. Yes, an idea! Even the thought of that tali-tali is enough to drive one mad.'

"I didn't have time to say a word. He had already gone and I was never to see him alive again.

"And this is the frightful tragedy which occurred the next day according to the police who with help from the dying Jacobini and Palmire's statements reconstructed the scene.

"At noon, Jacobini, who had not seen his wife since morning, went to the pavilion. He was filled with the darkest presentiments in spite of the fact that he tried to free himself of the idea of poison by trying to believe that his illness was due to swamp fevers which he had suffered from in the tropics.

"Luncheon was served there, and, as Jacobini entered, a door closed hurriedly at the end of the room. At the same time, he heard furtive steps and the sound of a box being closed. He ran to the door, half opened it and saw Olympe engaged in low conversation with Palmire. She seemed very much troubled.

"At that moment a terrible cramp seized him in the intestines and he let the door close, having only strength enough to drop on the sofa. With one hand he had unconsciously taken hold of Olympe's workbox, which was badly closed and showed bits of fine linen. Jacobini's fingers, clutching at the lid feverishly from pain, opened it and fumbled in the lace. Suddenly they struck a hard object and he stood up, haggard and mad…

"In his hand he held the fetish of death, the horrible phial, the hideous tali-tali which Olympe and Palmire had sworn was destroyed, burned before them. Olympe had lied. Olympe had poisoned him as she had poisoned the other two. He was to suffer the atrocious death which had tortured his predecessors.

"Overcoming the agony for a few minutes, Jacobini poured what was left of the poison into a bottle of wine on the table. There was enough left for a terrible dose, and then he waited for his wife.

"She was not long in coming. She kissed him and asked him how he felt this morning. He replied that he felt much better, but that the fever had not completely left him and that he was thirsty.

"'Then you must drink something, darling,' she said.

"He did not wait for her to pour the wine out and filled two glasses himself.

"'But you know that the doctors have forbidden me wine,' she said, 'and that I only drink water.'

"He insisted that she drink with him in the same glass, as they had often done. She turned her head away. He seized her brutally, threw her head back and savagely pinched her nostrils, thus forcing her to drink. As she cried with fear, he spoke. 'Perhaps you would have preferred another glass,' he said, and showed her the tali-tali.

"She cried for help, but suddenly put her hand to her abdomen and was taken with a horrible cramp. At the same time the pain clutched at him, and they fell together on the sofa. They shrieked together, agonized together, clutched and scratched, and bit each other. They pulled at each other like wild beasts. They twisted and writhed, contorting themselves in the same hell.

"Jacobini had still strength enough to insult her, naming the first victims. 'You won't kill any more. You are going to die. You are going to die with me.'

"But the pain was too great. It seemed as though there was hell within him. He pulled weapons down from the walls, and he tried to stab himself with a knife and so end the horror at one blow; but he only succeeded in making a terrible wound. Then he turned the steel toward Olympe and slit her open from top to bottom like an animal. The room echoed with her last howl.

"Possessed by a thousand demons he smashed her skull, pierced her like a pin-cushion, pulled out her eyes and cut her into pieces. She was nothing more than a bleeding, nameless horror when the servants rushed into the room.

"But Jacobini did not die until the next morning and in his few moments of lucidity narrated the hideous details of their abominable martyrdom. The assistant district attorney who at one time had hoped to marry her was present, and he returned home and went to bed ill. During the night he was so delirious that they thought he would lose his mind and so add one more victim to the list.'

Zinzin stopped. Perspiration beaded his temples. He let out a sort of groan.

"The most horrible part," he went on, "is the fact that she had done nothing."

"Oh !" the others exclaimed.

"Yes, she was innocent. I learned that the other day, only the other day."

"Palmire had done it all!" Gaubert exclaimed.

"As to her," said Zinzin with a terrible laugh, "the police took her and kept her. You can well understand that I did everything in my power to have her given full punishment. All she did was to say no, and to cry about Olympe. Concerning her mistress, however, she gave us explanations which dumbfounded us. They were so utterly stupid or naive. For example, when they asked her: 'If your mistress was innocent, she would not have told her husband that the tali-tali had been destroyed before the two of you.'

"'Bah, that is simple,' Palmire answered. 'We agreed between us to say that it had been because there were already rumors about and we did not want to be suspected; besides we did not know what had become of the tali-tali because we really believed that Monsieur Delphin had burned it all the day that he threw a few drops in to please Madame.'

"Yes, she said just that," Zinzin went on, "and she was hissed and hooted. I cried louder than the rest."

"And what was she sentenced to?" asked Chaulieu.

"Death," replied Zinzin in a whisper.

"But they don't execute women?"

"No…Her sentence was changed to life imprisonment. She died in her cell about ten years ago. I learned that the other day also."

"And did she repent? Did she confess?" Michel asked.

"No," Zinzin answered, looking at us like a madman, "and she had nothing to confess. . . She, too, was innocent!"

"Good God!" Chaulieu exclaimed.

"But then, who was guilty?" Gaubert asked.

"A man who has just died and confessed on his death bed. After the tragedy he left the town and settled not far from here. Yes, he died the other day at Mourillon. That man had owned some property which touched the edge of Olympe's estate in the far corner where the pavilion was."

"But who was the man?—one of the twelve?"

"Yes, one of the twelve—the twelfth, to be exact! He naturally could not ever hope to marry Olympe, because of course she would never go through with eleven husbands after such deaths, but he eliminated those who had been happier than he…and at the end he had fixed it so that the evidence all pointed to Olympe.

"Do you remember, when the twelfth suitor arrived that day when we were all lined up in the draw-ing-room—the arrival of Monsieur Pacifire, the regis-trar—what fun Olympe made of him and how we had all laughed when she placed him at the foot of the line? Yes, we made fun of Monsieur Pacifire when he came into the room! Well, he avenged himself, that man!"

Tales from Beyond

Horreur Sympathique

by Charles Baudelaire

May 1926 (vol. 7, no. 5)
Translated from the French by Clark Ashton Smith

"From this bizarre and livid sky, .
Tormented like your doom and mine
On your void spirit passing by.
What thoughts descend, O libertine?"

— Athirst for mortal things unsung,
In shadowy realms of lone surmise,
I will not whine like Ovid, flung
From out the Latin paradise.

Skies torn like strands of ocean-stream.
In you is mirrored all my pride!
Your slow, enormous clouds abide

The dolent hearses of my dreams;
Your glimmers mock with fluctuant lights
The hell wherein my heart delights.

The Long Arm

by Franz Nabl

October 1937 (vol. 30, no. 4)
Adapted from the German by Roy Temple House

I had been out of Germany for thirty-five years, drawn hither and thither by various glittering of will-of-the-wisps. When I returned to my native country, I was as poor in pocket as when I left, and much poorer in illusions.

The Berlin insurance company which I had represented with such mediocre success in Switzerland, Austria and Belgium agreed to let me sell for them at home, and by a curious coincidence there was an opening in the quaint old Bavarian city in which I had been born and bred.

I will pass over the strangely mingled feelings with which I rode in a twentieth century railroad train past the thousand-year-old walls of one of the most curious ancient cities in Europe, a town more-over whose every winding narrow street and sharp-gabled building had been the companion of my infancy and childhood.

No one seemed to know me, and I recognized no one. For several days I made no attempt to sell life insurance, but wandered in a dream, the bewildered ghost of my former self, about the spots which I had known in happier days.

One dull rainy afternoon I took refuge from the weather in a dingy little coffee-house in which, at the age of fourteen or fifteen, I along with certain boon companions, had learned the gentle art of billiards. It seemed as if every article of furniture was just as I had walked away from them, well toward half a century before. It was raining outside, and I sat alone in the gloomy, smoky old place, pondering the sweet and bitter mysteries of life.

While I sat thus, staring out with unseeing eyes at the rain which was by this time beating down smartly on the pavement, I became conscious that someone in the room was staring at me. I had not noticed that there was anyone else in the dark, low-ceilinged place except the obsequious proprietor who had served me my cigar and coffee. Now I realized that a man who sat in the corner diagonally across from me was studying me curiously from over his newspaper. His face was one that I had seen before. Suddenly, across all the years, I remembered him. And in that same moment he rose and came toward me with his hand held out.

We had been in school together, in the Gymnasium. He had been a strange fellow with few friends, but had enjoyed the reputation of being the best student in his class. But in his last year in the Gymnasium he had, for what reason I never knew, excited the animosity of a cantankerous old professor who had publicly declared that Gustav was not the kind of boy who should have a Gymnasium diploma and that he, the professor, was determined never to give him a passing grade. My father had admired the boy very much, and at one juncture when my marks looked perilously low, he had employed Gustav to tutor me. Gustav had been so successful that Father was delighted and made him a present of a silver cigarette case with Gustav's initials and mine engraved on it. I remembered all this very distinctly as we shook hands, but I was doing fast thinking, because for the life of me I couldn't remember his strange last name. I had a feeling that it was a very foreign name, Polish or Croatian or something of the sort. As he mentioned this and that, I fear I answered him a little absently and incoherently. The name was almost there. The syllables flitted tantalizingly just out of my reach. But I was sure the name began with a B. Wasn't it a Bam- or a Ban-something? Ah! I had it. Banaotovich!

From that moment the conversation went more easily. I was surprized and pleased when Banaotovich drew his silver cigarette-case out of his pocket to prove to me how highly he thought of my poor deceased father. We were soon launched on a cordial exchange of childhood memories. Banaotovich seemed a good-hearted fellow after all, and I wondered why in my childhood I had never been quite comfortable in his company. I remembered that other boys of the group had admitted to me confidentially that they were more than a little afraid of him.

The longer we talked the more intimate, the more in the nature of a mutual confession, our conversation became. I admitted to Banaotovich that the hifalutin fashion in which I had left the town to win fame and fortune years before, had been asinine in the extreme, and that it served me just right to have to sneak back unknown and penniless.

Banaotovich rejoined that for all his pride in his school marks he had remained a person of no importance, and that the pot had not the slightest intention of making itself ridiculous by calling the kettle black. He seemed almost painfully inclined to run himself down. I could feel in his manner a sort of pathetic reaching out for sympathy and consideration. And it began to seem as if he were about to tell me something or ask me for something. But whatever he had to tell seemed hard to say, and it was slow in coming over his lips.

Banaotovich ordered two bottles of the heavy native wine. I drank sparingly of it, because it goes to my head. But Banaotovich swallowed two or three glassfuls in hasty succession, and his cheeks grew flushed. There was a pause. Suddenly he leaned across the table toward me and spoke in a hoarse, excited whisper.

"Modersohn," he said anxiously, "I want to make a confession to you—a terrible confession. It may turn you against me completely. Maybe you don't want to hear it. If you don't, say so, and I'll go home. But it seems as if I've got to tell somebody about it. It seems as if I've got to find somebody who understands me and can excuse me, or it will kill me. Shall I tell you? Shall I?"

I was startled. I was reasonably sure that Banaotovich was no criminal, since he had lived half a century in his native city, undisturbed and from all he had told me solvent and respected. I had always known that he was a queer fish, a brooding, solitary sort of person, and I settled myself to listen to some harmless bit of psychopathy which meant nothing except to the unfortunate subject.

"My dear fellow," I said, no doubt a little patronizingly, "I am sure you haven't anything to confess that will make you out an outrageous rascal, but if it will do you any good to tell me your troubles, I am ready to listen to them."

"Thank you," said Banaotovich in a trembling voice. "I've done nothing that they can put me behind the bars for. But I—I—" He stared at me sternly. "But I've done worse things," he said solemnly, "than some poor fellows that have been strung up by the neck and choked to death!"

I laughed, a little nervously. "Tell me your story, if you like," I said, "and let me decide just how black you are. But I haven't a great deal of apprehension. We're all of us poor miserable sinners, as far as that's concerned. I could tell you things about myself—"

Banaotovich was not listening to me at all. He had fallen suddenly into a fit of black brooding. After a minute or two, he looked up and asked sharply: "Do you remember Wolansky?"

Wolansky was the Greek professor who had threatened to vote against Banaotovich when he was finishing his course at the Gymnasium.

"Of course," said I. "And I remember well how he abused you that last year. If there ever was a cantankerous old scoundrel, Wolansky was just that identical individual!"

"Maybe," he said absently; then after another pause: "Do you remember that Wolansky died suddenly, just a little while before the end of the school year?"

I nodded. "I imagine that was a great piece of good luck for you," I said.

"Yes," said Banaotovich. "If he had lived, I should never have had my diploma. As it was, I finished with honors. If Wolansky hadn't died when he did, I'd have been ruined. Don't forget that—ruined!"

I was puzzled at his insistence. "Yes, you would have been seriously handicapped," I agreed. "Ruined is the word, perhaps."

Banaotovich's face was purple with wine and some strange kind of suffering. "Do you remember another thing?" he said thickly. "Do you remember an old Hindoo who had a dark little hole away back of the shops and the beer depot and the livery stables between the Old Market and the river?"

"The old fellow that had love charms and told fortunes and helped people to health and wealth and happiness?" I said in a tone of slightly forced cheerfulness. It was hard to be cheerful with those somber eyes boring into you. "Yes, I remember him, all right. I wanted to go and see him once, when I was about fifteen or sixteen, but Father told me that meddling with the black art had sent more people to hell than it had helped. And Father was so terribly earnest about it that he frightened me. I never went. As a matter of fact, it was only a passing fancy, and I soon forgot all about him."

"That Hindoo," said my old school-fellow thoughtfully, "knew things about the secret forces in the universe that made him almost a god. And he taught me things that the wisest philosopher in the world doesn't suspect. Still, your father may have been right. I think it very likely that what he taught me may send me to hell!"

I shivered. I looked up nervously to make sure that the way was clear to the door. I began to suspect that my friend Banaotovich, though he was certainly not a criminal, might be a dangerous lunatic.

My *vis-a-vis* rubbed absently at a protuberance on his left side. I had noticed it when he first came across the room to speak to me. A deformity—I was sure it had not been there when he was a boy—or perhaps a tumor or some such thing as that.

"I kept very quiet about what the Hindoo taught me, because I knew most people felt about such things much as you say your father did. And I wanted to get on in the world. But I had an idea the Hindoo could help me get on. Perhaps he has—"

And he stared gloomily at space.

"Perhaps he has. And perhaps he hasn't."

He brooded. Then he took up the thread of his story.

"Wolansky nearly drove me to suicide. I read and studied and crammed, day and night. I tried everything I could think of to overcome the man's antagonism. I crawled in the dust before him like a whipped cur! Nothing did any good. And when I saw he hated me and was determined to smash me, I began to hate him, too. I came to hate him worse than I hated the devils in hell. There was a time when I had to hold myself back with all my strength to keep from sticking a knife into him or braining him with a chair. But the Hindoo and I made some experiments with telepathy, and I discovered that there are other ways of killing a man besides stabbing him or giving him poison.

"I learned how to make a man in front of me on the street turn around and look at me. I learned how to make you dream about me and come and tell me the dream the next morning" (when he said that, I jumped, for I remembered having done exactly that thing!). "I learned how to bring out a bruise on Wolansky's face although he lived on the other side of town; so that he went around asking people how he could have bumped his forehead without knowing it. And at last I went to bed one night, set my mind on Wolansky, and said over and over to myself a thousand times: Die, you dog! You've got to die! I order you to die!

"I said it over till I fell into a sort of trance. It wasn't sleep, I tell you. You can't sleep when you are in a state like that. And in my trance, I could feel another arm grow out of my side here and grow longer and longer, and grow out through the window although the window was closed, and grow out across the street and down the street and right through the walls and across the river.

"I had never known where Wolansky lived. But that night I knew. I had never known the street or the house number. I had never been there in my life. But I can tell you just exactly how his bedroom looked. The wash-stand between the two windows, the work-table against the west wall, the wardrobe, the old divan against the north wall. In a corner the blue-gray tiled stove with some of the tile chipped off. And against the south wall—the bed he lay in. I can tell you the color of the blanket he pulled up over his face. It was a dirty brownish red.

"But my hand seemed to go through the blanket and grip Wolansky by the throat. First he sighed and turned his head to one side and tried to wriggle free. Then he raised his arms and tried to get hold of something that wasn't there. His sighs turned into groans, and the groans changed to a death rattle. He threw his arms and legs wildly around in the air, his body bent up like a bow. But my hand held his head down against the pillow. At last he quit struggling and dropped down limp on the bed. Then the arm came crawling back in to my body, and I came out of the trance— and went to sleep—or perhaps I fainted.

"The next morning the director came into our classroom and told us Wolansky had died in the night of some sort of attack. You remember that, I am sure—"

When Banaotovich began to tell me this story, he had looked away from me, and his eyes never met mine during the telling. He had begun with a painful effort, but as he went on he grew more and more excited and more and more inflamed with hatred of the malicious old Greek teacher, till it almost seemed as if he had forgotten me and was living the astounding experience through for himself alone. When he was through, his ecstasy of indignation left him and he sat dejected and apprehensive, studying me pitifully out of the corners of his deep gray eyes.

When he stopped speaking, there was a moment of silence. Then I said something. I think what I said was, "Very extraordinary!"

He smiled, a strained, sarcastic smile. "Extraordinary?" he repeated, with an interrogation point in his voice.

"Your nerves were strained to the breaking-point," I said. "Your trouble with the old rascal had driven you half distracted. Then there was all that occultistic hodgepodge with the old Hindoo. And you were overworked and run down, anyway. No wonder you dreamed dreams and saw visions. And it may have been that there was some telepathic contact between you and Wolansky, and when he had his apoplectic attack—"

The sarcastic smile deepened on Banaotovich's face. "So you have it all explained, and I'm acquitted?" he inquired.

"Acquitted?" I cried. "You were never even accused. If the state were to bring action against every man who had a feeling that he would be happier if someone else were out of the way, the state would have a big job on its hands!"

"Very true," Banaotovich assented icily. "I see I haven't got very far with you yet. You are forcing me to continue my not very edifying autobiography—Did you know my father?"

I remembered his father, and I remembered that he had not enjoyed the best possible reputation.

"I think I knew him," I said hesitantly. "He was a—a money-lender, wasn't he?"

"Don't spare my feelings," said Banaotovich bitterly. "He was a usurer, and a cruel one. I had a feeling for years that his business was a disgrace to the family, and I made no bones about telling him so. There were ugly scenes. I thought several times of leaving home. Finally, Father told me one day that since I didn't approve of the way he got his money, he was doing me the favor of disinheriting me. I told him that was all right with me, that I'd rather starve than live on money that was stained with the blood of poor debtors.

"I thought at the time that I meant it. But about that time, I had become interested in a young woman. I had never had much to do with the girls, and very few of them seemed at all interested in me. But this one appeared to like me, and when I made advances to her, she didn't repel me. I am no connoisseur of female beauty, but I think she was unusually attractive, and at that time I was half mad about her. Still waters run deep, you know.

"Well, she had me under her spell so completely that I changed my mind about Father's money. I began to truckle to him, much as I had truckled to Wolansky. I began to feel him out to find whether he had made a will. He was very cold and non-committal. Finally I asked him outright if he would reconsider his decision to leave me penniless. He told me it was I that had made the decision, not he, and that he had no use for wishy-washy people that changed their minds like weather-cocks. He was very sarcastic. I lost my temper and answered him back. We had a terrible quarrel, and finally he—he struck me. I was twenty years old and a bigger man than he. And I think no man ever had more stubborn pride, at bottom, than I have.

"It was the Wolansky thing all over again. The humiliation, the effort at ingratiation, the failure, the long, eating, gnawing, growing hatred. And it—it ended the same way. The night of brooding that hardened into a devilish decision, the vision of the long arm, growing, stretching, crawling—but not so far this time, only through two walls and across our own house. You remember that Father died of an apoplectic stroke, just as Wolansky had done a year or two before."

"Yes, I think I remember," I said in considerable embarrassment. The thing did begin to look uncanny. I was thoroughly sorry for the poor, cracked fellow, but I would just as soon not have been alone with him in that solitary drinking-place in the twilight.

"Well?" he said, almost sharply.

"Well, Banaotovich," I answered with a show of confidence, "you have had a great deal of unhappiness, and you have my sympathy. This strange faculty you have of anticipating deaths, like the night-owls and the death-watch that ticks in the walls, has made these bereavements an occasion of self-torment for you. I think you should see a psychiatrist."

"Anticipating—anticipating?" Banaotovich had gone back and was repeating a word I had used, and as he repeated it, he drummed madly on the table with his fingers. "It's a curious coincidence that 'anticipating' is just the word my wife used when I told her about it."

"You—told—your wife—what you have just told me?" I stammered. "Do you think that was wise?"

"I couldn't help it," he said with a catch in his throat. "I thought I loved her, and I had to talk to somebody. I was miserable, and I had a feeling that she might understand and be brought closer to me by sympathy. Now that I think of it, I can see that I was an egregious idiot, but I discovered long ago that we aren't rational beings after all. We are driven or drawn by mysterious forces, and we go to our destination because we can't help it.

"My wife had always seemed a little timid with me. I never seemed to have the gift of attracting people. And I don't know whether she would ever have been interested in me at all if I hadn't used a little—a little charm the Hindoo taught me. Perhaps that didn't have much to do with it—but I had never been happy with her. However that may be, one evening when she seemed unusually approachable, I had just the same impulse that I had when I met you here tonight, and I told her about Wolansky and Father. She pooh-poohed it all just as you did. But she was afraid. I could see that.

She was more and more afraid of me as the days went by. For a long time, she tried to be cordial and natural in my presence, but it was a sham and the poor thing couldn't keep it up. Each of us knew as well what was in the mind of the other as if we had talked the situation over frankly for hours. We reached the point where we couldn't look each other in the face. No solitude could have been as ghastly as that solitude of two people who shared a revolting secret. For I had convinced her that I was guilty. I had succeeded in doing what I had set out to do, and I had ruined two lives in doing it. I have the faculty, it seems, of poisoning whatever I touch. Only today, my wife said to me—"

I started to my feet with a great rush of relief and thankfulness. "Ah, your wife is alive, then?" I cried.

"My wife is alive. That is—my second wife is alive," he said, with a horrible forced smile.

I sank back gasping. "What did you do with your first wife, you dirty hound?" I moaned in helpless indignation.

He closed his eyes, and a wave of bitter triumph played about the muscles of his mouth. "Have I convinced you too, at last?" he said.

Then I realized that I had been an insulting idiot. At worst, the man before me was a pathological case, and he certainly belonged in an asylum rather than in a prison.

"Forgive me, Banaotovich," I panted. "I don't know what made me—"

He looked at me sadly, almost compassionately. "There is nothing to forgive," he said, very quietly. "I am all you called me and a thousand times worse. Now let me finish my story."

"You don't need to," I said hastily. "I know all the rest of it."

All interest, I am afraid nearly all sympathy, had gone out of me. What I wanted most of all was to get away from this melancholy citizen with power and madness in his gray eyes.

"No, you don't know quite all of it yet," he insisted. "Perhaps if I tell you the whole story, even if you can't excuse me—and I don't deserve your excusing, I don't want your excusing— you can understand me a little better, and think of me a little more kindly.

"There was another woman. I couldn't help it, any more than any of us can help anything. A fine, sympathetic young woman, who loved me because she knew I was unhappy. I had been married to the other woman for four years. We were completely estranged. We could scarcely bear to speak to each other. I couldn't be easy one moment in the same house with her. I had a cot in my office out in town because I couldn't even sleep soundly at home. It was hell. The terror in her eyes made me physically sick. My wife learned about the other woman. My wife was a devout Catholic, and there was no possibility of a divorce. I could read in my wife's face just what went on in her mind. She knew the other woman had become my only reason for living. And one day I read in her eyes, along with the terror, a glint of desperate determination. She knew she was in danger, she knew I had a power that I could exercise when I chose in spite of all the courts and police and jails in the country. She knew her life was in danger, and her eyes told me that mine was in danger for that very reason. I didn't blame her. Half my grief through all the years had been grief for her. But the instinct of self-defense in me was strong—and—she went—too—like—"

He never finished his sentence. He dropped his head on the table and began to sob hysterically. I laid a gingerly hand on his shoulder.

"Banaotovich," I said unsteadily, "I'm sorry for you—"

He sat up and supported his chin in both hands. "I haven't been as—as bad as all this sounds like," he said after a while. "Before I was married a second time, I went to the chief of police and gave myself up. The chief listened to my story—I didn't try to explain it all, as I've done with you, but just blurted out the main facts; but the longer he listened the uneasier he became, and when I got through he asked me nervously if I didn't think I ought to go into a sanitarium for a while. Then he bowed me out in a big hurry. Perhaps if I had told him all the ins and outs of it, it might have been different—"

"But don't you think he's right about the sanitarium?"

"Right? I'm as sane as you are. I've killed three people, a crazy scoundrel, a hard man, and a pure, innocent woman. But I did it all because I had to. A sanitarium wouldn't do me or anyone else any good, and it would be a heavy expense. I have taken the responsibility for another pure, innocent woman, and

I must support her. The war and the depression swept away my father's fortune, and my present business has dwindled away till I am making only the barest living. I have applied for the agency for a big Berlin insurance company, and if I can get it, along with my other business, I shall be fairly comfortable. But I understand there is some talk of their sending in a representative from outside. If they do that, if they take the bread out of my mouth like that, it won't be good for the outsider!"

He was drunk, and his drunkenness was working him into an ugly mood. He was dangerous, and physical courage was never my strong point.

"What is the name of the Berlin company?" I asked timidly.

He named the firm I myself worked for. Then he fumbled for his bottle, and with stern and painful attention set about the difficult and delicate task of filling his glass again. I muttered something about being back in a moment, and made for the door. He was too busy to pay any attention to me.

When I had the door safely shut behind me, I sprinted through the rain to my hotel as if the devil himself were after me...

It was a long time before I got over waking up in the middle of the night with the feeling that an icy, iron-muscled hand was clutching at my throat. I don't have the experience often any more, but I have never seen the city of my birth since that awful night. I got out on the midnight train, and my company obligingly gave me territory on the other side of Germany.

Some time ago I happened to see a notice in the paper to the effect that a certain patient named G. Banaotovich had died suddenly in the Staatliche Nervenheilanstalt in Nuremberg. But I have met the name rather frequently of late, and I think it is a fairly common one. I didn't investigate.

A Passion in the Desert

by Honoré de Balzac

December 1936 (vol. 28, no. 5)

Translated from the French by Ernest Dowson

"The whole show is dreadful," she cried, coming out of the menagerie of Monsieur Martin. She had just been looking at that daring speculator "working with his hyena," to speak in the style of the program.

"By what means," she continued, "can he have tamed these animals to such a point as to be certain of their affection for—"

"What seems to you a problem," said I, interrupting, "is really quite natural."

"Oh!" she cried, letting an incredulous smile wander over her lips.

"You think that beasts are wholly without passions?" I asked her. "Quite the reverse; we can communicate to them all the vices arising in our own state of civilization."

She looked at me with an air of astonishment.

"Nevertheless," I continued, "the first time I saw Monsieur Martin, I admit, like you, I did give vent to an exclamation of surprize. I found myself next to an old soldier with the right leg amputated, who had come in with me. His face had struck me. He had one of those intrepid heads, stamped with the seal of warfare, and on which the battles of Napoleon are written. Besides, he had that frank good-humored expression which always impresses me favorably. He was without doubt one of those troopers who are surprized at nothing, who find matter for laughter in the contortions of a dying comrade, who bury or plunder him quite light-heartedly, who stand intrepidly in the way of bullets; in fact, one of those men who waste no time in deliberation, and would not hesitate to make friends with the devil himself. After looking very attentively at the proprietor of the menagerie getting out of his box, my companion pursed up his lips with an air of mockery and contempt, with that peculiar and expressive twist which superior people assume to show they are not taken in. Then when I was expatiating on the courage of Monsieur Martin, he smiled, shook his head knowingly, and said, 'Well known.'

"'How "well known"?' I said. 'If you would only explain to me the mystery I should be vastly obliged.'

"After a few minutes, during which we made acquaintance, we went to dine at the first restaurateur's whose shop caught our eye. At dessert a bottle of champagne completely refreshed and brightened up the memories of this odd old soldier. He told me his story, and I said that he had every reason to exclaim, 'Well known.'"

When she got home, she teased me to that extent, and made so many promises, that I consented to communicate to her the old soldier's confidences. Next day she received the following episode of an epic which one might call "The Frenchman in Egypt."

During the expedition in Upper Egypt under General Desaix,[1] a Provençal soldier fell into the hands of the Mangrabins,[2] and was taken by these Arabs into the deserts beyond the falls of the Nile.

In order to place a sufficient distance between themselves and the French army, the Mangrabins made forced marches, and only rested during the night. They camped round a well overshadowed by palm trees under which they had previously concealed a store of provisions. Not surmising that the notion of flight would occur to their prisoner, they contented themselves with binding his hands, and after eating a few dates, and giving provender to their horses, went to sleep.

---

1. Louis Desaix, a French commander present during the early phases of Napoleon's campaign of Egypt and Syria (1798–1801). Considered one of the greatest military leaders of the French Revolutionary Wars, he was killed at the age of 31 during the Battle of Marengo in 1800.
2. A term for inhabitants of Arabic-speaking western and central North Africa, derived from Maghreb, the name for that region. Applying this to Egyptians would be a misnomer, since they are widely considered to be inhabitants of the Mashriq, or the eastern region of the Arabic world.

When the brave Provençal saw that his enemies were no longer watching him, he made use of his teeth to steal a simitar, fixed the blade between his knees, and cut the cords which prevented using his hands; in a moment he was free. He at once seized a rifle and a dagger; then, taking the precaution to provide himself with a sack of dried dates, oats, and powder and shot, and to fasten a simitar to his waist, he leaped onto a horse, and spurred on vigorously in the direction where he thought to find the French army. So impatient was he to see a bivouac again that he pressed on the already tired courser at such speed that its flanks were lacerated with his spurs, and at last the poor animal died, leaving the Frenchman alone in the desert. After walking some time in the sand with all the courage of an escaped convict, the soldier was obliged to stop, as the day had already ended. In spite of the beauty of an Oriental sky at night, he felt he had not strength enough to go on. Fortunately he had been able to find a small hill, on the summit of which a few palm trees shot up into the air; it was their verdure seen from afar which had brought hope and consolation to his heart. His fatigue was so great that he lay down upon a rock of granite, capriciously cut out like a campbed; there he fell asleep without taking any precaution to defend himself while he slept. He had made the sacrifice of his life. His last thought was one of regret. He repented having left the Mangrabins, whose nomad life seemed to smile on him now that he was afar from them and without help.

He was awakened by the sun, whose pitiless rays fell with all their force on the granite and produced an intolerable heat—for he had had the stupidity to place himself inversely to the shadow thrown by the verdant majestic heads of the palm trees. He looked at the solitary trees and shuddered—they reminded him of the graceful shafts crowned with foliage which characterize the Saracen columns in the cathedral of Arles.

But when, after counting the palm trees, he cast his eyes around him, the most horrible despair was infused into his soul. Before him stretched an ocean without limit. The dark sand of the desert spread farther than sight could reach in every direction, and glittered like steel struck with bright light. It might have been a sea of looking-glass, or lakes melted together in a mirror. A fiery vapor carried up in streaks made a perpetual whirlwind over the quivering land. The sky was lit with an Oriental splendor of insupportable purity, leaving naught for the imagination to desire. Heaven and earth were on fire.

The silence was awful in its wild and terrible majesty. Infinity, immensity, closed in upon the soul from every side. Not a cloud in the sky, not a breath in the air, not a flaw on the bosom of the sand, ever moving in diminutive waves; the horizon ended as at sea on a clear day, with one line of light, definite as the cut of a sword.

The Provençal threw his arms round the trunk of one of the palm trees, as though it were the body of a friend, and then in the shelter of the thin straight shadow that the palm cast upon the granite, he wept. Then sitting down he remained as he was, contemplating with profound sadness the implacable scene, which was all he had to look upon. He cried aloud, to measure the solitude. His voice, lost in the hollows of the hill, sounded faintly, and aroused no echo—the echo was in his own heart. The Provençal was only twenty-two years old:—he loaded his carbine.

"There'll be time enough," he said to himself, laying on the ground the weapon which alone could bring him deliverance.

Looking by turns at the black expanse and the blue expanse, the soldier dreamed of France—he smelt with delight the gutters of Paris—he remembered the towns through which he had passed, the faces of his fellow-soldiers, the most minute details of his life. His southern fancy soon showed him the stones of his beloved Provence, in the play of the heat which waved over the spread sheet of the desert. Fearing the danger of this cruel mirage, he went down the opposite side of the hill to that by which he had come up the day before. The remains of a rug showed that this place of refuge had at one time been inhabited; at a short distance he saw some palm trees full of dates. Then the instinct which binds us to life awoke again in his heart. He hoped to live long enough to await the passing of some Arabs, or perhaps he might hear the sound of cannon; for at this time Bonaparte was traversing Egypt.

This thought gave him new life. The palm tree seemed to bend with the weight of the ripe fruit. He shook some of it down. When he tasted this unhoped-for manna, he felt sure that the palms had been cultivated by a former inhabitant—the savory, fresh meat of the dates was proof of the care of his predecessor. He passed suddenly from dark despair to an almost insane joy. He went up again to the top of the hill, and spent the rest of the day in cutting down one of the sterile palm trees, which the night before had served him for shelter. A vague memory made him think of the animals of the desert; and in case they might come to drink at the spring, visible from the base of the rocks but lost farther down, he resolved to guard himself from their visits by placing a barrier at the entrance of his hermitage.

In spite of his diligence, and the strength which the fear of being devoured asleep gave him, he was unable to cut the palm in pieces, though he succeeded in cutting it down. At eventide the king of the desert fell; the sound of its fall resounded far and wide, like a sigh in the solitude; the soldier shuddered as though he had heard some voice predicting woe.

But like an heir who does not long bewail a deceased parent, he tore off from this beautiful tree the tall broad green leaves which are its poetic adornment, and used them to mend the mat on which he was to sleep.

Fatigued by the heat and his work, he fell asleep under the red curtains of his wet cave.

In the middle of the night his sleep was troubled by an extraordinary noise. He sat up, and the deep silence around him allowed him to distinguish the accents of a respiration whose savage energy could not belong to a human creature.

A profound terror, increased still further by the darkness, the silence, and his waking images, froze his heart within him. He almost felt his hair stand on end, when by straining his eyes to their utmost he perceived through the shadows two faint yellow lights. At first he attributed these lights to the reflection of his own pupils, but soon the vivid brilliance of the night aided him gradually to distinguish the objects around him in the cave, and he beheld a huge animal lying but two steps from him. Was it a lion, a tiger, or a crocodile?

The Provençal was not educated enough to know under what species his enemy ought to be classed; but his fright was all the greater, as his ignorance led him to imagine all terrors at once; he endured a cruel torture, noting every variation of the breathing close to him without daring to make the slightest movement. An odor, pungent like that of a fox, but more penetrating, profounder—so to speak—filled the cave, and when the Provençal became sensible of this, his terror reached its height, for he could not longer doubt the proximity of a terrible companion, whose royal dwelling served him for shelter.

Presently the reflection of the moon, descending on the horizon, lit up the den, rendering gradually visible and resplendent the spotted skin of a panther.

This lion of Egypt slept, curled up like a big dog, the peaceful possessor of a sumptuous niche at the gate of an inn; its eyes opened for a moment and closed again; its face was turned toward the man. A thousand confused thoughts passed through the Frenchman's mind; first he thought of killing it with a bullet from his gun, but he saw there was not enough distance between them for him to take proper aim—the shot would miss the mark. And if it were to wake!—the thought made his limbs rigid. He listened to his own heart beating in the midst of the silence, and cursed the too violent pulsations which the flow of blood brought on, fearing to disturb that sleep which allowed him time to think of some means of escape.

Twice he placed his hand on his simitar, intending to cut off the head of his enemy; but the difficulty of cutting the stiff, short hair compelled him to abandon this daring project. To miss would be to die for certain, he thought; he preferred the chances of fair fight, and made up his mind to wait till morning. The morning did not leave him long to wait.

He could now examine the panther at ease; its muzzle was smeared with blood.

"She's had a good dinner," he thought, without troubling himself as to whether her feast might have been on human flesh. "She won't be hungry when she gets up."

It was a female. The fur on her belly and flanks was glistening white; many small marks like velvet formed beautiful bracelets round her feet; her sinuous tail was also white, ending with black rings; the over-part of her dress, yellow like unburnished gold, very lissome and soft, had the characteristic blotches in the form of rosettes, which distinguish the panther from every other feline species.

This tranquil and formidable hostess snored in an attitude as graceful as that of a cat lying on a cushion.

Her blood-stained paws, nervous and well-armed, were stretched out before her face, which rested upon them, and from which radiated her straight, slender whiskers, like threads of silver.

If she had been like that in a cage, the Provençal would have admired the grace of the animal, and the vigorous contrasts of vivid color which gave her robe an imperial splendor; but just then his sight was troubled by her sinister appearance.

The presence of the panther, even asleep, could not fail to produce the effect which the magnetic eyes of the serpent are said to have on the nightingale.

For a moment the courage of the soldier began to fail before this danger, though no doubt it would have risen at the mouth of a cannon charged with shell. Nevertheless, a bold thought brought daylight to his soul and sealed up the source of the cold sweat which sprang forth on his brow. Like men driven to bay who defy death and offer their body to the smiter, so he, seeing in this merely a tragic episode, resolved to play his part with honor to the last.

"The day before yesterday the Arabs would have killed me, perhaps," he said; so considering himself as good as dead already, he waited bravely, with excited curiosity, his enemy's awakening.

When the sun appeared, the panther suddenly opened her eyes; then she put out her paws with energy, as if to stretch them and get rid of cramp. At last she yawned, showing the formidable apparatus of her teeth and pointed tongue, rough as a file.

"A regular petite maitresse," thought the Frenchman, seeing her roll herself about so softly and coquettishly. She licked off the blood which stained her paws and muzzle, and scratched her head with reiterated gestures full of prettiness. "All right, make a little toilet," the Frenchman said to himself, beginning to recover his gayety with his courage; "we'll say good morning to each other presently," and he seized the small, short dagger which he had taken from the Mangrabins. At this moment the panther turned her head toward the man and looked at him fixedly without moving.

The rigidity of her metallic eyes and their insupportable luster made him shudder, especially when the animal walked toward him. But he looked at her caressingly, staring into her eyes in order to magnetize her, and let her come quite close to him; then with a movement both gentle and amorous, as though he were caressing the most beautiful of women, he passed his hand over her whole body, from the head to the tail, scratching the flexible vertebrae which divided the panther's yellow back. The animal waved her tail voluptuously, and her eyes grew gentle; and when for the third time the Frenchman accomplished this interesting flattery, she gave forth one of those purrings by which our cats express their pleasure; but this murmur issued from a throat so powerful and so deep, that it resounded through the cave like the last vibrations of an organ in a church. The man, understanding the importance of his caresses, redoubled them in such a way as to surprize and stupefy his imperious courtezan. When he felt sure of having extinguished the ferocity of his capricious companion, whose hunger had so fortunately been satisfied the day before, he got up to go out of the cave; the panther let him go out, but when he had reached the summit of the hill she sprang with the lightness of a sparrow hopping from twig to twig, and rubbed herself against his legs, putting up her back after the manner of all the race of cats. Then regarding her guest with eyes whose glare had softened a little, she gave vent to that wild cry which naturalists compare to the grating of a saw.

"She is exacting," said the Frenchman, smiling.

He was bold enough to play with her ears; he caressed her belly and scratched her head as hard as he could.

When he saw that he was successful, he tickled her skull with the point of his dagger, watching for the right moment to kill her, but the hardness of her bones made him tremble for his success.

The sultana of the desert showed herself gracious to her slave; she lifted her head, stretched out her neck, and manifested her delight by the tranquility of her attitude. It suddenly occurred to the soldier that to kill this savage princess with one blow he must stab her in the throat.

He raised the blade, when the panther, satisfied no doubt, laid herself gracefully at his feet, and cast up at him glances in which, in spite of their natural fierceness, was mingled confusedly a kind of goodwill. The poor Provençal ate his dates, leaning against one of the palm trees, and casting his eyes alternately on the desert in quest of some liberator and on his terrible companion to watch her uncertain clemency.

The panther looked at the place where the date stones fell, and every time that he threw one down her eyes expressed an incredible mistrust.

She examined the man with an almost commercial prudence. However, this examination was favorable to him, for when he had finished his meager meal she licked his boots with her powerful rough tongue, brushing off with marvelous skill the dust gathered in the creases.

"Ah, but when she's really hungry!" thought the Frenchman. In spite of the shudder this thought caused him, the soldier began to measure curiously the proportions of the panther, certainly one of the most splendid specimens of its race. She was three feet high and four feet long without counting her tail; this powerful weapon, rounded like a cudgel, was nearly three feet long. The head, large as that of a lioness, was distinguished by a rare expression of refinement. The cold cruelty of a tiger was dominant, it was true, but there was also a vague resemblance to the face of a sensual woman. Indeed, the face of this solitary queen had something of the gayety of a drunken Nero: she had satiated herself with blood, and she wanted to play.

The soldier tried if he might walk up and down, and the panther left him free, contenting herself with following him with her eyes, less like a faithful dog than a big Angora cat, observing every movement of her master.

When he looked round, he saw, by the spring, the remains of his horse; the panther had dragged the carcass all that way; about two-thirds of it had been devoured already. The sight reassured him.

It was easy to explain the panther's absence, and the respect she had had for him while he slept. The first piece of good luck emboldened him to tempt the future, and he conceived the wild hope of continuing on good terms with the panther during the entire day, neglecting no means of taming her and remaining in her good graces.

He returned to her, and had the unspeakable joy of seeing her wag her tail with an almost imperceptible movement at his approach. He sat down then, without fear, by her side, and they began to play together; he took her paws and muzzle, pulled her ears, rolled her over on her back, stroked her warm, delicate flanks. She let him do whatever he liked, and when he began to stroke the hair on her feet she drew her claws in carefully.

The man, keeping the dagger in one hand, thought to plunge it into the belly of the too-confiding panther, but he was afraid that he would be immediately strangled in her last convulsive struggle; besides, he felt in his heart a sort of remorse which bid him respect a creature that had done him no harm. He seemed to have found a friend, in a boundless desert; half unconsciously he thought of his first sweetheart, whom he had nicknamed "Mignonne"[3] by way of contrast, because she was so atrociously jealous that all the time of their love he was in fear of the knife with which she had always threatened him.

This memory of his early days suggested to him the idea of making the young panther answer to this name, now that he began to admire with less terror her swiftness, suppleness, and softness. Toward the end of the day he had familiarized himself with his perilous position; he now almost liked the painfulness of it. At last his companion had got into the habit of looking up at him whenever he cried in a falsetto voice, "Mignonne."

At the setting of the sun Mignonne gave, several times running, a profound melancholy cry. "She's been well brought up," said the light-hearted soldier; "she says her prayers." But this mental joke only occurred to him when he noticed what a pacific attitude his companion remained in. "Come, ma petite blonde, I'll let you go to bed first," he said to her, counting on the activity of his own legs to run away as quickly as possible, directly she was asleep, and seek another shelter for the night.

The soldier waited with impatience the hour of his flight, and when it had arrived he walked vigorously in the direction of the Nile; but hardly had he made a quarter of a league in the sand when he heard the panther bounding after

---

3. Meaning dainty, pleasing, small.

him, crying with that saw-like cry more dreadful even than the sound of her leaping.

"Ah!" he said, "then she's taken a fancy to me; she has never met anyone before, and it is really quite flattering to have her first love." That instant the man fell into one of those movable quicksands so terrible to travelers and from which it is impossible to save oneself. Feeling himself caught, he gave a shriek of alarm; the panther seized him with her teeth by the collar, and, springing vigorously backward, drew him as if by magic out of the whirling sand.

"Ah, Mignonne!" cried the soldier, caressing her enthusiastically; "we're bound together for life and death—but no jokes, mind!" and he retraced his steps.

From that time the desert seemed inhabited. It contained a being to whom the man could talk, and whose ferocity was rendered gentle by him, though he could not explain to himself the reason for their strange friendship. Great as was the soldier's desire to stay upon guard, he slept.

On awakening he could not find Mignonne; he mounted the hill, and in the distance saw her springing toward him after the habit of these animals, who cannot run on account of the extreme flexibility of the vertebral column. Mignonne arrived, her jaws covered with blood; she received the wonted caress of her companion, showing with much purring how happy it made her. Her eyes, full of languor, turned still more gently than the day before toward the Provençal, who talked to her as one would to a tame animal.

"Ah! Mademoiselle, you are a nice girl, aren't you? Just look at that! So we like to be made much of, don't we? Aren't you ashamed of yourself? So you have been eating some Arab or other, have you? That doesn't matter. They're animals just the same as you are; but don't you take to eating Frenchmen, or I shan't like you any longer."

She played like a dog with its master, letting herself be rolled over, knocked about, and stroked, alternately; sometimes she herself would provoke the soldier, putting up her paw with a soliciting gesture.

Some days passed in this manner. This companionship permitted the Provençal to appreciate the sublime beauty of the desert; now that he had a living thing to think about, alternations of fear and quiet, and plenty to eat, his mind became: filled with contrast and his life began to be diversified.

Solitude revealed to him all her secrets, and enveloped him in her delights. He discovered in the rising and setting of the sun sights unknown to the world. He knew what it was to tremble when he heard over his head the hiss of a bird's wing, so rarely did they pass, or when he saw the clouds, changing and many-colored travelers, melt one into another. He studied in the night-time the effect of the moon upon the ocean of sand, where the moon made waves swift of movement and rapid in their change. He lived the life of the Eastern day, marveling at its wonderful pomp; then, after having reveled in the sight of a hurricane over the plain where the whirling sands made red, dry mists and death-bearing clouds, he would welcome the night with joy, for then fell the healthful freshness of the stars, and he listened to imaginary music in the skies.

At last he grew passionately fond of the panther; for some sort of affection was a necessity. Whether it was that his will, powerfully projected, had modified the character of his companion, or whether, because she found abundant food in her predatory excursions in the deserts, she respected the man's life, he began to fear for it no longer, seeing her so well tamed.

He devoted the greater part of his time to sleep, but he was obliged to watch like a spider in its web that the moment of his deliverance might not escape him, if anyone should pass the line marked by the horizon. He had sacrificed his shirt to make a flag with, which he hung at the top of a palm tree, whose foliage he had torn off. Taught by necessity, he found the means of keeping it spread out, by fastening it with little sticks; for the wind might not be blowing at the moment when the passing traveler was looking through the desert.

It was during the long hours, when he had abandoned hope, that he amused himself with the panther. He had come to learn the different inflections of her voice, the expressions of her eyes; he had studied the capricious patterns of all the rosettes which marked the gold of her robe. Mignonne was not even angry when he took hold of the tuft at the end of her tail to count the rings, those graceful ornaments which glittered in the sun like jewelry. It gave him pleasure to contemplate the supple, fine outlines of her form, the whiteness of her belly, the graceful pose of her head.

But it was especially when she was playing that he felt most pleasure in looking at her; the agility and youthful lightness of her movements were a continual surprize to him; he wondered at the supple way in which she jumped and climbed, washed herself and arranged her fur, crouched down and prepared to spring. However rapid her spring might be, however slippery the stone she was on, she would always stop short at the word "Mignonne."

One day, in a bright midday sun, an enormous bird coursed through the air. The man left his panther to look at this new guest; but after waiting a moment the deserted sultana growled deeply.

"My goodness! I do believe she's jealous," he cried, seeing her eyes become hard again; "the soul of Virginie[4] has passed into her body; that's certain."

The eagle disappeared into the air, while the soldier admired the curved contour of the panther.

But there was such youth and grace in her form! she was beautiful as a woman! the blond fur of her robe mingled well with the delicate tints of faint white which marked her flanks.

---

4. A reference to *Paul et Virginie* by Jacques-Henri Bernardin de Saint-Pierre, published in 1788. The novel recounts the youth of two children raised as brother and sister by their mothers on the island of Mauritius, at that time a French colony. As they mature into teenagers, the innocent love of the children develops into romantic attraction. Sent away from the island, Virginie dies in a shipwreck on her return home, refusing the strip away her wet clothing in front of sailors. Paul and the children's mothers also die shortly after, of broken hearts. Often recommended to young readers for its themes of innocence and chastity, the novel was immensely popular (as well as criticized and parodied) during the 19th century.

The profuse light cast down by the sun made this living gold, these russet markings, to burn in a way to give them an indefinable attraction.

The man and the panther looked at each other with a look full of meaning; the coquette quivered when she felt her friend stroke her head; her eyes flashed like lightning—then she shut them tightly.

"She has a soul," he said, looking at the stillness of this queen of the sands, golden like them, white like them, solitary and burning like them.

"Well," she said, "I have read your plea in favor of beasts; but how did two so well adapted to understand each other end?"

"Ah, well! you see, they ended as all great passions do end—by a misunderstanding. For some reason one suspects the other of treason; they don't come to an explanation through pride, and quarrel and part from sheer obstinacy."

"Yet sometimes at the best moments a single word or a look is enough—but anyhow go on with your story."

"It's horribly difficult, but you will understand, after what the old villain told me over his champagne.

"He said, 'I don't know if I hurt her, but she turned round, as if enraged, and with her sharp teeth caught hold of my leg—gently, I daresay; but I, thinking she would devour me, plunged my dagger into her throat. She rolled over, giving a cry that froze my heart; and I saw her dying, still looking at me without anger. I would have given all the world to have brought her to life again. It was as though I had murdered a real person; and the soldiers who had seen my flag, and were come to my assistance, found me in tears.

"'Well, sir,' he said, after a moment of silence, 'since then I have been in war in Germany, in Spain, in Russia, in France; I've certainly carried my carcass about a good deal, but never have I seen anything like the desert. Ah! yes, it is very beautiful!'

"'What did you feel there?' I asked.

"'Oh! that can't be described, young man. Besides, I am not always regretting my palm trees and my panther. I should have to be very melancholy for that. In the desert, you see, there is everything, and nothing.'

"'Yes, but explain—'

"'Well,' he said, with an impatient gesture, 'it is God without mankind.'"

Siesta

by Alexander L. Kielland

November 1930 (vol. 16, no. 5)

Adapted by Charles Flint McClumpha, from a
German translation of the Norwegian original
by M. von Borch

I n one of those elegant bachelors' lodgings in Rue
Castiglione, a merry company lingered over the
dessert. Senor Jose Francisco de Silvis was a
Portuguese, short in stature, black as a coal. He was one
of those Brazilians who are wont to cross the ocean
with incredible fortunes, to lead incredible lives in
Paris, and to distinguish themselves, above all things,
by making the most incredible acquaintances.

At this little dinner-party there was hardly one
who was acquainted with his neighbor on the right, or
on the left; excepting, of course, those coming together.
The host himself had met them either at a ball, or at
table-d'hote,[1] or in the street.

---

1. A multi-course restaurant meal offered at fixed prices with few if any
choices in items, as opposed to à la carte.

Senor de Silvis laughed loudly, talked loudly, wherever he went, as rich foreigners always do. Not being able to gain entry into the Jockey Club, he collected around himself whatsoever he happened upon. He immediately asked for the address. The next day he sent an invitation for a small dinner-party.

He spoke all languages—indeed, even German. One could see that he was not a little proud when he called across the table, *"Mein lieber Herr Doktor!—wie geht's Ihnen?"*[2]

And there was, too, a real bodily German doctor in the party, with an exuberant beard, as red as fire, and that smile of Sedan,[3] worn by all Germans in Paris.

The temperature of the entertainment rose with the champagne. Fluent French and murdered French alternated with Spanish and Portuguese. The ladies leaned back in their chairs and laughed. The party was soon sufficiently acquainted to cast aside all embarrassment. Jesting and witty words flew over the table from mouth to mouth. The *"Lieber Doktor"* alone discussed seriously with his neighbor—a French journalist, with a red ribbon in his button-hole.[4]

---

2. "My good Doctor!—how are you?"

3. A proverbial expression for the smug sense of superiority evinced by Prussia following its victory in the Franco-Prussian War. The Battle of Sedan was fought on the 1st and 2nd of September 1870 and resulted in the capture of Emperor Napoleon III and over a hundred thousand troops. It effectively decided the war in favor of Prussia and its allies, though fighting continued under a new French government.

4. An indication that the journalist is a member of National Order of the Legion of Honor, France's highest order of merit, civil and military, established in 1802 by Napoleon Bonaparte. By the late 19th century, the award was relatively common, inspiring literary satire. Maupassant wrote a

And there was still another present who did not allow himself to be carried away with the general gayety. He sat at the right of Mademoiselle Adele. On her left sat her new admirer, the corpulent Anatole, who had been eating excessively of the truffles.

During the meal Mademoiselle Adele had attempted, by many harmless little devices, to enliven her neighbor on the right. But he remained quiet, answered courteously, but shortly and in a low voice.

She thought at first that he was a Pole; one of those most wearisome of creatures who travel about and play the despised. But she soon discovered that she had erred. That annoyed Mademoiselle Adele.

It was one of her many accomplishments to be able to distinguish, at the first glance, the many foreigners whom she encountered. And she was wont to declare that she could guess the nationality of a man as soon as he had exchanged ten words with her.

But this taciturn stranger was the source of much perplexity to her. If he had only been blond! Then she would at once have made him an Englishman, for he spoke like one. But he had black hair, a heavy dark mustache, and a fine petite figure. His fingers were remarkably long, and he had a peculiar way of crumbling the bread and playing with the dessert-fork.

---

parody of the phenomenon in his 1883 short story "Décoré". Despite being altogether undeserving of the title, the main character Monsieur Caillard dedicates his life to receiving the Legion of Honor. The story opens with Caillard recounting the results of yet another disappointing walk spent tallying the number of red-ribboned buttonholes he encounters.

"He is a musician," whispered Mademoiselle Adele to her corpulent friend.

"Ah," replied Monsieur Anatole, "I fear that I have eaten too many truffles."

Mademoiselle Adele again whispered some good advice into his ear, whereupon he laughed and appeared smitten with love.

Meanwhile, however, she could not neglect the interesting stranger. After she had enticed him to drink several glasses of champagne, he became livelier and more talkative.

"Oh," she suddenly cried out, "I perceive by your speech that you are certainly an Englishman!"

The stranger blushed and hastily replied, "No, madam!"

Mademoiselle Adele laughed.

"Pardon me," she said; "I know, Americans are always vexed when one takes them for English."

"I am not an American either," returned the stranger.

This was too much for Mademoiselle Adele. She bent over her plate and seemed very much embarrassed. Then, indeed, she observed that Mademoiselle Louison, sitting opposite to her, was delighted with her blunder.

The strange gentleman understood this, and added, half aloud: "I am an Irishman, madam."

"Ah," uttered Mademoiselle Adele, with a grateful smile, for she was easily reconciled.

"Anatole—Irishman! What is that.?" she whispered.

"They are the poor in England," he whispered in reply.

"So!—hem!" Mademoiselle Adele raised her eyebrows and cast a sly glance at her neighbor on the right. With one stroke he had completely swept away her interest in him.

De Silvis' dinner was excellent. They had been long sitting at the table. When Monsieur Anatole remembered the oysters, which had introduced the menu, they were to him like a pleasant dream. The truffles, on the contrary, continued to be to him a lasting reality.

The dinner proper was ended. Now and then someone lifted his glass again, or culled from the dish one of the choice fruits or little bonbons.

Tender-hearted, blond Mademoiselle Louison was lost in deep revery over a grape which she had dropped into her champagne glass.

"Look," cried Mademoiselle Louison, turning her great, liquid eyes toward the journalist; "see how the white angels bear a sinner toward heaven!"

"Ah, charming, mademoiselle. What a sublime idea!" cried the enraptured journalist in return.

Mademoiselle Louison's sublime idea made the circuit of the table, and was generally applauded. The frivolous Adele alone whispered to her corpulent admirer: "Really, 'twould take a whole host of angels to carry you to heaven, Anatole!"

The journalist, in the interim, knew how to grasp the opportunity and arrest the general attention of the company. Furthermore, he was happy at the prospect of escaping a wearisome political discussion with the German. And since he wore the red ribbon in his button-hole, and, in addition, had the matchless, important tone of a journalist, the entire party gave him audience.

He explained how small forces, when combined in operation, can bear such great burdens. And then he passed to the topic of the day: The magnificent collections of the press for sufferers from the floods in Spain and for the destitute in Paris.

He had much to relate. Every moment he spoke of the press as "we" while in the heat of his eloquence he talked of "these millions which we have raised with such enormous sacrifices."

But each of the others also had his story to tell. Innumerable traits, small or noble, were revealed on these days of festivities and pleasures. And all of them savored somewhat of self-sacrifice.

Mademoiselle Louison's best friend, an unimportant lady, whose place was almost at the foot of the table, related, despite Louison's protest, how three poor sewing-girls had come to her own lodgings, and how she had made them sew the whole night on her gown for the celebration at the Hippodrome.[5] Moreover, in addition to their wages, she had generously given these poor girls coffee and cake!

Mademoiselle Louison became suddenly an important personage at the table, and the journalist began to show her the most marked attentions.

---

5. The Hippodrome de Vincennes is a horse racing track located in Vincennes, an eastern suburb of Paris. It was first built in 1863 and then rebuilt in 1879, after being destroyed in the Franco-Prussian War.

These many noble incidents of benevolence and Louison's liquid eyes inspired the entire company with a feeling of repose, satisfaction, and sympathy for man-kind, which was most eminently fitting to the weariness following the fatigue of the meal.

Indeed, this feeling of comfort mounted even a few degrees higher, when they came to rest themselves in the soft arm-chairs of the little cool salon.

There was no other light here than the glow from the open fireplace. Its ruddy brightness stole softly across the English carpet and ascended to the golden cornices of the hangings; it played upon the gilded frames of the paintings, touched the piano which stood near the chimney; here and there it fell also upon a face, wonderfully illuminating and reclaiming it from the darkness. Otherwise nothing was visible except the red, glowing tips of cigars and cigarettes.

The entertainment began to flag; only a whisper now and then, or the clink of a coffee-cup disturbed the silence.

Every one seemed inclined to surrender himself distracted to the still enjoyment of his digestive powers and his philanthropic temperament. Even Monsieur Anatole forgot his truffles, while he stretched himself out in the low easy-chair near the sofa, on which Mademoiselle Adele had seated herself.

"Is there no one present who can give us a little music?" inquired Senor de Silvis. "You are always wont to be so obliging, Mademoiselle Adele."

"Oh dear, no—no!" cried Mademoiselle. "I've been eating too heartily!" At the same time, leaning back upon the sofa, she drew up her little feet, and, with a satisfied air, folded her hands across her breast.

But the stranger, the Irishman, emerged from his comer, and advanced to the piano.

"Oh! you're going to play something for us! Many thanks—Monsieur—hem. Monsieur—" Senor de Silvis had forgotten the name, a thing happening very often, indeed, with his guests.

"You see, he is a musician!" said Mademoiselle Adele to her friend. Anatole answered with a grunt of admiration.

There was something else. The others also perceived it at once, noticing the manner in which he sat down and struck a few chords here and there to awaken the instrument, as it were.

He then began to play—sportively, flightily, frivolously—just as the mood was upon him.

The melodies of the day whirled away into gay waltzes and tuneful glees; all those insignificant popular tunes hummed by all Paris for the past week he snatched up and executed with spirit and fluency.

The ladies cried out with astonishment, sang a few bars in accompaniment, beat time softly on the floor. The entire company followed him with intense interest. He had gained their sympathy, and carried them away with him from the very beginning. The "*Lieber Herr Doktor*" alone listened with that Sedan smile. Such things were too simple for him.

But soon there was something for even the German. He nodded now and then somewhat approvingly.

A bit of Chopin burst forth and wonderfully accorded with the general temperament—the pungent fragrancy filling the air, the gay women, the men so frank, so unconcerned, each strange to the other, lost in the obscurity of the dusky salon, each following his own most secret thoughts, borne along by the mysterious, half-distinct, half-confused music, while the light of the open fireplace brightened now, now sank back again, causing everything golden to glimmer with a faint, trembling glow.

And now there was still more for the doctor. From time to time he turned to-ward de Silvis and motioned to him whenever the harmonious sounds suggested "our Schumann," "our Beethoven," or, indeed, "our famous Richard".

Meanwhile the stranger continued playing, slightly inclined to the left, though without effort, in order to put more force into the bass. It sounded as if he had twenty fingers all of steel. He knew how to assemble a multitude of tones, so that the instrument itself produced one powerful, united, distinct sound. Not stopping, not marking the transitions, by ever newly recurring surprises, imitations, happy combinations he fixed their attention so firmly that even the most unmusical person was forced to follow him with rapture.

Wholly unnoticed, the music changed its character. The artist played the deep tones uninterruptedly. He then inclined himself more and more upon the left, and there arose a wonderful commotion in the bass. The Anabaptists of *The Prophet*[6] approached with heavy steps; a knight from the *Damnation de Faust*[7] mounted from the depths below with that desperate, hobbling, diabolical gallop.

More and more it rumbled and thundered in the deeper tones, and Monsieur Anatole began to feel the truffles anew. Mademoiselle Adele leaned half forward from the sofa; the music would not allow her to rest in peace.

Here and there the chimney-fire was reflected in a pair of black eyes staring fixed upon the player. He had bewitched them; they could now no longer detach themselves from him; he led them ever deeper down, down, down, where the sound was muffled and gloomily muttered with lamentations and threats.

"He manages his left hand marvelously," said the doctor. But de Silvis did not hear him; like the others, he sat in breathless suspense.

A mysterious, oppressive fear stole out from the music and brooded over the whole assembly.

The artist seemed to clench his left hand into a fist, which could never again relax, while with his right he cast hither and thither descants of sounds leaping aloft

6. *The Prophet* is a grand opera in five acts by Giacomo Meyerbeer. It premiered in Paris on 16 April 1849. The plot is based on the life of John of Leiden, an Anabaptist leader and self-proclaimed "King of Münster" in the 16th century.

7. Another grand opera, written by Charles Gounod to a French libretto by Jules Barbier and Michel Carré, from Carré's play *Faust et Marguerite*, in turn loosely based on Johann Wolfgang von Goethe's *Faust, Part One*. It debuted at the Théâtre Lyrique on the Boulevard du Temple in Paris on 19 March 1859.

like sparkling flames. It sounded as if something dismal, horrible had been committed in the cellar, while those upstairs were dancing, laughing, and amusing themselves under the resplendent candelabra.

There was heard a sigh, a low cry from one of the ladies who felt unwell, but no one took notice of it. The performer was now wholly occupied with the bass, on which he was playing with both hands. His tireless fingers rapidly mingled the sounds together, so that cold chills ran up and down the backs of his hearers.

There was, however, a gradual ascension from the threatening, tumultuous lower sounds to the higher notes. The tones ran into each other, over each other, past each other, upward, ever upward, but never seeming to advance. There arose a wild tumult, a struggle to reach the top. They swarmed like little black demons, fighting, wrangling, full of raging wrath, feverish hurry, climbing, clinging, clenching with hands and teeth, each kicking, crushing the other with its feet, cursing, shrieking, praying— and, meanwhile, his hands glided along the keys so slowly, oh, so painfully slowly!

"Anatole," whispered Mademoiselle Adele, as pale as a ghost, "he is playing the Poverty!"[8]

"Oh, dear!—those truffles!" moaned Anatole, beginning to writhe with pain.

The salon suddenly became as bright as day. Two servants entered from behind the portiere with lamps

---

8. The editors of this volume worked under the impression that this statement was another allusion to 19th century popular music, rather than just a general commentary about the condition of the Irish under British rule, but the latter rather than the former seems more likely.

and candelabra. At the same moment the strange musician stopped playing, with all the might of his steeled fingers striking a discord so impossible, so startling that the entire party instantly sprang to their feet.

"Away with the lamps!" cried de Silvis.

"No, no!" shrieked Mademoiselle Adele; "come in with the light. I'm afraid in the dark. Oh, the horrible creature!"

"Who was he?—yes,—who was he?" And they involuntarily thronged round their host. Nor did they notice that the stranger had slipped out behind the servants.

De Silvis tried to laugh it off by saying: "I think it was the devil. Come, let us go to the opera!"

"To the opera? Not for the world," cried Louison. "I won't listen to any music for a fortnight. Ugh! think of that crowd on the opera stairway!"

"Oh, my truffles!" howled Anatole.

The company broke up. They all suddenly realized that they were strangers in a strange place. Each one desired to steal away home and be alone by himself.

On accompanying Mademoiselle Louison to her carriage the journalist said: "There, you see, that's the result of allowing one's self to be persuaded to accept the invitations of one of those half-barbarians. One never knows what sort of a crowd one will meet."

"Oh, dear, yes! He has quite put me out of humor," replied Louison, plaintively, all the time lifting her liquid eyes appealingly to him. "But won't you accompany me to Trinity? I know that a quiet mass will be read there at midnight."

The journalist bowed acquiescence, and took his place beside her in the carriage.

While Mademoiselle Adele and Monsieur Anatole, on the other hand, were passing the English apothecary in Rue de la Paix, the latter bade the coachman stop, and said, "No," beseechingly to her, "I think I must be put down here and have them give me something for my truffles. You won't be angry with me? But, you see—the music—"

"Please do not let it trouble you in the least, my friend. To be frank, I think that neither of us is in a specially happy mood tonight. Well, good-night! *Auf Wiedersehen* tomorrow!"

She leaned back in the cushions of the carriage. She felt relieved. She was alone. And the frivolous creature wept, as if she had been whipped! She was then driven home.

Of course Anatole was suffering extremely from the truffles, but it seemed to him that he felt better the moment the carriage rolled away.

Since the time that they had become acquainted they were never so satisfied with one another as at this very moment of parting.

But the one who had best recovered from the affair was the "*Lieber Herr Doktor*," for, being a German, he had become inured as far as the music was concerned.

Siesta

Notwithstanding this, however, he resolved to stroll off to the brasserie Müller in Rue Richelieu, to drink over it a good square pint of German beer, with a bit of ham, perhaps.

A Ghost

by Guy de Maupassant

November 1930 (vol. 15, no. 2)
Translated from the French by Anonymous

We were speaking of sequestration, alluding to a recent lawsuit. It was at the close of a friendly evening in a very old mansion in the Rue de Grenelle, and each of the guests had a story to tell, which he assured us was true.

Then the old Marquis de la Tour-Samuel, eighty-two years of age, rose and came forward to lean on the mantelpiece. He told the following story in his slightly quavering voice.

"I, also, have witnessed a strange thing—so strange that it has been the nightmare of my life. It happened fifty-six years ago, and yet there is not a month when I do not see it again in my dreams. From that day I have borne a mark, a stamp of fear—do you understand?

"Yes, for ten minutes I was a prey to terror, in such a way that ever since a constant dread has remained in my soul. Unexpected sounds chill me to the heart; objects which I can ill distinguish in the evening shadows make me long to flee. I am afraid at night.

"No! I would not have owned such a thing before reaching my present age. But now I may tell everything. One may fear imaginary dangers at eighty-two years old. But before actual danger I have never turned back, mesdames.

"That affair so upset my mind, filled me with such a deep, mysterious unrest that I never could tell it. I kept it in that inmost part, that corner where we conceal our sad, our shameful secrets, all the weaknesses of our life which can not be confessed.

"I will tell you that strange happening just as it took place, with no attempt to explain it. Unless I went mad for one short hour it must be explainable, though. Yet I was not mad, and I will prove it to you. Imagine what you will. Here are the simple facts:

"It was in 1827, in July. I was quartered with my regiment in Rouen.

"One day, as I was strolling on the quay, I came across a man I believed I recognized, though I could not place him with certainty. I instinctively went more slowly, ready to pause. The stranger saw my impulse, looked at me, and fell into my arms.

"It was a friend of my younger days, of whom I had been very fond. He seemed to have become half a century older in the five years since I had seen him.

His hair was white, and he stooped in his walk, as if he were exhausted. He understood my amazement and told me the story of his life.

"A terrible event had broken him down. He had fallen madly in love with a young girl and married her in a kind of dream-like ecstasy. After a year of unalloyed bliss and unexhausted passion, she had died suddenly of heart disease, no doubt killed by love itself.

"He had left the country on the very day of her funeral, and had come to live in his hotel at Rouen. He remained there, solitary and desperate, grief slowly mining him, so wretched that he constantly thought of suicide.

"'As I thus came across you again,' he said, 'I shall ask a great favor of you. I want you to go to my chateau and get some papers I urgently need. They are in the writing-desk of my room, of our room. I can not send a servant or a lawyer, as the errand must be kept private. I want absolute silence.

"'I shall give you the key of the room, which I locked carefully myself before leaving, and the key to the writing-desk. I shall also give you a note for the gardener, who will let you in.

"'Come to breakfast with me tomorrow, and we'll talk the matter over.'

"I promised to render him that slight service. It would mean but a pleasant excursion for me, his home being not more than twenty-five miles from Rouen. I could go there in an hour on horseback.

"At ten o'clock the next day I was with him. We breakfasted alone together, yet he did not utter more than twenty words. He asked me to excuse him. The thought that I was going to visit the room where his happiness lay shattered upset him, he said. Indeed, he seemed perturbed, worried, as if some mysterious struggle were taking place in his soul.

"At last he explained exactly what I was to do. It was very simple. I was to take two packages of letters and some papers, locked in the first drawer at the right of the desk of which I had the key. He added:

"'I need not ask you not to glance at them.'

"I was almost hurt by his words, and told him so, rather sharply. He stammered : 'Forgive me. I suffer so much !'

"And tears came to his eyes.

"I left about one o'clock to accomplish my errand.

"The day was radiant, and I rushed through the meadows, listening to the song of the larks, and the rhythmical beat of my sword on my riding-boots.

"Then I entered the forest, and I set my horse to walking. Branches of the trees softly caressed my face, and now and then I would catch a leaf between my teeth and bite it with avidity, full of the joy of life, such as fills one without reason, with a tumultuous happiness almost indefinable, a kind of magical strength.

"As I neared the house I took out the letter for the gardener, and noted with surprize that it was sealed. I was so amazed and so annoyed that I almost turned back without fulfilling my mission. Then I thought that I should thus display over-sensitiveness and bad taste. My friend might have sealed it unconsciously, worried as he was.

"The manor looked as though it had been deserted the last twenty years. The gate, wide open and rotten, held, one wondered how. Grass filled the paths; I could not tell the flower-beds from the lawn.

"At the noise I made kicking a shutter, an old man came out from a side door and was apparently amazed to see me there. I dismounted from my horse and gave him the letter. He read it once or twice, turned it over, looked at me with suspicion, and asked: 'Well, what do you want?'

"I answered sharply: 'You must know, as you have read your master's orders. I want to get in the house.'

"He appeared overwhelmed. He said: 'So—you are going in—in his room?'

"I was getting impatient. '*Parbleu!*[1] Do you intend to question me?'

"He stammered: 'No—monsieur—only—it has not been opened since—since the death. If you will wait five minutes, I will go in to see whether—'

"I interrupted angrily: 'See here, are you joking? You can't go in that room as I have the key!'

"He no longer knew what to say. "'Then, monsieur, I will show you the way.'

"'Show me the stairs and leave me alone. I can find it without your help.'

"'But—still—monsieur—'

---

1. By God!

"Then I lost my temper. 'Now be quiet! Else you'll be sorry!'

"I roughly pushed him aside and went into the house.

"I first went through the kitchen, then crossed two small rooms occupied by the man and his wife. From there I stepped into a large hall. I went up the stairs, and recognized the door my friend had described to me.

"I opened it with ease and went in.

"The room was so dark that at first I could not distinguish anything. I paused, arrested by that moldy and stale odor peculiar to deserted and condemned rooms, of dead rooms. Then gradually my eyes grew accustomed to the gloom, and I saw rather clearly a great room in disorder, a bed without sheets, having still its mattresses and pillows, one of which bore the deep print of an elbow or a head, as if someone had just been resting on it.

"The chairs seemed all in confusion. I noticed that a door, probably that of a closet, had remained ajar.

"I first went to the window and opened it to get some light, but the hinges of the outside shutters were so rusted that I could not loosen them.

"I even tried to break them with my sword, but did not succeed. As those fruitless attempts irritated me, and my eyes were by now adjusted to the dim light, I gave up hope of getting more light and went toward the writing-desk.

"I sat down in an armchair, folded back the top, and opened the drawer. It was full to the edge. I needed but three packages, which I knew how to distinguish, and I started looking for them.

"I was straining my eyes to decipher the inscriptions, when I thought I heard, or rather felt, a rustle behind me. I took no notice, thinking a draft had lifted some curtain. But a minute later, another movement, almost indistinct, sent a disagreeable shiver over my skin. It was so ridiculous to be moved thus even so slightly, that I would not turn around, being ashamed. I had just discovered the second package I needed, and was on the point of reaching for the third, when a great and sorrowful sigh, close to my shoulder, made me give a mad leap two yards away. In my spring I had turned round, my hand on the hilt of my sword, and surely had I not felt that, I should have fled like a coward.

"A tall woman, dressed in white, was facing me, standing behind the chair in which I had sat a second before.

"Such a shudder ran through me that I almost fell back! Oh, no one who has not felt them can understand those gruesome and ridiculous terrors! Your soul melts; your heart seems to stop; your whole body becomes limp as a sponge, and your innermost parts seem collapsing.

"I do not believe in ghosts; and yet I broke down before the hideous fear of the dead; and I suffered, oh, I suffered more in a few minutes, in the irresistible anguish of supernatural dread, than I have suffered in all the rest of my life!

"If she had not spoken, I might have died. But she did speak; she spoke in a soft and plaintive voice which set my nerves vibrating. I could not say that I regained my self-control. No, I was past knowing what I did; but the kind of pride I have in me, as well as a military pride, helped me to maintain, almost in spite of myself, an honorable countenance. I was making a pose, a pose for myself, and for her, whatever she was, woman, or phantom. I realized this later, for at the time of the apparition I could think of nothing. I was afraid.

"She said: 'Oh, you can be of great help to me, monsieur!'

"I tried to answer, but I was unable to utter one word. A vague sound came from my throat.

"She continued: 'Will you? You can save me, cure me. I suffer terribly. I always suffer. I suffer, oh, I suffer!'

"And she sat down gently in my chair. She looked at me.

"'Will you?'

"I nodded my head, being still paralyzed.

"Then she handed me a woman's comb of tortoise-shell, and murmured : 'Comb my hair! Oh, comb my hair! That will cure me. Look at my head—how I suffer! And my hair—how it hurts!'

"Her loose hair, very long, very black, it seemed to me, hung over the back of the chair, touching the floor.

"Why did I do it? Why did I, shivering, accept that comb, and why did I take between my hands her long hair, which left on my skin a ghastly impression of cold, as if I had handled serpents? I do not know.

"That feeling still clings about my fingers, and I shiver when I recall it.

"I combed her, I handled, I know not how, that hair of ice. I bound and unbound it; I plaited it as one plaits a horse's mane. She sighed, bent her head, seemed happy.

"Suddenly she said, 'Thank you!' tore the comb from my hands, and fled through the door, which I had noticed was half opened.

"Left alone, I had for a few seconds the hazy feeling one feels in waking up from a nightmare. Then I recovered myself. I ran to the window and broke the shutters by my furious assault.

"A stream of light poured in. I rushed to the door through which that being had gone. I found it locked and immovable.

"Then a fever of flight seized on me, a panic, the true panic of battle. I quickly grasped the three packages of letters from the open desk; I crossed the room running; I took the steps of the stairway four at a time. I found myself outside, I don't know how, and seeing my horse close by, I mounted in one leap and left at a full gallop.

"I didn't stop till I reached Rouen and drew up in front of my house. Having thrown the reins to my orderly, I flew to my room and locked myself in to think.

"Then for an hour I asked myself whether I had not been the victim of an hallucination. Certainly I must have had one of those nervous shocks, one of those brain disorders such as give rise to miracles, to which the supernatural owes its strength.

"And I had almost concluded that it was a vision, an illusion of my senses, when I came near to the window. My eyes by chance looked down. My tunic was covered with hairs, long woman's hairs, which had entangled themselves around the buttons!

"I took them off one by one and threw them out of the window with trembling fingers.

"I then called my orderly. I felt too perturbed, too moved, to go and see my friend on that day. Besides, I needed to think over what I should tell him.

"I had his letters delivered to him. He gave a receipt to the soldier. He inquired after me and was told that I was not well. I had had a sunstroke, or something. He seemed distressed.

"I went to see him the next day, early in the morning, bent on telling him the truth. He had gone out the evening before and had not come back.

"I returned the same day, but he had not been seen. I waited a week. He did not come back. I notified the police. They searched for him everywhere, but no one could find any trace of his passing or his retreat.

"A careful search was made in the deserted manor. No suspicious clue was discovered.

"There was no sign that a woman had been concealed there.

"The inquest gave no result, and so the search went no further.

"And in fifty-six years I have learned nothing more. I never found out the truth."

End

* 9 7 9 8 9 8 7 5 6 2 6 3 5 *